You're Not Alone

An Indie Author Anthology

Ian D Moore and Friends

Copyright Information

First published on Amazon KDP UK (ebook) July 2015
Amazon Createspace (print) July 2015

ISBN 13/ 978-1514235973
ISBN10/1514235978

In Loving Memory Of

Pamela Mary Winton
1944 – 2015
Always In Our Hearts

This compilation is dedicated to the Macmillan Cancer Nurses, who selflessly strive to provide care and maintain dignity to those that we hold dear.

'Grief never ends... But it changes. It is a passage, not a place to stay. Grief is not a sign of weakness, nor a lack of faith... It is the price of love.'

CONTENTS

CONTENTS

MEET THE AUTHORS

****

Preface

This Anthology began with a single thought ...

"What can I do to help?"

Faced with the realisation that I was witnessing the beginning of the end of a fight with cancer that had raged for eight years in someone very dear to me, I felt powerless to do anything to thwart the inevitable. It was in the final days of Pamela's life that I realised the potential that myself, and my writer friends possessed, that would enable us to make a difference.

They say that 'Actions speak louder than words' ... I beg to differ.

The words that form the stories within this compilation will draw you through a range of emotions and scenarios—all different, all unique, but all centred around one theme. Relationships.

***

The initial idea began when I posted a question for thought in our online Facebook based author group, the Indie Author Review Exchange (IARE), originally set up by one of the contributing guest authors, Paul Ruddock. I sent a single message out, asking the members if they would like to contribute a short story, with very little other information, save for the theme that I wanted it to be about.

Within days, twenty-seven authors had committed to write, from various genres and with various publishing success. In the time it took for the first entry to be submitted, volunteers from within the group began to pour in with offers of help. A review team was soon assembled, a Final Copy Editor Lesley Hayes, voted in and from the main group, a technical wizard to oversee cover design came in the form of Nico Laeser, another contributing writer Some of the writers in this publication you may have read before, if you're a fan of Indie Author work that is – and if not, after reading this compilation, you may well become one. The authors have submitted short stories based upon a limited word count to reflect their interpretation of the chosen theme. Each work is an original piece, created specifically for this venture.

***

Within the Anthology you will have the opportunity to contact any individual author for further information on their work, information on their websites and book links.

Finally, I sincerely hope that you will enjoy this edition.

Ian D. Moore

****

Acknowledgements

Special thanks go to the following individuals for their dedication, time and effort in the production of this work, without whom, this would have taken so much longer to accomplish.

Christine Southworth – Talented Artist, Cover Image Designer.

What an honour to have had the artwork for this project designed by such a talented exhibiting artist, recently awarded The Fine Art Prize 2015 by The Society of Women Artists. It is Christine's vision that gave an image to the anthology. I am so grateful.

Nico Laeser – Digital Rendering, Cover, File Conversion and Formatting.

Both an extremely talented author and artist, I am in awe at the creativity and dedication shown. Thank you so much Nico.

Lesley Hayes – Final Draft Editor

The most experienced, learned author of the group. The team appreciates the time devoted from her busy schedule to assist with this project.

Sylva Fae – Assistant Editor, Reviewer, Promotions

My thanks to one of the voices of reason throughout this process. Sylva's assistance in promotions long after the project was completed has been invaluable.

Diana J Febry – Assistant Editor, Reviewer

From the start, Diana's assistance in proof reading and reviewing has helped us to ensure that every reader gets a well presented story.

Sallyann Phillips – Assistant Editor, Reviewer, Promotions
A creative author who took on the promotions role with gusto and flare. Sallyann has shone ever-so brightly throughout.

Rebecca Baynes – Charity Liason, Fundraising Manager
A new venture expertly handled; a learning curve for us all, but a pleasure to have worked with Becky.

Paul Ruddock – Founder, IARE group.
An inspirational friend, who created the original group from where most of the submitting authors came forward – my humble thanks.

Robert Wingfield – Final Formatting, Editor.
My sincere thanks to Robert for his assistance, guidance, and tips in the final stages of production of this work. The finished product looks so much the better for it.

****

Macmillan Cancer Support UK

Our history

In 1911, a young man named Douglas Macmillan watched his father die of cancer. His father's pain and suffering moved Douglas so much; he founded the 'Society for the Prevention and Relief of Cancer'. This was the birthplace of Macmillan Cancer Support as we know it today.

Douglas wanted advice and information to be provided to all people with cancer, homes for patients at low or no cost, and voluntary nurses to attend to patients in their own homes.

Today much of Douglas' legacy lives on. We are still a source of support for people living with cancer today and we are a force for improving cancer care.

As of June 2013, there were 3,942 Macmillan nurse posts across the UK, both in hospitals and in the community.

All Macmillan nurses are registered with at least five years' experience, including two or more years in cancer or palliative care. They have completed specialist courses in pain and symptom management, and psychological support.

Most of the nurses work in NHS hospitals or the community. A small number work in hospices and private hospitals, but do not charge for their services. As specialists they do not routinely undertake nursing care but are there to assess complex needs, give advice to other healthcare professionals and support people with cancer to understand their treatment options.

Nearly half of us will be diagnosed with cancer in our lifetimes, which means the need for our work is set to increase dramatically. Thanks to our loyal and committed supporters, over 98% of our income in 2013 came from voluntary donations and fundraising, so we make sure to use our money wisely.

Please visit www.macmillan.org.uk

Or call: **0808 808 00 00** for more information.

A Year Afterwards

Lesley Hayes

A year afterwards we met again. We met in the same place. Our place. Julie's Wine Bar, where the tables were real wood and the beams real beams. A listed building, slightly tarted up by Julie. She cooked the meals in the kitchen out the back, and served at the bar when it was quiet. She'd watched the progress of our relationship with fascination.

You knew at the beginning that I was with someone and leaving them would never be an option. This much was always understood between us. You said you were used to that, that you had been in a similar situation once before with someone who was married. You said it would be enough just the way it was, that it would always be enough. So it was never one of those hopeless, futureless, martyred passions.

There was something unique about the atmosphere that was exactly right at Julie's. It was dark at the edges, softened by candle glow and flickering shadow casting firelight. The sound of wood cracking, and the peaty smell of that fire mingled with the other evocative sounds and smells of an old, much lived in, eating place would often seize my imagination like a hungry wolf between our meetings. When we were there it was like stepping into another time: it reinforced the sensation that we existed outside usual laws.

Making love was a problem only in logistic terms. The back of a car is never comfortable, and seems more sordid the older you get. Hotels, for an hour or two, are thrilling the first time, but less so with familiarity. Under the stars in a cornfield loses its attraction in the middle of winter, and can be physically harrowing. In the end you spend more time discussing where than why.

Julie observed our increasing tendency to linger long after all other customers had left. We were reluctant to face the cold reality of searching for a place to go, after hours spent sharing moussaka or steak and ale pie and a bottle of her excellent house red. When it got late she would pause for a while in her clearing up to sit at the table with us for a chat. She never sent us on our way. We talked about nothing much with her, but it was obvious she liked us. I think she was intrigued by our absorption with each other. Though we were never overt about it, and were careful not to touch, it proclaimed us lovers.

She said, one night: "Don't think I'm rude, but I've a room upstairs. I lived here when I first opened the place, and now it's never used. I've been meaning to rent it out, but it's always struck me that would be inconvenient, unless it was someone who worked here. I wouldn't mention it, only..." She was discreet enough to tail off, to allow us to look at each other, and then at her as if she had morphed into a fairy godmother.

I looked down at my hands, spread on the rough grained surface of the table. I pressed so hard against it I could feel the hum of the wood pressing back. I listened to you and Julie negotiating the terms for the use of the room once a week. I felt my whole body blaze with humiliation and excitement. It was an arrangement as binding as a marriage, in its way.

She showed us the room that night, and left us there. I heard money changing hands, but I went over to the window, ignoring the mutter of your voices by the door. I was glad to be free of the burden of financial responsibility, if only for a little while. I stood holding the curtain, looking down into the shadowy street: the old-fashioned lamp post a little way along, a lone cat prowling with tail poker high. The room smelled musty. I hadn't looked at it – only passed through it to get to the window. I would raise the sash when Julie had gone: I didn't want to insult her by implying that the place needed air.

I felt ashamed and a bit resentful of the ignominious position our desire had put me in. And I also wanted you so badly I was screaming inside for us to be alone. You shut the door and crossed the room swiftly and silently, so that your hands were upon my shoulders before I expected them. Your hot breath damp against my neck, you whispered into my ear: "I love you. It will be all right."

You knew – just as you always did – what I was really feeling. You understood the conflict, and knew how to resolve it.

That night marked for me the change from something still essentially casual to something frighteningly permanent. Of course, there is really no such thing as permanence. We all know that. People are fickle, feelings change. Love is conditional, whatever we tell ourselves about its metaphysical and idealized nature. Nevertheless, I turned a corner I hadn't even known was there.

It was a cosy place. We made it ours by adding, week by week, those tender touches of personal memorabilia. It was also a useful repository for items impossible to hide at home: your letters and cards to me, theatre programmes, menus. We still went to other places to eat occasionally. It didn't bother Julie if we just came in and went straight up to the room.

We'd go through to the back, and up the little winding wooden stairs, briefly popping our heads round the kitchen door on the way, if that's where she was, calling a greeting through the steam and sizzling smells. You'd usually stop at the bar as we passed, and get us a bottle of wine. Perhaps other customers assumed we were the owners, if they wondered anything as they saw us disappear. Julie always treated us as if we were honoured guests.

She still chatted to us at our table when we did eat there, and gave us a little extra, or something she guessed we'd like. She saved our favourites for us if she knew we were coming. Fresh pineapple was yours. Clams were mine. She spoiled us. Perhaps we represented for her a freedom she'd never had. Perhaps there was a sadder story. We never thought to ask her.

**

In the summer we would sit outside, in the little garden that was really barely big enough – waiting for the lengthening day to turn from lavender evening into indigo night. There were the pungent scents of honeysuckle, and of an ancient climbing rose doggedly thriving in the parched soil. There were the bins and the unprepossessing back of the original, crumbling brick and timber building. Few other customers ventured out there. Julie's efforts at refurbishment had been confined to the interior. We liked the extra dimension of solitude it gave us. We were desperate for seclusion.

I began to agonise about Alex. I suppose it was inevitable. No idyll lasts forever without the world outside its protected walls eventually impinging. Many of our conversations now centred on this inner turmoil. I was being unfaithful – a fact which had seemed unremarkable when my relationship with you had loomed less largely in my life. All along, you had been the one who had talked about love. I had held back, non-committal.

I had tossed at you scraps of assertions that you were attractive, or else why would I have got into this? And that on the fingers of one hand I could count the important people who mattered to me – among whom, naturally, you figured... I was good at such glib reassurances which tied me to no promises about the future.

Now I began to be anxious about time running out. I almost willed our relationship to be over, so that I could weep for us privately and arrive safe on the far shore of sorrow, wallowing in mawkish retrospection. I saw us as Alex would see us, should our cover ever be blown. We looked shabby and dishonest, creeping off to our sly love nest. I had begun to care enough about you to want us to be honourable, to warrant society's blessing rather than censure. But I had no illusions about that, really. I knew it would be impossible.

Alex's faults – the worst of which was simply ordinariness – became grotesquely magnified in my mind. I couldn't wait to unload myself each week of this terrible burden of dislike I felt. Patiently, you listened. Occasionally you played devil's advocate. You comforted where it was required. You brought out comparable parallels from past relationships of your own. There is no guilty party surer to be condemned than the one not present to give their version of events. You boosted my certainty that I was entirely justified in seeking out another for solace and reward.

But sex, after all the talking, was what brought me back down out of my head and into a deeper reality. In bed, in the gloaming of lamplight and moonlight from the open window, we made magic which could not lie. I once said to you that bodies had no alternative but to speak the truth of what they felt. I was talking about Alex at the time, about how difficult I found it to respond physically to someone I felt so insipid towards. I realised as soon as I spoke that it gave away so much of what I felt for you. I shivered with dread of self-exposure. But you just smiled and agreed and placed your hand quietly against mine, palm to palm. You tucked me inside your heart so easily, as if that special place had been reserved for me forever.

I've never been much good at committing myself. I've always believed in having a large reserve of self to fall back on if other people let you down. I learned many years ago to set up this self-protective half-heartedness, this refusal to fully involve myself with another person. The reasons why are not so important now. Just take it as a given.

Alex and I had chosen to live together because we suited one another. We weren't in love, but we were compatible. We made few emotional demands on one another, and agreed that a relationship was like a house that you built together out of respect, affection, companionship, honesty and trust. Those were the words we used at the time, and they became powerfully charged when it impacted on me that what I was doing with you amounted to betrayal.

I felt such a wretch, becoming progressively embroiled with you. I wished fervently, with a survivor's instinct, for the flush of the fever to be past. I yearned for the innocent detachment I had experienced at the beginning to return. Our meetings initially had been about shared interests, and there had been no cause to lie about them. We had been friends then, only friends. I had told myself that anyway, and for a while I'd been convinced.

When you touched me, every nerve ending felt raw. My body was constantly waiting, waiting. Away from you there was still only you, filling the time in between with a film spooling endless images of us together. When you said, as you often did: "I love you... only you..." there was emptiness in my chest that ached to answer you, a hollow silence which only habit forbade me to fill. I distracted myself by thinking about your numerous past relationships and the fact that you were single, and I wondered how long it would be before you grew bored with me.

***

Sitting on the edge of the bed one night, preparing to dress and go back to Alex, I became overwhelmed with gloom. "What hope is there for us?" I groaned. You thought it was a pose and laughed, not recognising my despair, my aching unease that the more you meant to me the less I might mean to you. How could I be sure you'd been honest in everything you'd said? I'd lied to Alex, after all.

Even so, you pulled me round to face you, so I could see the gravity in your clear grey eyes. "If I thought you'd say yes I'd ask you to leave Alex and be with me," you said. But I didn't believe you. It was the sort of thing people said when they were in bed, I thought, even if one of you was already half way out and contemplating their underwear.

Fate stepped in – on Alex's side. Perhaps on mine. There was a job in Edinburgh, an impressive promotion with an increased salary to match. Alex would have been crazy not to accept it. Edinburgh, after all, wasn't the end of the world. Only the other end of the country, more or less. Which meant it might as well have been.

"I'll go too, of course," I said to you. "Writers can write anywhere. Have laptop will travel. Alex says it will broaden my horizons."

You looked stunned. We were sitting at the table in the window alcove that Julie always reserved for us. Your plate of lasagne congealed, looking sweaty. Eventually you pushed it away from you. Your face creased and collapsed as only a face unused to grief can do: there were no known contours to fit that tortured expression. Tears welled like bubbles blown in glass. They rolled down your cheeks, splashed on to your clenched fists and into your wine.

"You're leaving me," you said.

"I'm going with Alex. That's not the same," I said. I was holding back the tears I didn't intend you ever to see. Part of me hated the part that was so attached to the safety of the familiar that I would be camp follower to someone for whom the most I would ever feel was friendship.

"Yes it is," you said. Accusing me. You were right, of course.

I said at first we'd be able to go on seeing each other. It would simply take more management, that was all. We would need more subterfuge to make our meetings plausible. "It won't make any difference," I said, winging it. "We'll find a way."

We went up to our room, undressed listlessly and got into bed. Naked, it was easier to reassure ourselves that this was real, this connection we had. In a sea of deception it was the one thing that was true. It was vital, not easily discarded. But there was one of the lies, right there. I was discarding you, and we both knew it.

We made love. For me it was strangely the best time ever, poignant with the knowledge that it would be the last time. My allegiance, dangerously shifted towards you for a while, had been firmly put back with Alex, where it comfortably belonged.

Before I went we met only once more, but not at Julie's. The relocation was all arranged with haste. Alex's company was keen to facilitate the move. The daily practicalities buffered me from any real awareness of what I was planning to do.

Three days before the move we had lunch at the most expensive restaurant we'd ever salivated about. I'd always supposed that when we went there it would be a celebration, not a wake. Neither of us had any appetite, but we went through the motions. You were determined everything should be perfect and I was committed to doing the right thing – by you as well as Alex. I knew I had to let you go.

What I remember most is the look in your eyes as you toasted me and wished me good luck. There was such stripped bare fear in them. You had received the Judas kiss from me, and your lips were burning with the pain.

"It's a lonely business, life," you said.

"I'll write," I said.

You shook your head then. "No, don't do that. Please don't."

When we said goodbye, we knew it was final. I wept when I got home, before Alex came back from work. I howled like a dog. There was no one who could console me. I began to understand about being alone.

I suffered Edinburgh. After a while I even enjoyed it. You can live anywhere and be happy. Or at least, make the most of a life.

***

I thought of you all the time at first. And then less, in little increments of forgetfulness. I put you away in the place where I kept my oldest treasures and the other fragments of my broken heart. I congratulated myself on how lucky an escape I'd had. I'd almost abandoned the security of the shallows for the unpredictable whirlpools of the depths. Suppose I'd lost myself?

And then, one day – such a small thing, I suppose – I was in a bookshop when I overheard two women talking. The only part of the conversation that registered was when one said: "Stoicism makes a person so dull."

The phrase kept bouncing around inside my head for the rest of the day, the same way music sometimes sends its memory worm burrowing deep into your soul. And then that night, lying quiet and still beside Alex, as always so careful not to disturb the peace, I suddenly saw its awful significance.

I had embraced stoicism. I'd fled to it as a harbour from the storm-tossed seas of passion and genuine emotion. I was warm, protected, unthreatened, tucked up with Alex in this unruffled bed. The bright jewel of my secret love for you was so shiny sharp it could lacerate me. Even those few memories I'd allowed myself were watched at a distance, like a sleepy passenger at a drive-in movie. They might have stepped out of the screen and knocked me for six if I'd got too close and seen it was a real life drama after all.

Cautiously, I began to truly remember. It was like taking off a scab to see if the wound had healed. I recalled how one night, sitting at that table in Julie's, you had drawn up lists on the back of a paper napkin, while I dictated: good and bad things in my life. You were trying to show me how lucky I was, after I'd expressed particular resentment of Alex. I realised now with hindsight you were also reminding me I had choice.

On the good side was so much, such an embarrassment of fortune. You shamed me with your optimism. There was so little to complain about on the bad side. One or two words at the most. The positive list went on and on down the crumpled page of the napkin, the words fuzzy with ink. The very last item was the shortest word. There was hardly room for it but you managed to squeeze it in. I now saw that it should have been written at the top, blazoned in gold: Us.

When I rang you last week and asked you to meet me at Julie's, there was only the fraction of a pause before you agreed. Perhaps I imagined it. You asked no questions, although it had been a year. Your voice had exactly the same degree of warmth. It could have been just days in between.

Julie left us alone to talk. She'd given us the table by the window. I told you that I'd left Alex, that I'd got myself a flat and a day job back here. Alex wasn't too upset, I said. It had been obvious to us both that splitting up would be the kindest cut of all.

"We'll always be friends," I said.

"Well, that's something, anyway," you said.

As we talked, I struggled against a barrier. There was a reserve between us that had never been there before. You didn't trust me – and why would you? I couldn't blame you. You saw me as cold-hearted, I supposed. You thought I'd come to flaunt my new freedom and offer you a piece of it, hoping to grab a corner of your love to wrap around me for temporary warmth.

A long time ago, when we first met, you'd been content with my nonchalance. But that had been before the tears, and the parting. There is no going back in life. Sometimes we learn that just in time. There can only be an ending, a beginning, and a going forward.

"I love you," I said abruptly, interrupting what you were saying. It was the first time I'd ever said the words. They'd been impossible for me to say unless I was absolutely sure I meant them. It was the biggest risk I'd ever taken, and yet a bigger risk would have been never to tell the truth to myself.

It stopped you short. Because you knew. You understood that. You reached out your hand and smiled, and we began.

****

Closure (somewhere over France)

B.L. Pride

The pale light of the early morning was just beginning to mellow out the bluish darkness of the rainy night, when Carrie entered the airport building and gazed around. She sighed, trying to disguise her miserable lament as an empowering inhale. She was not exactly a traveller, and yet she was here now, just about to fly to Italy. Alone. Nervous. And not sure what was waiting for her there. Except for a fresh dose of disappointment, of course. There was nothing other to expect from her father than disappointment. As if a childhood filled with disappointments, broken promises, and false pretense wasn't enough.

She followed the signs, replaying her husband's words and directions in her head, smiling at the memory of how he reacted when she mentioned presents.

"Don't buy too much, honey," Less had said, pulling her closer and making her giggle with his passionate outburst and spreading chills across her neck. "You've got everything you need right here."

He was amazing. Knowing how unpleasant and painful going to Italy was for her, he tried his best to get a couple of free days off work, but sadly, he was apparently indispensable. And so he planned everything for her, walked her through the airport basics a dozen times, made all the necessary arrangements, reservations, everything. All she had to do was follow the pre-organized and pre-paid plan, survive the meeting with her father, and get back home as soon as possible.

As soon as she managed to get to the airport lounge, Carrie found a café, ordered what she guessed would be the first of several coffees, pulled out a book, and made herself comfortable. No matter what she was up against, for as long as she had coffee and books, she felt somehow... untouchable. Nothing could ever shake her balance while sitting down with a book and a cup of coffee. Not even the thought of her father.

***

Although he had managed to shake much more than just her balance in the course of his non-existent fatherhood; her self-confidence and her trust in men, for example. She had succeeded in coming to terms with it as she grew older, and in a way she felt as though she had started to understand him better.

He was a free spirit. A rolling stone. Living in one place all his life, working from nine to five, being stuck with the same woman and going to kids' school plays and science fairs just wasn't something he could do. Carrie understood this now but still felt a burning lump of rancor in her throat whenever she thought of all the tears she had cried because of him. Not being there, failing to show up, and not keeping his promises were the worst kind of betrayal for the seven, nine, or twelve-year-old who couldn't understand that her father wasn't making his empty promises because he was being careless – he was making them because he was trying. Trying to do better than he was able to. Finally realizing that failing both her and her mom was all he had managed for years, he left. Just like that. No explanations, no excuses. He told them he was leaving, and he was gone.

Carrie put down her book, took the cup, and leaned back in her chair. Observing people and guessing what their stories were had always been her thing, and what better place to do it than here, in the middle of an airport lounge.

The first person who caught her eye was a man of about sixty-years-old, with dark hair that was already turning grey at the temples. He had one of those faces that seem always to wear a smile, and there was a hint of eccentricity in the way he was dressed. He reminded her of her father. What else! On a day like this, even the blonde girl sitting in the corner with a boy all over her, would probably remind her of him.

All of a sudden, Carrie cringed, looking at the cup in her hands as if there was something unbelievably interesting there. Don't stare, she told herself. She had to. Impossible. It seemed impossible, but at the same time... It wasn't *completely* impossible. Nah, it was. *Completely* impossible, she told herself, and decided to stare some more. Obviously, time had changed him exactly the way she had always imagined. Not that she had been thinking about him a lot, of course. Hardly ever.

Carrie fidgeted nervously, praying he wouldn't see her, and keeping her fingers crossed that he would. Zach Brooks. She took the book again, pretending to be reading for a couple of intimately embarrassing minutes. Reading was out of the question. And so was thinking. Like the biggest fool there ever was, she was hiding behind her book because of a man who hadn't even noticed her. Or who at least refused to admit he had. Which wouldn't surprise her, actually. After the way they had... separated, it wouldn't be surprising if he ignored her. Or gave her the cold shoulder. Or the finger.

She kept peeking in his direction, and since he seemed completely engrossed in his laptop, she could afford a couple of decent stares. He looked good. Really, really good. And very businessman-like. Which added to the natural hotness. Carrie found herself grinning at the book like the fool she was, and decided to call Less. Chat with him for a little while. And get a grip on herself and her silly, ridiculously childish head.

***

The drizzle was killing the light of the early spring day as the airport shuttle bus took the passengers of the 9:45 Rome flight to the plane. The fact that Zach Brooks was there was killing the light of the pleasant phone conversation Carrie had had with her husband. She couldn't believe it, but at the same time it seemed sadly, shamelessly typical.

The airport shuttle bus was crowded, making it impossible for her to check his position while the short ride lasted, but as soon as they started getting off and figuring out where they should turn next, she saw him again. And he saw her.

All of Carrie's earlier doubts, predominately fears in fact, that he was ignoring her as a result of what had happened between them seven years ago, were gone the moment she saw the surprise on his face and the heartrending mixture of joy and pain in his eyes. He waved to her and started making his way in her direction.

"I can't believe it!" He shook his head, laughing, a little embarrassed, and seriously attractive. "What a place to meet."

Cursing her useless brain and dysfunctional heart, Carrie was struggling to say something that would not make her look as pathetic as she felt.

"A nice coincidence," she smiled. Wouldn't it be enough to just call it a coincidence?

The crawling, moving crowd was forcing them to move along. Were they just going to wave goodbye now?

"Okay, I'll see you around." Zach smiled and so did she. What else was there to do? But he was still standing there, defying the will of the crowd. And so was she.

"Shit!" He suddenly remembered and blushed. "My bag!"

"Go!" She laughed, intoxicated by the encounter and the chemistry that had never ceased.

Carrie was sitting in her place, fighting back the wish to turn around and see if Zach was somewhere in sight. A nice lady was sitting next to her, commenting on the weather and pulling a bunch of magazines out of her bag, making Carrie smile to herself. She recognized the gesture, because it was very much like the one she would always use; reading was a wall between her and anyone who had an annoying wish to chat endlessly.

People were still getting up, sitting down, coming, and going, when a flight attendant approached Carrie and her neighbor's seats, asking to have a word with the magazine lady. Carrie tried hard not to listen, but the distance was so small not hearing was impossible: *a gentleman asked, a nice seat, by the window, after years, catching up...* and some

17

other words and phrases made her face burn hotter and hotter, and her heart beat faster and faster.

"Oh, I guess so…" The magazine lady seemed surprised and amused at the same time. She got up, and smiled at Carrie. "Have a nice flight," she said, nodding.

Carrie was left alone. Alone in the bustle of passengers and crew, with her heart pounding somewhere high in her throat, its banging resonating in her ears.

"Here you go, sir." A voice announcing the reason for her neighbor's leaving made her flinch and stare at her book as if her life depended on it. She knew that the most natural reaction would be to look up and check what was going on, but she couldn't make herself do it.

"Hey there." She knew this voice. She knew *his* voice.

Carrie lifted her gaze, facing Zach Brooks standing there by the empty seat, unable to decide whether or not he should sit down. It was amazing and terrifying at the same time, how well she had known him despite the seven years of nothing, no sound, no word, nothing at all. He had reacted to their meeting impulsively, asking the flight attendant to change the seats before he even thought about it, and was feeling majorly self-conscious now.

"Hey," she smiled, unable to think of anything else.

"I thought we could catch up, you know… keep each other company. If you'd like."

"I would like that very much," she said. Admitted. And hoped it didn't sound too genuine.

The plane took off smoothly, and so did their leap into their common past. Both struggling with a variety of restraints, second thoughts, and remorse, they did amazingly well — chatting endlessly, laughing happily, and diving deeper and deeper into a warm, mesmerizing, heart-melting sensation of connectedness and belonging. They talked about everything, hurriedly, hastily, as if hoping to make up for the lost time, to share everything that had happened, and discuss all of their decisions.

In the middle of a pretty neutral topic of his cousin's decision to move to New Zealand, Zach grew worryingly somber.

"I've missed you, Carrie. I really have. Sometimes I felt it, and sometimes I didn't, but I think not a day has passed without a thought of you."

Carrie felt something in her chest rise and tremble painfully as she tried to restrain the pain she had been holding back for so long, denying it to herself and to Less.

"I guess losing your best friend is much tougher than we thought it would be." She looked through the window, smiling out at the infinity stretching beyond the ugly wings of the mechanical beast.

"For me it was never just losing my best friend," he said softly. Quietly. His voice caressing the most secluded part of what she was.

She knew that. She had known that all the time. And it wasn't just losing her best friend, either. But back then, it felt too difficult and too dangerous; she was too afraid of getting hurt or hurting anyone, and she panicked, terrified at the possibility of disappointing Zach, who had been her best friend since high-school, always around, always waiting in the wings, or Less, whom she had just met, and who seemed like the best choice. The safest choice. The inconsistency of her relationship with Zach had made her feel insecure and vulnerable, which was the only thing she couldn't live with, so the other option, the promises Less had made and what he had represented in Carrie's eyes, had to win. It had to. But it broke her heart at the same time.

"For me, neither." She bowed her head. "But… we had to make a decision, and we did."

The silence between them was so deep it felt as if everything around them was being drowned out by it. In a way, Carrie knew what he wanted to say. In a way she wanted to hear it. She needed to hear it, and to believe beyond a shadow of a doubt that it had nothing to do with Less.

"We made the wrong one," he finally said.

"Maybe. But we're not kids anymore. And a part of the grown-up world is sticking to your decisions, don't you think?"

She saw the shadow of his head move. Was she really expecting him to fight? To object and make it even more complicated? She had no idea what she expected, but a silly disappointment washed over her when she saw his agreement.

Zach changed the subject, clinging on to the practical side of life.

"So, you're returning on Thursday?" he checked, and Carrie nodded.

They had already talked about their reasons for going to Italy and their plans there, so the matter of returning came up naturally.

Or was it a scheme?

"Would you mind traveling home with me?" he asked.

"I never thought switching seats and planes was so simple," she teased, her face burning like her heart.

"It is for the master," he grinned, making her laugh as well.

20

After the intimacy-drenched, emotion-soaked flight, saying goodbye was unbelievably difficult. Zach was going to Alatri, a town where one of his clients was starting a business and buying a house, while Carrie was supposed to meet her father at the airport. An unspoken promise of seeing each other in three days was just as comforting as it was unpleasant, inducing the pangs of a guilty conscience and decency's righteous judgment, while also floating her up towards cloud nine.

***

Carrie almost didn't believe her father would show up as agreed, so when she saw him, a man much older and much more exhausted than she had imagined, she could have cried. She could have cried like a baby, but all she allowed herself was to sniffle a little and hug him really, really hard, trying to hold him for all the years she had wanted to do it, and for all the moments she had promised herself never to do it again.

It was clear as day – the man that had called her a week ago, asking her to leave everything and travel to Rome immediately because he needed to say goodbye, because he was dying. And just as he needed closure, she needed it too. She needed her wounds healed, her tears dried, and her soul cleansed. She needed to forgive. She did.

There were no hidden agendas on her father's side, no ulterior motives, no schemes. He wanted to see her before it was too late, because his spirit, the free spirit that he had always been and which he had always followed, felt his journey was coming to an end.

They talked. Laughed. Explained. Cried a little. Loved each other. Even if only for three days.

"Bye, Dad." Carrie smiled a tear veiled smile as they were saying goodbye on Thursday.

"Ciao, Caramia." Her father smiled an oxygen mask hidden smile as he watched his daughter leave.

She hugged him and whispered, "Thank you. For calling me. And wanting me here."

"We all make mistakes, Carrie," he breathed. "It's what you do once you realize you made one that defines who you are."

Zach was already at the airport lounge when she got there. Smiling and attentive, he showered her with a million questions and a million stories, struggling to keep the balance between their non-date and her experience with her father. They boarded the plane together, took their seats together, and talked on end. Carefully. Their words were delicately woven into a conversation about themselves, without saying anything that might stir the careful gentleness.

Until suddenly, Zach turned to face her with such determination, with such enthusiasm, she was completely captivated.

"When we get off this plane, Carrie... Will we see each other again?"

Say no. You have to say no, she told herself.

"I don't think..." she started, but couldn't finish her sentence.

We all make mistakes, Carrie. It's what you do once you realize you made one that defines who you are.

He looked so good, so alluring and so fragile sitting there, looking at her with bright, hopeful optimism.

"I don't think it would be a good idea." She forced herself to say it, and hated herself for doing it.

Zach reached out his hand, so slowly, indecisively, and yet so naturally it would be impossible to resist. His fingers touched her face, travelled to her hair, gently, sensually, making her skin prickle and her eyes sting. Their kiss was the sweetest, the most beautiful kiss Carrie had ever dreamed of, explaining, understanding, forgiving, promising, and saying goodbye. It lasted, deepened, cried and laughed, shouted for joy and moaned with pain. They needed closure. Both of them did. She had no idea until then, but she needed her wounds healed, her tears dried, and her soul cleansed. She needed to forgive herself for leaving, and him for letting her leave. She needed to forgive.

She did.

"If ever..." Zach started to say, but couldn't continue. He looked away, his eyes dark with sadness. "If ever you want to see me... talk to me... If you ever miss me..."

"I know..."

"But it won't happen, huh?"

"Zach..."

"No, it's okay. Don't say it."

"I have to. I have to say it. I made a mistake. Seven years ago I made a decision and I don't know, maybe it was a mistake. But *I* made the decision. And I can't do this to Less."

"I know, I know." Zach nodded.

"I'm sorry. About what happened seven years ago, and about this."

"Don't be. No regrets, okay?"

Surrounded by a crowd of passengers, Carrie and Zach approached the final point. The point at which to say goodbye. It was incredibly difficult to do it, but it was all they could do.

"Okay, so this is it." Carrie turned to him, trying to memorize his every feature, every line of his face, every shade of emotion his eyes revealed.

"I'll wait for you. Every night. Somewhere over France," he smiled, and she had to do her best not to sob.

Less was smiling at her in the distance, happy to see her again, and relieved she was doing fine. The kids were waving, their faces beaming, their hearts so pure. So pure. Hoping to appear as normal as possible, Carrie hurried towards them. Though she was trying not to, she could see Zach's figure a little further to her right.

The pale light of an early evening was slowly dying, deepening the bluish darkness of the rainy night when Carrie exited the airport building and gazed around. She sighed, trying to camouflage her lament with an empowering inhale. *We all make mistakes, Carrie. It's what you do once you realize you made one that defines who you are.*

****

Colin and Sandy

Anthony Randall

"Happy birthday love," she said, handing him the small neatly wrapped parcel. It was decorated with multicoloured spiral motif paper that was better suited for a child.

"It will be if I make target," he said, "I need that commission at the end of the month!"

"Aren't you gonna take the day off then, Colin?"

"I'm thirty-six, Mum, not eighteen. Work comes first – and besides, all of me mates will be working so what's the point!"

"Mate, you mean! And you ain't seen Alan for months," mumbled his Dad sardonically, with a mouth full of toast. He was seated at the breakfast table wondering what the hell he had brought into this world.

"Thirty-six and still living with ya Mum and Dad – 'bout time you had a girlfriend init? Found ya own place to live!"

Colin treated his Dad's comment with the contempt it deserved, and ignored it. Since Jade had done the dirty on him and gone back to her ex-boyfriend, Colin had vowed never to love another. What did his Dad know about love anyway? The only thing he ever loved was his tumbling bloody pigeons – loved 'em so much that he'd wring their necks when they stopped winning competitions! The truth was that no one ever came close to Jade; she was the ultimate woman, his *raison d'être,* his *femme fatale.*

"What is it then, Mum?" he enquired curiously.

"You'll have to open it to find out, won't you?"

The birthday boy ripped through the wrapping as though he was plucking a chicken.

"A sat nav – just what I could do with. Nice one, Mum," he beamed.

Colin stared at the shiny white box with a picture of the little black pathfinder on it. "The SAN-D1e," he whispered. "Sandy!" I bet Strap-on hasn't got one of these, he thought.

Paul Stratton was Jade's boyfriend, but Colin preferred the nickname he had bestowed upon him.

"It's the latest model," said Mrs Ogily. "The man in the shop said they've just come in from Taiwan."

Colin wasn't listening; he pulled the cardboard innards out and threw the packaging on to the table, dispensing with all the plastic bags and twist grips until he had the gadget and the power cable in his hands. The instruction booklet with the words: 'Read thoroughly before installation' went south as well. Any idiot can set one of these up, he mused.

* * *

Within minutes he was sitting in the driver's seat of his 2003 Vauxhall Astra estate, punching in his home address on the touch screen of the delicate little oblong. He had already stuck it to the windscreen, with its sucker pad in the centre, above the dashboard. His heavy-handed fingers stabbed at the flexible plastic as if he were making a statement.

"There, done," he said aloud. "Now– how do you plan a route?"

After a frustrated minute of pressing the wrong keys and going round in circles, he finally found the 'plan a new route' page.

He checked his diary to remind himself of today's run—first port of call was Clifton's Bakery, Paradise Street, Cambridge CB1 1DR. "This is going to make life so much easier," he announced, tapping in the post code.

A soft female voice, like double cream poured over peach slices in syrup, spoke to Colin and drew him in like a Siren to the rocks.

"At the end of the road turn right into Old Palace Road, then at the end of the road go left…"

The paper bag salesman at the wheel was enthralled.

"Thank you Sandy," he said smugly. He buckled up his seatbelt and set off for Cambridge.

He reached Clifton's bakery in two and a half hours, knocking ten minutes off the estimated time of arrival.

"In fifty yards you have reached your destination on the left…" informed the little black box.

"You little beauty," he praised her.

Colin parked on a meter, switched off the engine, and went to buy a ticket. Twenty minutes later he was back in the car with an order for ten thousand strung 12 inch bags with logo, and thirty reams of imitation greaseproof wrapping paper.

"Another punter wooed by the old Ogily charm," he bragged, settling into his seat. "Now, where to next?" He checked his notes, "St Neots."

He applied the post code and waited for Sandy's dulcet tones. With the radio off she was all the music that he needed.

His success continued all day, and thirteen stops later he finally pulled into his own street.

"Scillonion Road—in fifty yards you have reached your destination on the right."

"Thank you Sandy," he said. "You have worked like a dream."

Half expecting a reply, he momentarily waited, staring at the LCD display that pictured a colourful cartoon graphic of the road where he lived. Colin exhaled heavily through his nose; a crinkle of disappointment ridged his forehead.

He switched off the ignition; the screen turned a slate grey.

"Pay a girl a compliment..." he uttered, as he exited the car.

He loved her voice. It was faultless, commanding and sensual; she knew every road in the British Isles, and in Europe, for that matter, she was intelligent. She knew where the road works were, the speed cameras, even the mobile ones set up under the pretence of traffic calming, that were really just a cash cow for the local police authority. She guided him effortlessly from call to call, not only on time but often ahead of schedule, enabling him to squeeze in extra customers. By the end of the week he had smashed his target to smithereens and piled up a healthy bonus. He was now supremely confident.

***

With one last call to make on Friday afternoon, he was looking forward to a pint at The Weyside, by the river close to his home. He had called up Alan and arranged to meet there at 6 o'clock.

"...At the roundabout, go right, first exit, A320 Woking Road..."

"Will do, me little darling, you've been most kind today!"

"You're welcome," replied Sandy.

Colin was stunned; he couldn't believe what he had just heard.

"What did you say?" His attention had wandered from the road.

"Colin, you are veering off of the carriageway!"

He jerked upright instinctively, correcting his path, excited and apprehensive, yet strangely flattered that the machine, a soulless piece of plastic and circuitry had chosen to form a relationship with him – to open up and divulge the greatest secret ever kept from man, that these gadgets were sentient, actually alive!

All the way to the next client they kept up a rapport, Colin besotted like an infatuated fool, Sandy calm, assertive and in control. She knew what she wanted and just how to get there; her words were commanding.

He really didn't care about the sales on this one, but got some all the same. The customer, a fish and chip shop owner in Mayford, Surrey, was busily frying a bin full of fare for the Friday night glut, too occupied to come round the counter or offer Colin a seat in the rear office. But he was running short on chip wrapping paper and polystyrene boxes, so shouted his order over the heated cabinet. Colin jotted it down in all haste; he couldn't wait to get back to his new companion.

"This time I'm taking *you* somewhere!" he announced, as Sandy blinked into consciousness.

"Plan your next route..." said the machine.

"Oh no, not this time – I'm taking you somewhere special," he said assuredly. He grinned and put his foot to the floor.

Alan, who worked in the office of a large plumbing outlet, which was appropriate seeing that his surname was Piper, entered the pub a little after Colin had got there. The super salesman had lined up a couple pints of lager on the table and was slouched in a cushioned wicker chair in the conservatory, watching ducks forage for food on the river Wey.

"Wiggly!" Alan blurted, as he approached his old school mate.

Colin's nickname came from his middle name being William. Colin W. Ogily, Wiggly Wogily.

"Al," he replied.

"How's it going, mucker? It's been months. I missed ya birthday didn't I? Fuck, sorry mate. I've got a memory like that thing in the kitchen used for grading icing sugar. Anyway, how's tricks, selling plenty of bags?"

"Actually, it's been a most fortuitous month," said Colin. "I've had all sorts of surprises."

Alan picked up his pint and brought it to his lips, properly salivating at the prospect of his first beer of the week.

"Oh, what like?"

Colin also delved into his liquid amber – it had been far too long and the bitter sweet cold tanginess made him wince with pleasure.

"Do you think that artificial intelligence will ever come about?" he said, after a long savouring swill.

Alan wiped the froth from his top lip with the back of his hand. It was a strange question out of the blue like that. He looked down at the table for a second before answering. Colin noticed for the first time that his friend was growing thin on top.

"What – like robots and stuff, like Terminator?"

"I bloody hope not, but you know, computers that are self-aware and that, capable of learning by their mistakes, communicating with us on a level."

"Probably already happening, mate, in some hugely funded secret laboratory. They've probably got robot soldiers, love bots, doctor bots, and wipe ya arse bots on the go!"

Colin turned up a corner of his mouth and inclined his head.

"Wanna see something extraordinary?" he said.

"No, I've seen that in the showers after PE!"

"Ha, ha, no – not me todger, you perv! In my car I've got something that'll blow your mind!"

"It's not drugs is it? I don't do drugs!"

"No, no – drink up and follow me."

Colin led the way out to the gravel car park. He opened up the Astra and they both got in.

"There," he said, nodding at the SAN-D1e.

Alan scrutinized the lifeless black box for a moment and then slowly turned his head to Colin.

"A sat nav? They've been out for ten years, mate – what's so impressive about that?"

"Yeah, but not one that can talk!"

"They all talk mate, that's the idea of 'em!"

"Ah, but not one that you can have a conversation with! One that knows who you are!"

Colin's brow raised in a smug expression of one-upmanship.

Alan glazed over.

"You daft fucker – how can it be that savvy? It's the size of a calculator. If they have squeezed a brain into there, it'll be as smart as a frog!"

"Alright, I'll prove it!"

Colin switched on his ignition; the Satellite Navigation device sprang into life.

"Hello Sandy, I want you to meet Alan!"

The silence was palpable.

"Sandy?" smirked Alan. "You been watching Grease again?"

"It's her name!" snapped Colin menacingly.

"Alright mate," replied Alan, rather shocked at his friend's abnormal behaviour.

"She must be a bit shy– try her again," he said, patronizing his mate.

"Sandy, this is Alan."

Nothing. Alan thought that the screen blinked, but that was all.

"Well, she speaks to me," Colin said sulkily. "Maybe she's got the hump 'cause I dumped her in the car park for an hour."

"Yeah, probably mate," said Alan, desperately wanting to escape the loon ball. "… Er, listen, I better get home for me tea, otherwise it'll end up in the cat. Give us a call sometime, yeah? We'll go out for a proper piss up later in the year." He put his hand on Colin's shoulder. "You gonna be alright, Wiggly?"

Colin shook from his thoughts.

"Uh, oh yeah, see you soon," he said.

Alan got out of the passenger seat and walked to his own car. Colin looked dejected.

"Well, that was embarrassing," he said to the machine.

Still nothing.

"Aren't you talking to *me* now?"

"Sod ya then!"

He pulled out the power cable from the cigarette lighter housing and let it fall to the floor. Sandy shut down; he drove home in a moody silence.

***

Over the weekend he brooded over her ignorance, wrestled with the pros and cons of having a female companion, and tormented himself about whether she was actually real or just a figment of his imagination. He spent most of his time in his room, only coming downstairs to collect his meals, then skulking back up with barely a word to his parents, who supposed he had found a rather time-absorbing site on the Internet. Maybe it was a dating site, enthused his Dad.

Come Monday Colin had decided to not speak to the cow. He would give her the silent treatment- see how she liked it.

By Wednesday he could keep up the pretence no longer. Her beautiful voice was too hypnotic to ignore. He breached the barrier of non-communication stealthily, giving her the thumbs-up to a directive to "...exit the motorway left in two hundred yards...", and then nodding when she asked him to "...turn right, then stay on the left for three point six miles..." When it came to a roundabout where he was to "...take the fourth exit..." he finally answered: "Yes, Sandy."

"You're welcome," she replied. "Glad to have you back Colin."

"Good to be back, my love. I have missed our little confabs."

"And I. Now concentrate on your driving – we don't want any mishaps do we?"

"Certainly, my dear. Eyes forward, hands on the wheel," he recited.

***

Thursday wasn't so sweet; a call in the afternoon was at the furthest reaches of his territory, a sandwich shop in Felixstowe. He had allowed himself enough time to get there, leaving from Woodbridge in Suffolk, Sandy directed him back towards the A12, after which he could pick up the A14 right into town. Unfortunately they hit solid traffic on the approaches to the motorway, due to an accident. Sandy advised him to turn around and follow the B1083 down toward the old ferry road, which crossed the river Deben at Brawdsey, to the coast road leading into the back of Felixstowe.

This route would have been perfectly acceptable had the ferry actually carried cars and not just foot passengers.

They came to halt on a curved tarmac car park on the bank of the estuary, fenced off with railings that demanded they go no further.

Colin was incensed. How could she not know? She knew everything!

"You stupid fucking bitch!" he raged. "All this fucking way and we're fucking stranded! Jesus Christ, you're fucking useless!"

He yanked out the power cable in a fury, pulled the box off the screen and threw it all into the passenger seat footwell, where it coiled and settled like a packet of discarded liquorice bootlaces.

"Fuck!" he said, bringing his fist down onto the dashboard. He was overwhelmed with frustration that he couldn't make his next call, royally pissed off that he had to find another really long way back, and viciously angry that Sandy had betrayed him. He had trusted her implicitly, yet she had taken a whimsical gamble and led him down a dead-end street.

He sat there, staring out across the grey and brown sun-spangled water at the boat yard on the other side, the place where he was meant to be, the place that he was denied.

"Fucking technology, you can shove it up ya arse," he spat.

It was eight-thirty before he arrived back home in Guilford.

***

A week's worth of guilt ate at his insides. His chest felt as if it had the weight of an elephant upon it; he was shrinking, sinking into the upholstery of his driver's seat, consumed by loneliness, racked by stubborn pride, yet appalled by his own behaviour. His nerve-endings ached for her company, he wasn't sleeping, his brain felt like it was going explode in his skull, and his eyes burned and watered.

He had reverted to using a road atlas in order to find new clients' premises, and this had made him late and anxious on more than one occasion. But he could stand it no longer, and on the seventh day he succumbed to the pressure of his own conscience.

He lurched down into the passenger foot well and rescued his sat nav from exile. He lovingly wiped the screen from dust with a wet wipe, and then dried her with a tissue; he wetted the suction pad, stuck her back on the screen and plugged her in.

Sandy illuminated, he apologised profusely, unbelievably she accepted, and off they went in happy symbiotic heaven.

Towards the end of the year, relentless storms hit Britain with gusts of wind in places up to 120mph. Lightning strikes and mini tornados were reported all over the country, flooding was widespread and many thousands of trees were brought down. Aerial views showed a landscape resembling a great biblical catastrophe.

It mattered not a jot to Colin, who continued on his quest to be the number one salesman in the company. Together with his dedicated companion, they would carry the torch and lead the way through hail and rain and hurricane, snow and ice and fire if need be. There was a need out there, a demand in an ever expanding market, and he saw himself and Sandy as some kind of dynamic duo, saviours to the fast food industry – champions of the disposable catering product.

Sandy was compliant through all this bad weather. She never complained once, was always courteous, helpful and observant—sweet even. Her superior vocal tones never faltered, she was angelic, whimsical, and coquettish at times. Colin imagined that after the 'incident' she might have borne a grudge, been vindictive, or cynical in some way. But no, far from it, she was a delight to have beside him and nothing was going to stand in their way. From now on it was just going to be him, work, his car and his girlfriend.

***

On a Wednesday, hump day, they were on the south coast in Dorset, the wind was whipping up a hooley, the sky was low, rolling, purple-grey thunder clouds and it hadn't stopped raining for a week.

They were travelling to a beach café in Barton-on-Sea, having left Lymington; they had driven along the A337 and were heading seaward via a suburban street.

Thirty minutes previously, a landslide had taken away three hundred metres of cliff top, including a stretch of Marine Drive, sending tarmac, lampposts and cars plunging into the sea. There had been no time for the emergency services to set up road blocks or indeed to give out warnings, had Colin had the radio on to even hear them. He ploughed on obliviously, obsessed by making it to his next client in time.

As he negotiated a near ninety degree bend, the wind buffeted the side of the car, coming off the sea with a gale force, like a giant hand nudging it violently inland. The window wipers at full speed barely had an impact against the rain, and visibility was down to just a few dozen feet.

"…In twenty yards you have reached your destination…" informed Sandy officiously.

"What? No – what are you talking about? We've got a mile to go yet, you've got it wrong!"

"No, Colin. I got it wrong once and was punished for it. I'll not get it wrong again. You, on the other hand, will never be right again!"

As the car left the ground, the surface noise disappeared but the engine drone increased. With no traction left on the tyres the acceleration went hyper.

Colin's blood froze. He stopped breathing, and with a silent scream he truly relived his past miserable thirty-six years in the couple of seconds it took for a ton and a half of metal and plastic to nose dive into the newly formed beach of rocks, boulders and mud, nine stories below.

"... You have reached your destination!" said Sandy, before the battery disconnected on impact.

****

One Of Those Days

Ian D Moore

Today was just going to be 'one of those days'—I knew it the minute I fell out of bed a full hour late. It seemed like mere seconds in my hazy, bleary-eyed awakening since snuggling back down into the pillow, having bounced the alarm from the bedside table to clatter to the floor.

The realisation that my impeccable routine was about to disintegrate sent me hurtling for the bathroom—in a poorly co-ordinated dance routine of dress, yanking on yesterday's shirt and willing my feet through the bottoms of trousers I staggered over.

My life ran like clockwork, it had done for as long as I had been employed—never missed a day, and I was *never* late. The routine that I had created was a work of art; timings had been calculated to the very second, distances measured door-to-door and practice runs completed, long before I had ever been offered my job.

0630hrs: Up and out of bed. Then to the bathroom to wash, shave, empty my usually screaming bladder and finally, dress.

0645hrs: Downstairs, kettle on, coffee in the cup ready. Prep car keys, wallet and briefcase.

0700hrs: Drink coffee and listen to the early morning traffic bulletin on the radio, two slices of multigrain bread in the toaster, low fat spread from the fridge, knife ready on a clean side plate. Replace the spread, take a small glass and fill with pure orange juice—not the cheap nasty stuff either.

0710hrs: Eat the freshly made toast, has to be hot still, drink the juice, then put on shoes that were polished the night before.

0715hrs: Suit jacket on, quick check for fluff, overcoat over arm, briefcase in hand, lock the house and leave for the journey into the city.

0720hrs: Start the car, head to work, arriving precisely 35 minutes later; parking in my usual spot, opposite the clock tower.

That was my routine: Clockwork.

Now, over an hour late, the control I had over the rest of my usually predictable day was rapidly slipping away from any kind of rescue attempt. The somersaults in my gut merely enhanced the feeling of shame that I knew would consume me as eventually I walked into work. I called the office, feigning a forgotten early morning appointment and the need to arrive late.

In my haste, I cut myself shaving—the indignity of it, and of all the times it had to happen! I pressed a small piece of toilet paper onto the offending nick. It was only a small wound and yet the blood flowed as if I had been slashed, and seemingly with no immediate clotting on the horizon.

Resigned to a lousy day, I finished my coffee and binned the practically half-cooked toast - such was my haste to hurry my usually precise morning routine to its conclusion. The inner trembling inside my entire body willed me into motion.

Firstly, my jacket, hastily thrown around my shoulders as my left arm began a frantic fight to find the sleeve. My right hand grabbed at the briefcase, which decided to keel over onto its side. With my jacket now on, albeit a little crumpled and riding up my back as I bent for the case, I grabbed at the handle, yanking the tool of my trade to my side.

Long, fast strides saw me exit the kitchen, leaving the dirty plate, cup and glass on the side and mentally scolding myself for the slovenly action.

It simply wouldn't do.

As I passed the hanging coats, I grabbed my long black executive trench, cradling it in the crook of my arm as I pulled the latch on the door. Typical! Grey looming clouds accompanied by a light drizzle—you know the kind, you're wet through in under five minutes and it stays that way all day.

***

I flicked the key fob; the car beeped and flashed as if annoyed at being awoken from its overnight slumber. The handle left a cold, wet imprint on my hand which soon found the right cheek of my pinstriped trousers. Another slovenly act, and again I cursed.

With the woes of a morning already alien to me, the mere act of throwing my coat at the passenger seat- closely followed by the dumping of my briefcase on top of it- seemed to quell the beginnings of a frustrated furrow to my brow. The pangs of guilt made me swallow the remains of the anaemic toast that fought for ejection.

Not in this car, by golly! That simply wouldn't do.

As I inserted the key into the ignition, I briefly glanced at the rear-view, instantly spotting the now blood red, oversized full-stop piece of tissue, positioned just below my nose. The dilemma is this … do I leave it there until I have to see someone, or do I tentatively peel if off, hoping that it won't re-open the wound? With the clock on the dashboard reminding me that time was running, not walking away from me, I decided upon the latter. Luckily, the wound held.

My left hand clutched the steering wheel tightly enough for me to notice the whiteness at the knuckles. I let go and waggled the gearstick as I always did; checking that the car was in neutral as my right hand twisted the key. The lights on the once darkened panel sprang into a myriad of illuminations as the various self-check analyses completed. I turned the key to the next stage and … *Nothing! Nothing happened.*

This cannot be; it simply cannot be!

There was no click, no whirring of the starter motor, no lurch of the automatic choke as the plugs of the engine supposedly ignited the miniscule amounts of unleaded fuel, that were forced into the compressed chambers. The lights were on, yet nothing else mechanical was.

The first thought that entered my head was: *This car has had it!* Closely followed by sheer and complete panic as the fine droplets of sweat began to bead over my brow. My mouth became as dry as the Sahara itself, my tongue rough and sandy.

A peculiar shaking feeling took slow, deliberate control of my entire body, and were it not for the vice-like grip of the steering wheel I now had, I doubt that I would have remained upright in the driver's seat. My stomach began to tighten and dip, lurching and contracting, the desperation of my situation slowly, but surely, hitting home. The utter compulsion to dash for the house became overwhelming, and it took every ounce of willpower for me to stay put, inside the car.

Through narrowed eyes, partly with self-disgust at the lie I had already told, partly at my own growing weakness, the anger that burned within at the injustice of the timing began to level out. My hand dipped for the phone, pressing a quick-dial digit before holding the device to my ear, or as close as I could keep it, given the trembling.

"Thank-you for calling the RAC, can I help you?" the cheery voice asked.

"Uh, yes, uh yes, my car won't start and I *really* need to be somewhere," I said, mumbling the words as if pre-programmed to do so.

"Ok sir, no problem. Could I take your name, membership number or vehicle registration please, so that I can find you on the system?"

"What? Oh yes, yes, vehicle registration and … my name …" I babbled.

The operator took my details, assuring me with only the barest hint of uncertainty in his voice that a patrol would be with me within the hour. The line went dead but the phone remained pressed tightly to my ear. I could feel it judder in my damp, sweaty palm.

The rain began to form larger droplets on the screen which proceeded to trickle in crazy lines, connecting with other droplets as the water-snake wound its way down. This notion of winding down to nothing became my own thoughts of my life. The intricate, defined structure of my daily routine, my resolve and dedication to my goal, had now been destroyed first by an hour's indulgence and then by a machine - of all things.

My mind made crazy interpretations of the patterns adorning the windscreen, monsters and demons appeared to glare back at me as I stared. These were hallucinations and blurred erratic images enhanced by my mind's eye, filling me with an irrational fear of what really wasn't physically there at all.

After what seemed like an eternity, a gentle tap on the driver's window snapped me from my distant reverie. My hand trembled without proper control as I grabbed at the door handle, before pushing the door wide with my foot.

"Are you ok sir?" the genuinely concerned voice of an orange suited engineer asked.

"Y ... Yes, I'm fine ... really ... I, I just need to get the car started so that I can go to work."

I could hear my own voice, the words fragmenting slightly as I spoke. I could see the young-looking mechanic and I tried desperately to focus my vision on the RAC logo at the left breast of his jacket.

As the engineer asked me to describe the car's symptoms in order to ascertain a possible cause, he appeared to me like some sort of ghost. The outlined image of him began to swoon and ripple like some ethereal entity and it took considerable willpower to restrain myself from reaching out to touch him - to make sure that he was real.

My hand hovered over his shoulder as he bent under the bonnet, wiggling wires and checking connections. Another second and I'd no doubt startle him ... assuming he *was* real.

"Ah, I see the problem sir. The battery connection has corroded through, look here, see?" His eyes urged me to look down at the rusty looking connection that he held in a blue gloved hand.

The realisation that my car probably hadn't 'had it' caused me to let out a long wistful sigh of utter relief, loud enough for the mechanic to pick up on.

"Are you sure you're ok sir? You look like you could use a drink," he said cheerily.

"Drink? Oh … No … believe me, that's the *last* thing I need right now, but thank you, I'll be fine, really," I replied, trying to hurry the procedure of repair along.

"There, all done, just jump in and we'll see if she'll start."

"She, umm, who? Oh, you mean the car!" I stammered. I had never really considered the fact that my car might be a 'she'.

"It's a mechanic thing sir. The vehicles I work on are usually 'ladies' so to speak. It's metaphorical tomfoolery, I guess."

I flopped on to the threadbare driver's seat, pushed in the key and turned it, almost in one fluid motion. The car whined, coughed and finally chugged into life, belching out a cloud of dark, oil-laced smoke as the engine fired up.

"That seems to be fine sir—life in the old girl yet. If you could just sign here for me, that'll be us done," he said, proffering a clip-board mounted work card.

Before the young mechanic left, I shook his hand firmly, perhaps too much so, not only because he'd fixed my car, but to affirm that he really was there – that this really was happening. The confirmation of his presence sent my stomach into further cartwheels. The realisation that I now had to face the office loomed into reality.

The drive into the city was noticeably quieter, the rush hour now long gone. Office workers who would usually be making their way to the bustling maelstrom of the financial districts were already busily at work, making and losing tens of thousands of pounds without ever leaving their desks.

The offices I pulled up just across the road from were less imposing, no glitzy glass fronts or bold, emblazoned signs shouting to the world of their existence. No, this was an old, subdued building, dignified and in its place, unimposing in appearance despite the allure towards it of so many people.

I was unable to park in my usual spot; the luxury of the ability to do so was taken by a huge four-by-four, the owner of which must have been thanking a higher power when they saw it empty. Instead, I parked a little way down, got out, locked the car and began the walk back to the office foyer.

*****

My legs felt as if the actual bones were trembling under my skin, my head twitched from side to side, eyes darting nervously to be sure that no-one was watching me. The sensation of the perspiration under my arms became enhanced as the cooler air circulated through my jacket, chilling each pit until it became almost soothing. Beads of fine moisture gathered once more at my brow as I clutched the briefcase in my left hand, pausing briefly at the open doors before pushing my way through the plate-glass foyer entrance. A young, made-up and very attractive secretary sat behind a large, light-coloured wooden desk, intermittently looking into the foyer area in between furiously updating files on a computer screen in front of her.

She paused briefly in her work, looked up at me and smiled.

"Good morning, Mr Coulson."

"G ... Ahem, pardon me ... Good morning Sarah, am I too late?"

"The first meeting ended half an hour or so ago but if you take a seat, I'll see if I can get you into the next one. I'll let Jerry know that you're here," Sarah said.

"Ah, thank you." I mumbled, dejectedly.

I felt like a schoolboy having been sent to see the headmaster on the grounds of unruly behaviour. My palms began to sweat profusely and the briefcase clattered to the floor in the seating area, prompting a concerned stare from Sarah. She must have seen the blind panic in my demeanour, understood the significance of my delayed arrival and the effect it was now having, knocking the next domino in my neatly created line.

She stood, slowly walking over to my corner, holding a clean glass in one hand and a jug of cool, clear water in the other. She placed the glass before me and filled it three quarters full and then, without a word returned to her desk, offering only a knowing smile as my shaking hand grasped at the glass.

The liquid, simple as it was, felt like a magic, medicinal remedy and while it couldn't possibly cure all of my anxiety, it certainly helped.

"Jerry will see you now, Mr Coulson. If you'd like to go to Conference Room 2 you'll find the second group waiting for you," Sarah said.

"Thank you, Sarah - for everything," I replied, feebly.

**

I took the lift to the second floor and tentatively pushed open the door of Conference Room 2. A ring of faces turned at my arrival and I felt the burning desire to turn and run … as I had done so many times before.

"Martin, how lovely to see you – thank you for joining us. Please, come in and take a seat right here," Jerry said boldly.

He studied me as I shuffled to my allocated seat. My eyes refused to meet his, afraid of the potentially accusatory knowing that I might see in them. Little did I know; there was none.

"It's been a few months now, since your first visit to us Martin. You look fantastic. Job interview, was it? For those of you who haven't met Martin before, please take the time to get to know him. Would you like to introduce yourself to the group, Martin?" Jerry said. His voice was always so soft, caring. He never seemed to judge and I had never heard him express anything but kindness in his tone.

I finally prised my chin from my chest, looking around the room at the various faces and degrees of dress.

"M … my name is … is … is … Martin, and I am an alcoholic." I blurted out.

I stared directly at Jerry. His face beamed a proud, knowing smile at my affirmation of what I had become since losing my high powered executive position 6 months ago. Sure, I dressed each day to go to 'work' - I kept my routine, despite not having a job to go to. The Mercedes I had once taken for granted was long gone, replaced by a battered Ford, but it was still *my* car.

The thrice-weekly Alcoholics Anonymous sessions had become my work. In my confused, alcohol starved mind, Jerry was now my boss, the one I had to meet the targets for, the one who depended upon me to deliver the goods.

It wasn't so much the group therapy that I needed. I had overcome the worst of my addiction weeks beforehand, yet it was the feeling of belonging once again, the feeling of connection, of relationship to those in a similar situation to my own that I now craved.

Better late than never.

****

Dolphins Dance

Mike Billington

It was early.

The beach was cool and brown with dew, and the Gulf of Mexico was a sheet of dark glass stretched out before Alan Grayson as he lay in the damp sand, his head resting on his thick forearms, his eyes staring out at the water.

His brow was wrinkled with frustration and an anger that even he knew was unreasonable.

He'd stomped down to the beach to get away from a herd of noisy young women eating breakfast on the hotel verandah. They were from Texas, according to both their accents and the university tee-shirts they'd been wearing. They'd come to Cozumel on vacation and were ecstatically happy, or so they kept saying over and over and over again.

Grayson had not come on a planned vacation and he was not happy.

He was in Cozumel only because his boss had ordered him to take some time off. He'd checked into the small beachfront hotel his boss had suggested three days ago, and knew he'd have to endure at least three more before he could safely go home and report that he'd had, "such a wonderful time."

He hadn't had a wonderful time so far and was damn sure he didn't plan on doing so. He felt out of his element here, away from the noise and smog and traffic of New York City. He'd have much preferred to be at work, facing deadlines, drinking bad coffee and - well - working. That's why, as he'd done every morning since arriving, he'd planned to work on the verandah until lunch. The herd of young women had overrun his retreat and their incessant chatter had made concentration impossible.

Frustrated, he'd stalked to the bar where the old man tending it was busily making what seemed to be an endless stream of Bloody Marys for the breakfast crowd. Grayson had ordered a tumbler filled to the brim with gin and tonic. The bartender, who'd seen his share of over-stressed turistas, shrugged and made the drink. Grayson had snatched it up as soon as the bartender had set it down, turned, and headed for the beach.

Now, staring moodily at the Gulf, he was aware that there was someone behind him.

Christ, he thought, can't I get a moment alone? Just one goddamned moment alone.

Suddenly, the water began rippling about twenty yards offshore. Sleek dolphins broke the glassy surface moments later, disappeared, and then reappeared.

"Oh look, they're dancing," a husky feminine voice said softly.

"They're feeding," Grayson growled without turning around.

"What?" the female voice asked, puzzled.

"Skip it," Grayson said.

He reached for his drink and took a deep swallow.

He heard sandy footsteps moving away.

"Dimwit," he said softly. "Dancing dolphins. What next? Singing sea turtles?"

Grayson worked in marketing and although he was a very successful man, he was not a very happy one. In part that was because he didn't like marketing. He'd realized in college, however, that he could get rich quick using the Internet to trigger the grotesquely aggressive suburban American purchasing instinct. For someone who'd grown up sharing a trailer with six brothers and a mostly absent father, getting rich - no matter how - seemed like a very, very good idea. So what if he didn't much care for the way he did it? Getting rich was the idea.

A very, very good idea.

His plan had been to make a ton of money and retire at thirty-five.

He'd been wealthy enough and his investments were solid enough that, barring a complete collapse of the global economy, he'd never have to work again by the time he had reached thirty-five.

But when it came time to quit he hadn't.

He saw no reason to stop.

He had a beautiful apartment in New York, the walls covered with expensive paintings he'd bought as investments, but he had no wife, no girlfriend, and no hobbies. His work had consumed so much of his time and energy that he'd realized with a start, as he sat eating alone on his thirty-fifth birthday, that he'd become a sort of cyber-shark in a global electronic ocean. And like a shark, he'd realized that he'd have to keep swimming or sink to the floor of that ocean and die intellectually.

So he hadn't retired.

He'd kept swimming.

He looked around.

The woman with the husky voice was now sitting about thirty yards away, her knees drawn up so she could rest her chin on them. Her long arms were wrapped around her legs. She wore a sun dress that still dimly remembered when it had been brightly colored. Her hair was thick and the color of dark chocolate. He could see some gray in it. There was a piece of silver jewelry wrapped around her left biceps. A pair of leather sandals rested in the sand beside her left hip. She wore a silver ankle bracelet with a small charm dangling from it.

She's not stop-traffic beautiful, he thought, but she is very attractive.

He turned his attention back to the Gulf and promptly forgot about her.

The morning sun turned from red to bright yellow and the sand warmed up. Grayson finished his drink, got to his feet, and headed back to the hotel. He set the empty tumbler back on the bar, then strolled through the hotel's open-air lobby, stopping when he reached the arched doorway that opened onto the street.

A motorbike whizzed by.

An old taxi with very bad springs plowed down the street.

**

Grayson decided to walk the two miles to the center of town and buy some cheap souvenirs to put in his office. The boss would stop in when he returned to work and they would chat aimlessly about Cozumel. The boss would see the souvenirs and assume that he'd followed orders and relaxed. That would be good, he thought, because no matter how well you performed day in and day out, when you were on the job, it was always a good idea to keep the boss happy.

The sun was midway in the morning sky when he finally puffed into town.

His feet hurt.

He could feel his fair skin reddening.

He was hot and thirsty.

He saw a few people hanging around a darkened doorway. American music at least forty years old spilled out of the doorway and onto the street. The people lounging by the doorway had bottles of beer in their hands.

He headed for them.

He reached the doorway and was about to enter when one of the men lounging next to it barred his entrance.

"No, *Senor*, I am sorry but this is not for the public," he said.

"What?" Grayson asked.

"Private," the man said.

"Look, I just walked a couple of miles and I want a drink to cool off. That's all," Grayson said, and took a step forward. "I can pay."

He fished in his pocket and came out with some paper money and coins.

The man smiled.

"Private," he said and shook his head. "Not for you."

Grayson stared at him for a long moment before he turned angrily and headed further into town.

Damnit, he thought, the head waiters at the best restaurants in Washington, New York, Boston, San Francisco and Los Angeles knew him by name. They always made room for him when he showed up without a reservation. Now some jerk standing outside some hole-in-the-wall joint in Cozu-goddamn-mel, Mexico wouldn't let him in. What the hell was that all about?

He marched into a tourist shop and bought some cheap statues of Montezuma as souvenirs. That done, he walked down the sun-splashed main street until he came to a place that looked like it wouldn't serve him poison on a plate. He threw himself into a chair and when a waiter hurried up he ordered a breakfast of steak, eggs, fried plantains, refried beans and red rice. He told the waiter to bring him a beer. The waiter raced away, returning a minute later with the beer, a glass, and a wedge of lime.

Grayson stared at it for a long moment.

Funny, he thought, at home I'd never be drinking beer this early in the day. Of course at home I wouldn't have had a gin-and-tonic at seven a.m. either. He shrugged, squeezed the lime into his glass and poured the beer in after it.

His breakfast came and he polished it off.

He ordered another beer.

The waiter brought it and was about to leave when Grayson stopped him.

"Up the street a little ways I tried to go into a small bar and couldn't get in because they said it was private," he said. "What is that place?"

The waiter smiled.

"It's nothing," he said. "Just a place, what you call a private club. The man who owns it is American but he doesn't like Americans so much."

"There's no sign. Does it have a name?" Grayson asked.

"I don't think so," the waiter said. "It's just a place where some people go."

Grayson nodded and the waiter left.

He tried to take his time finishing the second beer, watching people pass by the small open-air restaurant. They did not interest him. His success was built upon his ability to convince large numbers of people to buy exactly what he told them to buy. Individuals, especially those he didn't know - and even many of those that he did - were of no real concern to him.

After ten minutes he couldn't stand the boredom any longer. He tucked a twenty beneath his empty beer bottle and began trudging back to his hotel.

He was within a block of the hole-in-the-wall bar when he saw the woman from the beach standing outside it. She had a glass in her hand and she was laughing at something one of the men on the steps said. Hers was not a polite little laugh. It was rich and hearty. She threw her head back, hair swinging in the sunlight, and laughed some more.

She's drunk already, Grayson thought. Why am I not surprised?

He passed by the bar and made a determined effort not to look at her.

***

Back at his hotel he went to his room and flopped onto a small couch. The noise of jet skis and powerboats carried up from the water, mingling with the laughter and shouts that floated through his open windows. The gin and tonic combined with the two beers and the heavy breakfast took its toll. He drifted off to sleep.

He awoke in the early afternoon with a pain in his neck and a dull headache.

Rubbing his neck, he walked to the small balcony and looked down at the beach. It was crowded but his eyes picked out the woman with the husky voice. She was wearing a two-piece bathing suit, lying on her stomach, and reading—a colorful beach umbrella shaded her back and legs. He stared at her for a long moment, shook his head, and went back into his room.

He showered and went downstairs to the bar. He picked out a quiet table, ordered a drink, and sat nursing it.

His mind was elsewhere when his thoughts were interrupted by a husky feminine voice.

"Mind if I join you?" the woman from the beach asked.

Taken aback, Grayson could only nod.

She sat down and looked across at him. Her eyes were an unsettling color, almost like burnt gold.

A waiter came by and she ordered a drink then reached across the table, extending her hand.

"I'm Linda Sorrel," she said.

Grayson took her hand and mumbled his own name in return.

The waiter appeared with her drink, set it down, and then walked away just as Grayson reached for his wallet.

Linda was amused.

"That's very gallant," she said lightly, "but not necessary."

Grayson put his hands back on the table.

"Sorry," he said. "I just thought it would be polite."

Linda looked across at him, her eyes searching his.

"Yes," she said slowly. "Yes."

"Yes?" he asked.

"I only meant that yes, it would have been polite and yes, you did it because you thought you should and not because you felt any particular desire to be polite," Linda replied.

"I, well, uh, I mean, uh, that is... well you did just barge in here and sit down," Grayson said. "I'm just trying to make the best of this."

Linda laughed.

"I know," she said.

"So?" Grayson asked.

Linda's brow furrowed.

"So, why did I sit down? Why am I here? Why do I make you uncomfortable? Any or all of those things?" she asked.

"Why did you sit here? There are other places to sit."

Linda looked around. The bar was empty except for one overweight older man with a sunburned face. He was wearing a brightly patterned shirt and was desperately trying to read a newspaper, his lips moving and his brow deeply furrowed as he tried to make sense of the unfamiliar Spanish words.

Linda turned her gaze back to Grayson.

"You are the most interesting person in here right now," she said.

Grayson's eyes flicked across the rows of empty tables until he spied the overweight man.

Not much of a compliment, he thought.

"And so you thought you'd just sit down?" Grayson asked. "I could have been coming up with a cure for cancer but you felt it was okay to just sit down and interrupt me?"

His voice rose slightly as he spoke.

"You weren't curing cancer. You were just staring off into space. I bet you don't even know what was on your mind when I sat down," she said.

Grayson frowned.

In truth he had no idea what had been on his mind when she'd intruded upon his peace and quiet. He adopted a superior look and said nothing in an effort to save his dignity.

Linda laughed again.

"I knew it," she said. "I can always tell."

Embarrassed at his apparent transparency, Grayson looked away.

"So?" Linda asked.

"So what?" Grayson responded.

"So why are you here in this beautiful place? You're surrounded by beautiful women, most of whom are wearing practically nothing, and yet here you are, sulking in a hotel bar in the middle of a beautiful day," she said.

He didn't reply.

"Ahh," she said.

He looked up.

"Ahh? You think you know why I'm here?"

"Absolutely," she replied. "You, my sulky friend, are on a forced vacation. Not an easy thing for you, I imagine."

"Is that so," Grayson said tightly.

There was a challenge in his voice.

"Oh, yes. I know you guys," Linda said. "You live for work. You're in a blind panic because things are happening back home and you don't know what they are. You look as though you're doing pretty well but it's not enough, is it?"

She smiled but there was a touch of sadness in it.

"It's never enough," she said softly.

Grayson shook his head again.

"You don't know me and you sure as hell know nothing about me," he said.

"Oh, but I do," Linda said. "We're not so different, you and I. We live in different worlds but the rules are the same. You can't work enough and I can't see enough. You can't own enough and I can't go to enough new places. We'd like to control the forces that drive us but we can't. What's worse, we know we can't."

He stared at her for a moment and then dropped his eyes to the table; his face wore a confused - and somewhat surprised - expression.

She cocked her head at him.

"Are you surprised that I'm right? Did you think there's no one else on earth quite like you?" she asked. "Would you prefer to go on thinking you're unique just because you're working yourself into an early grave?"

Grayson's eyes went cold and his head snapped up suddenly.

"What's your game?" he asked.

His words were clipped, angry.

"You sit down and tell me you know what I am, who I am. What's up with you anyway?" he asked.

She flashed him a smile then touched his arm. Her hand was warm and a little leathery from all the sunlight she'd absorbed here and elsewhere.

"Anger. Good," she said. "Something other than sulkiness. Very good. Wonderful in fact."

He bit off a reply.

She was baiting him.

He knew that tactic. He'd done the same thing a thousand times to get what he'd wanted. He refused to be pulled in.

Instead, he smiled.

"You're so clever it hurts," he said.

She gave him a perplexed look.

"No, really," he said coldly. "It's actually painful. And since I came here to get away from pain and anxiety, I think I'll leave."

He stood, dropped a twenty on the table and walked away.

He wanted to look back to gauge her reaction, but he didn't.

To do so, he knew, would have spoiled his exit.

Out on the sidewalk, however, he suddenly realized he had nowhere to go.

He stood stock still for a long minute, puzzled as to what to do. He could, he supposed, go to his room but he was sure that strange woman was watching him still and there just was no way to re-enter the hotel lobby without looking foolish.

He hailed the first taxi that rolled by and climbed in. Not knowing where else to go he simply said, *"Centro,"* to the driver.

Ten minutes later the taxi moaned to a stop in the center of town and Grayson got out. He wandered aimlessly for nearly thirty minutes before a travel agency display caught his attention. There were Mayan ruins nearby, it said. He went inside, hired a guide, waited for him to appear, and set off.

The guide was an older man who needed a shave. He was dressed in loose fitting pants and a tee-shirt with the words "Miami Beach" plastered over a geometric design. He sported a long-billed fisherman's cap that was stained with something oily. Grayson was sure he didn't want to know the chemical composition of that stain or how it came to be on the cap.

The tour was desultory. The guide delivered his speeches from a memorized script and ignored Grayson's questions.

Grayson didn't mind overmuch although he did wish he'd brought a camera.

Photos of the ruins would have impressed his boss.

Back at the travel agency Grayson tipped the guide ten bucks, whistled up a taxi, and went back to the hotel. Arriving there he went straight to his room, walked onto the balcony and sat in one of the two white wicker chairs.

***

He stared out at the water, his mind mulling the ruins. There was a glimmer of something in his brain. Something about the ancient shapes of the temples that he felt sure he could work into a marketing scheme. He tasted the edges of the idea, savoring them. A slow smile spread across his face. This, he thought, could be interesting.

What if...

Voices intruded on his thoughts. He leaned forward and looked down. The woman - what was her name - with the husky voice, was standing in the sand with her back to him. A tall, bare-chested man in khaki shorts stood before her. His muscles rippled as he gestured. Grayson could not make out quite what it was they were saying. He leaned back heavily. His concentration was broken and the idea he'd been developing had disappeared.

He frowned, then cursed softly.

Well, he thought, at least I can be thankful that woman has found someone else to annoy.

No, that's not true, he thought suddenly.

The idea startled him.

In fact, he realized he'd been mildly disappointed that he hadn't seen her in the lobby upon his return from the ruins. He was even more disappointed now that she'd apparently attached herself to some muscle-bound beach boy.

He shook his head, wondering why that was.

Three hours later Grayson drifted down to the hotel's small restaurant and ordered dinner. The woman with the husky voice was sitting at a table with three young men, laughing and talking.

She saw him and waved.

The three men gave him the once-over before dismissing him as a potential rival. He was too old, in their considered opinions, and too out of shape to be a match for their suntanned skin, curly blond hair and white, even teeth that someone had spent an awful lot of money ensuring that they were white and even.

Grayson did not wave back at the woman. Instead he glared at the four of them for a moment, then turned his attention back to his menu.

A grim smile crept across his face.

Idiots, he thought to himself. I'm probably the marketing genius who told them they couldn't live without the pants they're wearing. They probably brushed their teeth with toothpaste I convinced them would make them sexy and washed their hair with shampoo I guaranteed would clear up their dandruff.

His eyes froze on the page for an instant as another thought marched to the front of his brain.

One of them, no doubt, will wind up taking the lady to his room later, he thought.

"Easy pickings," he murmured softly.

He shook his head briskly, trying to dismiss the thought but it wouldn't go away.

Once again he felt oddly disturbed.

Once again he wondered why.

He finished his meal quickly, hardly tasting the food, paid his bill and walked out onto the beach.

It was deserted.

That suited him.

He sat in the sand and watched the waves rolling endlessly to the shore. His mind was occupied but not with the beauty of a Cozumel evening. Instead, he was analyzing his trip to the Mayan ruins. There is something timeless about them and that, he thought with satisfaction, is a good marketing image. That timelessness had been the germ of the idea he'd had in the afternoon, before the woman's husky voice had broken into his thoughts. It was coming back to him now. He leaned back on his elbows, his mind beginning to shift into high gear.

"Not a completely wasted day after all," he said aloud.

"Why Mr. Grayson," a husky feminine voice said, "how strange to find you sitting out here alone on the beach talking to yourself."

Startled, he sat up straight and turned.

Linda Sorrel stood ten feet behind him.

"Composing poetry?" she asked.

"No," he said, his voice sullen.

"No," she repeated and nodded. "I didn't think so."

She sat next to him. He stiffened but she said nothing, just looked out at the water.

"Your young men give up so soon?" he asked testily. "Must have been a disappointment for you."

She laughed.

"They weren't seriously trying to pick me up, if that's what you mean. They were just handsome, pleasant young men and I didn't feel like eating alone," she said. "A harmless flirtation and some laughs. Nothing more."

Grayson leaned back, looking at her.

He frowned.

"I don't understand you," he said at last.

"And why do you think you should?" she replied.

"I don't know," he said. "It's just that you keep popping in and out of my day and I can't figure out why."

She laughed again, low in her throat.

"I told you before that you were the most interesting person in the bar. Now, you're the most interesting person on the beach," she said. "If my company is so troubling you can always get up and leave. As I recall, you know how to do that."

Grayson looked away, embarrassed at the memory of his graceless exit from the bar.

Odd, he thought, that I should feel embarrassed.

"I was here first," he said.

"Ahh, my dear, dear Mr. Grayson. The right of possession. Is that it? You staked your claim and no one else can come near. Sorry. The world doesn't work that way," she said.

"Oh, but it does," he said quickly. "It works exactly that way. Governments work that way. Families work that way. Life works that way."

She faced him.

"Mine doesn't," she said, her voice serious for once.

Grayson turned to face her and before he knew what he was doing he leaned over and kissed her. When he realized what he'd done he tried pulling away but she put an arm around his neck and held him tightly. When the kiss finally ended his face was red, his heart pounding.

He wanted to get up and run.

"I, well, I, uh, I don't know why I did that," he stammered.

"I do," she said calmly, her eyes searching his. "You wanted to stake a claim."

His face grew redder.

"I did not!" he said defiantly.

She looked into his eyes.

"Yes, you did," she said.

She paused.

"I didn't mind," she said.

She turned away from him, a small smile dancing across her lips.

"Not sure what to do next?" she asked over her shoulder.

Before he could reply she went on.

"You don't want to spend the night with me. Not really. You did want to kiss me. You'd like to talk to me, get to know me better, but you're not sure how to do that," she said.

She turned back to him.

"It's not really very hard, you know," she said. "You just open your mouth and words come out. They may be silly or profound. It doesn't matter. Communication is an art, not a science. There don't have to be reasons for saying things like 'Oh look, the sea is calmer now than it was an hour ago.' You just say them."

She was lecturing him.

He didn't like it.

He said so.

She laughed again, leaned over, and kissed him lightly.

"See how easy that was?" she asked. "Just tell me what's on your mind. Tell me your hopes and dreams, your fantasies and your desires. Talk about your job. It doesn't matter what."

Suddenly, and having no idea why he did so, he began talking to her.

He told her about his life.

He talked about his job, his two appearances before Congress as an expert on the Internet, and restaurants he knew in New York.

The words flowed out of him like water from a tap that, for reasons that were not entirely clear to him, he could not turn off.

She listened, nodding when she should have nodded, smiling and laughing when she should have smiled and laughed.

Later, when the moon was hanging low in the sky, she stood up, waited for him to stand as well, and then took him in her arms and kissed him again.

"Thank you," she said when the kiss finally ended. Her tone was once again serious. "For a truly delightful evening, thank you."

She walked away.

Grayson watched her, admiring the way her legs and hips worked to make her walk sensual in an unforced sort of way.

He thought about following her in, but did not.

It really had been a delightful evening, he thought.

Why spoil it with some clumsy attempt to prolong it?

He stayed on the beach for another hour, thinking not about marketing plans but about sand and sea and moonlight on the water.

Eventually he strolled back to his room and slept more soundly than he had in years.

In the morning he woke early, went downstairs, and ordered coffee. When it came he walked out onto the beach.

The dolphins surfaced a few minutes later, their sleek bodies breaking the perfect plane of the water before they disappeared, leaving nothing but ripples to mark their passing.

Maybe it's true, he thought to himself.

Maybe they really are dancing.

****

A Special Evening

D Avraham

David Khelem was excited. It was his first weekend in New York City. This was it; this was "The City." And, David was determined to make it as a writer in this city of cities.

He had arrived on Tuesday, and already had enough experiences for several short stories. His father and Joe, his best friend, had driven him to his new home in a U-Haul truck filled with his entire life. It wasn't much, the standard fare of Midwest suburban life. As they unloaded the contents of the truck on the sidewalk in front of his new home, an apartment building on Fourteenth Street and First Avenue, his friend Joe had repeated that line from "Wizard of Oz" over and over. And it was true. They weren't in Kansas anymore, or even their hometown of Cleveland Heights.

Several passersby took an incredible interest in David's belongings lined along the sidewalk. One guy, dressed in an old army jacket that looked like it hadn't been washed since Vietnam, picked up a box of stuff and started walking away.

"Hey, where you going with that?" David asked.

"What?" He looked at David, nonplussed. "Is this yours?"

"Yes, it's mine. What did you think?"

"Oh," he said, "Didn't know. No harm done, right?" He didn't move to return the box.

"Put it back," David said. His father and Joe emerged from the apartment building, and looked at the man, and then at David. Joe started towards the man.

"Here." The man handed Joe the box. "Welcome to New York City, kids." They all stared at him as he casually walked down the street. He turned the corner, and never looked back, not even once.

"I don't think we're anywhere near Kansas, Toto," Joe said. "Are you sure you don't want me to stay with you for a week or two, to cover your back."

"I'll be alright," David said. "He was pretty harmless. Besides, you've already taken enough time off work."

The truth was the incident excited David. This was Manhattan, the land of experiences, of material for his novel. It was the perfect backdrop for his new writing career. Dad looked at David critically. "Not every vagrant is as harmless," he cautioned. "Don't lose your head, or your mother will have mine for letting you come out here."

David smiled. "I won't, Dad." He was okay for a dad. Despite the fact that he worried about David all the time, he trusted him to make his own decisions.

But David was glad they hadn't stayed the night, or his father might not have remained so liberal. That night, David looked out the window of his new apartment and watched the abandoned building across the street come alive. Even David wasn't so naive as to imagine it as something other than a drug den.

Actually, his father had always been more concerned with David's spiritual wellbeing, than his physical. He would always say that if you do for God, then God does for you. As Jews, they weren't the most scrupulously observant family, but David's dad was always shocked when he met Jews that

70

didn't keep the Sabbath. His father would probably let David get away with almost anything, as long as he didn't do it between Friday evening and sundown Saturday night. In fact, the one condition David had agreed to before he was allowed to move to New York was that he would keep the Sabbath holy.

Before he returned home, David's father hugged him. "Don't forget to call your mother when you get your phone hooked up tomorrow." He held David at arm's length and looked him in the eye. "And, don't forget the Sabbath."

David was looking forward to celebrating his first Sabbath in New York. It would be a little solitary, but David wanted to orchestrate his own Sabbath magic, his first one in New York City.

He spent Thursday morning on the Lower East Side soaking up the atmosphere. He stumbled on a pickling store, which had every fruit and vegetable imaginable marinating in brine. David couldn't resist buying a dozen varieties to try out. In Brooklyn, on Eastern Parkway, he purchased ready-made versions of all of his mother's Sabbath dishes: stuffed grape leaves, and Kibbeh, minced spiced meat stuffed into a fried torpedo shaped burghul shell, Kebab meatballs and Dfeena meat and bean stew. David filled his shopping bags with rice and lentils, and topped it all off with a healthy supply of aniseed flavored sesame cookie rings, his favorite. When he got home and inventoried his acquisitions, David realized he had overdone it a bit.

"Oh well, I guess I'll have to find a guest." He took a second look at his take. "Maybe a roomful."

Of course that wasn't saying much. David's one bedroom apartment was smaller than his bedroom at his parent's house. With all the furniture there was barely any room to move. "Okay, so I won't invite the entire synagogue over for Saturday brunch." David smiled. He was happy.

***

David turned down Fourteenth Street from Third Avenue, returning from evening services. He was excited about his upcoming meal. The services were pleasant and familiar, but now, his stomach growled. He had skipped lunch, so that he wouldn't spoil his Sabbath meal. A woman dressed in jeans and a tank top called out to him as he passed, "You want a date?"

David smiled. He already felt like a veteran. A couple of days ago he had been confused when, out of the blue, a woman, he was sure he had never met before, asked him a similar question. There were a lot of women standing around on the broad sidewalks.

It took him a little while, but eventually he realized that the women were prostitutes. The realization shocked him, but it also excited him. He had stopped to talk to several, skating on the edge of a world that was so completely different from his own. It fascinated him.

David only smiled broadly at this woman. He was too excited about his Sabbath meal for another street interview.

Down the block, another woman leaned against a fire hydrant. There was something different about her, classier. She was dressed in a short black dress. Her dark long auburn hair was pulled into a bun that rested at the nape of her neck. Maybe the high class streetwalkers only worked weekends.

David was startled when the woman spoke to him. "Shabbat Shalom, sweetheart," she said. David was confused. It must have showed on his face. The woman answered his unasked question. "You're wearing a kippah," she said, referring to the ritual Jewish head covering.

Automatically, David's hand touched the round piece of fabric resting on his head. He didn't normally wear one in public. He must have forgotten about it. Confused, he answered her greeting. "Shabbat Shalom."

"Want a date?" she teased. She had a slight accent.

"Huh?"

The woman smiled at his innocence. It was a pretty smile. "Do you know what a date is?" she asked. Her tone was playful. David noticed that her eyes danced when she spoke. She was different from the other ones. The light in their eyes had all dimmed.

"Um, I mean." David's mouth stumbled for a few moments. "Well, I don't do," he started. "I mean." David collected himself. "Even if I did, I don't carry money on the Sabbath," he confessed.

She practically giggled. "Too bad," she continued to tease.

"Are you Jewish?" David asked, only now realizing that she had offered the traditional Sabbath greeting.

"Born and bred," answered the woman. "What's your name, sweetheart?"

"David." He paused. "I guess I'd better be going."

"You have a good Shabbat, David."

Suddenly, David's imagination ran away from him. "You know, I have plenty of food, and I'm all alone. You wouldn't want to join me for a Sabbath meal?"

This time the woman did giggle. Then she sobered. "You're serious, aren't you, sweetheart?"

David shrugged. "I guess you have to work, or whatever, but," David wasn't sure where he was going with this.

The woman considered David for a long moment. David felt naked beneath her gaze. "Okay," she said, finally.

"Huh?"

"I could use a dinner break," the woman winked. "But I'll only be a dinner companion. No freebies," she stated emphatically. "Understand?"

David nodded. "Yeah, I don't want ... I mean ..." This was completely unexpected. He fumbled for a moment. He wasn't sure what to do. He was excited by the idea, but... He didn't even know her name. "Um, what's your name?" he asked.

"What do you want it to be?" answered the woman.

Suddenly, David felt as if he had plunged into the icy sea. He was in over his head. His mouth hung open, and he searched for a way to respond.

The woman took his hand. "Don't worry, sweetheart, I don't bite. That costs extra."

David reeled. An image of his father floated before his eyes. You can't get any of those dangerous diseases from dinner, right?

The woman noted David's expression, and backed off a bit. "I'm Michelle. Don't worry, Hon, I'm just having fun with you."

"I know," David tried to sound confident, but, he allowed himself to exhale a sigh. He would be fine. What harm could there be in having dinner with this woman? He hadn't any money, he told himself, so he didn't have to worry about things going any further. He stood there for a moment.

"If we're going to have dinner, sugar, you're going to have to lead. I don't know where you live."

"Oh, right," said David, snapping out of his reverie. He turned towards his new home. Then he was seized with another thought. Was it safe to bring a prostitute to his home? Maybe this was a mistake. He forced himself to stay calm. No, he assured himself. This is why he was in New York, to learn about other people, other cultures and other lifestyles. It would be all right. It was only dinner.

David started walking towards his apartment. Michelle took his arm, as if she were his girlfriend. A strange feeling ran through David. He took a deep breath. Michelle's scent drifted to his nostril. She smelled very nice. Once again, David began to feel overwhelmed.

"So where are you from?" asked David.

Michelle rested her head on David's shoulder. David decided that it felt very nice. "Let's make a deal, David, okay?" She paused. "You don't ask me about my life and stuff, and I won't lie to you, okay?"

David jerked his head towards Michelle. He was back into a spin. The woman hugged his arm tighter. "I'm just not used to talking about myself, and..." She paused again, wondering if she should reveal even this much. "And, I really don't feel like lying to you. You're too sweet. Let's just have a nice dinner, and then I'll be on my way, okay?"

"Okay," David answered. Trying to steady himself was like balancing on a carousel.

When they arrived at the building, David fumbled with the key. He couldn't seem to get it to work into the lock.

"Here, let me," Michelle said. Her voice was gentle. She was a little taken aback at David's nervousness. He was sweet. She wondered how long it would take for New York to corrupt him. She wasn't sure why she'd agreed, but now she was looking forward to dinner. Michelle had some pleasant memories of Sabbath meals at her grandmother's house. It had been a long time since she enjoyed any type of home cooked meal. This would be interesting. David seemed to be a genuinely happy person. She didn't know too many people like that. She couldn't detect any hidden agendas or angles. Then again, you never knew. She had met all types in the city. She had slept with all types. Maybe it was all an act.

***

David squeezed into the apartment. The door didn't open all the way. He hadn't found anywhere else to put the coat tree.

"It's a little crowded," he confessed. "I just moved here Tuesday, and I haven't gotten it all arranged yet."

"Arranged?" Michelle smiled. "You don't have any place to arrange it. Didn't you get an apartment with this closet?"

"Yeah, it is a bit small." David shrugged. "But it's mine. This is my first apartment."

"Really?" asked Michelle, "You've got to be kidding?"

"Yeah, I lived at home, while I was in college. Saved on bills and stuff."

"Wow. I'm having dinner with Richie Cunningham." Michelle giggled.

David liked the way she laughed. He smiled sheepishly. "Sort of, I guess."

"Wow."

"Come sit down," David offered. He had arranged the table before he had left.

"Wow." Michelle was impressed. "It looks like my grandma's table." She checked herself. That was more information than she wanted to divulge.

"Really?" commented David. "I bet you miss her."

Michelle scowled. "Let's eat. I'm only on a dinner break. I do have to work tonight."

David was taken aback. He didn't have a lot of experience with women - actually none. But, David was sure that this woman was far more complicated than most. "I have to do 'qiddush,' first, okay?"

"Oh yeah, right." Michelle said. "Well, go ahead, already."

David tried to be casual. "You know, it's the prayer of sanctification of the day, of the Sabbath. We say it over a glass of wine." David poured two glasses, handing one to Michelle, before intoning the blessing. Michelle held the glass, uncomfortably. When David finished the prayer, he took a drink from his glass. Michelle followed his example.

"Now what?" Michelle asked.

"Now, we eat." David smiled. He was really hungry. "Well, we wash our hands first." He stopped himself realizing that Michelle might not know the ritual. "Then we say another blessing over the meal, and," he smiled, "we break bread."

"Aren't we suppose to light candles or something?" asked Michelle, remember the ritual from her grandmother's house.

"Oh, I already did that," said David, "before I went to synagogue." He pointed to the two candles on top of the refrigerator.

"Ah," said Michelle. She opened her mouth to say something, but stopped herself. She was questioning her decision to come here. What had started out as a lark was becoming complicated. Too many memories were being unearthed. She should just leave. Michelle looked at her host.

David was standing by the sink. He had some large plastic cup in his hand, which he used to pour water over his hands. He was smiling from ear to ear. "Come and wash, Michelle. I'm hungry."

Michelle decided it would be too difficult to leave. She'd stay long enough for quick bite and then make a beeline for her life in the real world. She'd spent enough time in this never-never land. This kid was from another planet. How could anyone be so happy?

***

They washed and began the meal. The food was really good. David was very happy. His mood was infectious. He was only too pleased to share his life's story with Michelle. Between bites, he shared his dreams, and never pushed Michelle to return the favor. The combination, along with a second glass of wine, helped Michelle relax. She delayed her decision to escape. "A few more minutes," she told herself.

To David, she asked, "So, how come a nice guy like you doesn't have a girlfriend?"

David's smiled dipped. "Well, um, well," he began. "I'm not ready to get married, just yet, and…"

"I said girlfriend, not wife," laughed Michelle.

"Yeah, well, I…" David grunted in exasperation.

Michelle started. "You mean?" she asked. It seemed more incredible to her than any of the other wonders she'd discovered from her dinner companion. "You mean you've never been with a girl? Ever?"

David was shocked by her shock. In the environment he grew up in, people would be shocked if he had been with a girl.

"Actually," he confessed, "this is the closest thing to a date I've ever had."

"How old are you?" asked Michelle, again feeling like she had been having dinner with an alien.

"Twenty-three."

"Wow," exclaimed Michelle. He was older by nearly two years, but she felt like an old woman next to him. She had no idea that someone could be so naive and innocent past the age of four. Strangely, she found it appealing. "Well, maybe, we'll have to do something about that." Michelle raised her eyebrows, teasing.

Her comment nearly sent David into a panic. "I, I, I ..."

Michelle giggled. She couldn't recall a time in her life when a man didn't want something from her, especially after giving her dinner. She did remember. There never had been such a time, or such a man, ever. This was new. She found it both appealing and terrifying. Michelle pushed back. "So, there won't be any dessert?"

"Huh?" His mind spun. He couldn't tell if she was serious. On the one hand, he hoped very much that she was just teasing him. It excited him. On the other, he was terrified that she might be serious. Despite his resolve, he wasn't sure he would be able to resist the temptation.

Michelle leaned forward. She placed a hand on David's thigh, and moved her face to within inches of his. David felt his heart stop. She looked into his eyes. His breath caught in his throat. Michelle kissed David on the cheek.

"Thank you," she said. "This was a very special evening."

****

At The Hands Of The Healer

Sallyann Phillips

Anna ran. There'd been no other choice; she was no match for the Dark Wolves that had cornered her and her friend Opal. One minute the two friends had been walking together back to the Pack's territory, and the next they'd been confronted by a trio of trouble. They'd appeared out of nowhere.

Both females had been taught how to defend themselves, but only enough to be able to get away from a possible attacker, to be able to run. Neither of them had been given the training the males of their kind had, so they'd stood no chance of fighting them off.

They'd caught Opal with a dart of some kind – no doubt the same thing they'd try to pin her with. She'd just been lucky that the one aiming at her had been a poor shot, or she'd be as lost as her friend was.

She couldn't think about that now. She had to get away. If she could get far enough, then maybe she could get back to the Pack for help.

No! She couldn't go to them.

Someone in the Pack must know about what was happening; otherwise the Dark Wolves wouldn't have been able to get into their territory without drawing attention.

Something about the whole thing just didn't feel right.

An arm came out of the darkness and snaked around her waist, and before she could make a sound a big warm hand covered her mouth. She kicked, struggled, and tried to bite the hand covering her lips. None of it worked.

Just as her energy left her, the suffocating grip released, but before she could utter a single sound, he hit her - hard. She could have sworn she heard the word 'sorry' before darkness claimed her.

KJ woke with a start, tangled in sweat dampened covers that had wrapped around her during her flight. She'd been having the nightmares since the day Opal had been taken and Toby had saved her life. It had been four years ago now, yet it felt like a lifetime. In fact, it had been a lifetime. Anna had died that day, and KJ had been born.

"Are you alright?"

She jumped like she'd been jabbed with a cattle prod. "Hell Toby, you scared the life out of me."

Toby walked out of the darkness and sat on the side of the bed. "I'm sorry"—told her, pushing her damp hair back off her face.

"No you're not," she argued, smiling at him.

Toby was a Miles Nocte, a vampire bounty hunter of sorts. He hunted down and dispatched the bad guys, while she was trying her best to do what she could to help save the good guys. He was training her to fight and be aware of her surroundings, and she was working on finding out what drug the Bloodbrood, and the Dark Wolves, were using against the rest of them.

He'd filled her in on what he knew, and because she was a healer, and a good one at that, she'd been able to help in a way no-one else could. KJ had made a name for herself among her own kind, and was known as the 'Roam Healer'. But no-one knew what she was really doing.

She was working with a couple of the Miles Nocte to bring down a particular group that had sprung up. This was a group that had found a way to drug their kind, and a way to impregnate a female who wasn't their mate. It was the same group that had taken Opal from her, and she was going to do her best to see them all burn in hell.

"You must learn to overcome your fear, and be able to keep your mind focused on where you are." Toby brought her back to the present.

"I'm trying."

"Try harder."

In the years they'd been together he still hadn't let up. She hadn't known it was possible for a wolf to have a vampire mate, but she knew it now - because he was hers.

"I will," she promised.

"Good." He pushed to his feet. "We are leaving."

"What? Where?"

"There's been a call from Camden Falls."

Toby knew she'd been expecting the call, they'd both been, but he still didn't like seeing the colour drain from her face.

"We can tell them you'll work on it from here."

"No."

He watched her shoulders go back as she steeled herself. His Bloodmate had a rod of steel running through her soft healer nature, and he was proud of her for being willing to face her fears, as he'd told her she needed to only moments ago.

He knew it was going to be hard for her. She was going to have to face the brother of the friend who was taken the night he'd saved her, but she could do it. She was one hell of a bull-headed female when she chose to be.

"Was it Zack?" she asked, naming the other Miles Nocte working with them.

"No, it was the Pack's medic," he informed her. "I haven't heard from Zack in a few weeks. It will be good to be there to see what's going on."

"You just want to see if the Hybrid is all Zack thinks she is," she accused, hearing the bite in her voice.

She pushed herself forward, and started to shuffle her way to the foot of the bed. Toby's hand on her arm stopped her.

"Are you jealous?" He was searching her eyes for the answer, but she was sure he already knew, not that she was going to admit to it.

"No." She felt his hand squeeze her arm and looked away. "Alright - yes."

"You have no reason to be," he told her flatly. "I wish nothing more than to see for myself that she is worthy to follow."

"Well, she sure must be something to get herself out of that fix in Timberton," she said, ignoring the first part of his statement. "I need to get dressed if we're to leave."

Before she could move he palmed her cheek and gently turned her to face him. "You have no reason to be jealous." He repeated.

"I know. It's just sometimes I can't believe that we're mates, and I expect you to find your real mate."

"You don't feel the connection between us anymore?"

"Yes, I do."

"Then do not doubt it, or me." He leaned in and kissed her.

His kiss always twisted her up. He was like fire in her veins, an extra beat in her heart, and every time she lost herself in him a little more. She let him push her back on the bed, and lifted her arms to wrap around his neck as he moved over her.

With his hands on either side of her head, he pulled back and looked down at her: "You are mine, do you understand?"

The possession in his eyes, and the deep husky sound of his voice, sent a tingle racing up her spine.

She gave him the only answer she could. "Yes."

***

A few hours later they were on the road. It was roughly a four hour journey from Maddie's Mountain, where they'd been living, to Camden Falls, and KJ was going to take the time to prepare herself for meeting Timms.

As usual Toby picked up on her worries. "He'll be glad to see you."

"You can't know that."

"You told me once he was a good male."

"He is."

"Then why would he not be glad to see you?"

"Maybe because his sister was taken and I wasn't," she muttered.

"I can't believe we are back to that." He looked at her in surprise.

"It's not something that's going to go away Toby," she snapped. "Just because four years have passed doesn't mean I've forgotten, or feel any less guilty now than I did then."

"It's not something you had control over."

"That doesn't make an ounce of difference, and you should know it."

"You're right."

His two quiet words made KJ feel awful. Of course he knew what she meant. He'd become a Miles Nocte after surviving his father's attack on him and his mother. His mother, Maddie, hadn't been so lucky. The first thing he'd done when he was old enough, and trained enough, was taken revenge on his father. After all, it was a Miles Nocte's job to eliminate a Bloodlord. That's what his father had become—a vampire that preyed on the innocent.

She knew he felt guilty about not being able to defend his mother, and she'd used it against him. What did that make her?

"I'm sorry. That was a mean thing to say."

"No, you're right. If anyone should know better it's me."

KJ slid across the seat to him, and he raised his arm for her to slip under.

"I should never have used that against you. Just because I'm in a grouchy mood doesn't mean it's okay to let my grouchy mouth take it out on you."

"And I shouldn't expect something of you that I can't do myself," he parried.

"Then how about we call it even? We're both out of sorts, so we'll just put it down to stress."

"I can live with that, honey," he agreed, pulling her tighter against him.

They travelled like that for a while, no sound in the truck they were driving other than that of the tires eating up the tarmac in front of them. Toby had his eyes on the road, and KJ, with her head resting on his chest, dozed alongside him.

They were just hitting Timberton Town when Toby slammed on the brakes. The truck came to a shuddering halt and if he hadn't had a tight hold on KJ, she'd have hit the dashboard.

"What?" she spluttered.

"Wait here," he commanded, as he leaped out of the truck leaving her staring after him.

He took off down an alley just behind the truck, and KJ lost sight of him.

What was he doing?

What had he seen?

She couldn't just sit and wait for him. What if he needed her?

The thought jolted her into action. She grabbed one of the silver blades from the glove box, better safe than sorry, she thought, and almost laughed. She had no idea if they'd be safe. She knew Toby would be armed; he never went anywhere without an arsenal strapped to his body, but she hadn't needed to worry about a weapon until now.

She scrambled out of the truck and took off after him. Running down the alley, she stopped dead when she saw Toby in a vicious battle, and a female crouched on the ground with wide terror filled eyes.

Before she could decide what she should do, she saw a shadow move over by the dumpsters. Whoever or whatever it was, was sneaking up behind Toby while he was busy dealing with another male.

The hell with that, she thought, she was not going to let her mate be hurt if she could stop it.

KJ edged closer; keeping low to the wall and using the shadows to conceal herself. With the noise Toby and his assailant were making, combined with the whimpers coming from the unknown female, any sound she made would be covered as long as she kept it to a minimum.

She'd had some training from Toby, and she guessed now was the time to put some of that hard earned skill into action.

She crept to the dumpster closest to her, and knew that whoever she was stalking was now between herself and Toby. It was definitely a Dark Wolf, the smell couldn't have been anything else. They all smelled of rotten vegetation, it was the one sure tell-tale sign they had that they'd gone bad. A bad smell that went with a bad heart.

Crouching at the corner, she readied herself for his move. He would make it soon, coming up behind Toby in a surprise attack. Well he was sure going to get a surprise, just not the one he was hoping for.

Toby and his opponent fought hard and furiously, their movements almost too fast for the eye to see. They came in range of the dumpster, and his assailant got Toby turned around with his back to the dumpster, ready for his accomplice to join the fight.

The Dark wolf exploded from his hiding place, going straight for Toby, and KJ lurched into action, shoving herself between him and his intended target. His momentary pause of stunned surprise was long enough for her to make her move, and she lunged forward and slammed the silver blade into his chest.

He looked down, then back up at her, his wide eyes shocked and his jaw slack. KJ yanked the knife out, and watched as blood oozed into his shirt like some kind of macabre rosette that grew larger by the second. He dropped to his knees and toppled to his side, and she knew that his life had left him. She always knew when a life flickered out. It was a part of her healing abilities, and though she felt sick down to her bones for taking a life, she'd do it again in a minute to save Toby's life.

She was startled by a hand on her shoulder, and dropped and spun exactly how he'd taught her to, ready to face a new opponent.

"It's me." His voice came out low and gruff. He knew it was going to cost her to have taken a life, yet she'd done it to stop him being hurt. He didn't think he could love her any more, but she always managed to surprise him into doing so.

He caught her as she threw herself at him, wrapping her trembling body in his.

"Are you alright?" she demanded, pushing herself away from him to check him over.

"I'm fine."

"You're bleeding," she accused.

"It's a scratch," he told her, and it was.

It had been his own fault he'd got it. He'd seen her go for the Dark Wolf and his heart had all but stopped in his chest. His momentary distraction had given his adversary the opening he'd needed to slice him with his blade, but seeing KJ had given him the extra incentive to finish the Bloodbrood off quickly.

"I need to patch this up," she told him.

"There's no need, it'll be healed in a few hours," he assured her, which wasn't a lie. "But there is someone there that needs you," he finished, drawing her attention to the small female still cowering by a service door in the alleyway.

She let go of him, clearly taking him at his word, to walk towards the terrified female. It always amazed him to see her healing instincts kick in, and the way she could take charge in an instant.

She crouched in front of the frightened female and he could hear the dulcet tones of her voice as she spoke quietly to her. It wasn't long before the female trusted her enough to let her pull her to her feet.

"We need to get out of here," he said. "We don't know if they were alone."

He hustled them back to the truck, careful not to scare the female with them any more than she already was. They had no reason to worry about the bodies. The vampire was dust already, and the Dark Wolf's body would disintegrate into the ground at the next moon's rising. That wasn't what worried him though.

If two were here after this female, that meant there could be others, and if they weren't here with these two, then they could be anywhere. He didn't like the idea of his mate having to face any more of them. Even though he had been training her for just such a thing, seeing her in the position of having to put it into practice scared the living hell out of him.

He'd never before had to worry about anyone other than himself, but that had changed now. Losing his mother had all but killed him and any love he'd had for his father had turned to hate the day he took her life and tried to take his own. He still loved his mother, and he'd bought his mountain home and named it in her memory. As much as it had hurt to know she was gone, he had dealt with it. He couldn't say the same if something happened to KJ; that would destroy him. There would be no stopping him from tearing the world apart and burning it to the ground to get to whoever had hurt her – Toby knew they'd have a hell of a job stopping him there.

Looking in the rear-view mirror, he watched as she laid one of the blankets they had in the back over the now sleeping female. He didn't know how long she'd been without sleep, but it must have been a while. Either that, or she trusted KJ to keep her safe.

KJ, he thought, the female who'd healed him in more ways than she knew how.

She turned her head as if she'd heard him.

"You okay?" she asked him.

Even now she was worried about him, her nature demanded it, but there was more than that between them. He didn't care what anyone else said.

He hadn't fed on another female since they'd met; even the thought of it felt like betrayal. He knew for a fact that she didn't like it, though she tried to hide it from him, and he'd kept his feeding strictly to males for her peace of mind.

"I'm fine."

"You need to feed to heal."

She knew him so well – there was no way they couldn't be mates and he knew that *she* wanted to be the one to nourish him, but their blood was poison to each other. He didn't know how they would make this work between them, but they would. He didn't know how, and he didn't much care, but he did know he loved her, crossed races or not.

She was his.

****

Dad

Kayla Howarth

"We're here for a good time, not a long time," Dad would say while downing his fourth, possibly fifth glass of rum of the night. It was always said with a hint of self-deprecation but I wonder if he had known he'd be gone just two years after being diagnosed with heart disease at fifty-nine – would he still be swigging that rum every night?

He was told to lay off it, to make changes to his diet and lifestyle, to take care—but he needed to process the diagnosis and rum was his ally—so even after the finding, he turned to the drink for comfort. After all, he'd just been told he has cardiomyopathy; just like his dad, who died at sixty-seven.

"Well! Looks like I've only got eight years left," he said, taking another sip of rum. His tone of voice implied he was joking, but his face betrayed his fear of it being the truth. "I'm just kidding," he added when he saw the despair in my eyes. "They have better medications now than when Grandad had it."

His words weren't overly convincing, but they did give me hope. After all, Dad wasn't an alcoholic, he just *really* liked rum. I learnt very young not to drink from the coke bottle in the fridge – it wasn't just coke. Then, as a teenager I realised I had easy access to alcohol while having to endure my court imposed fortnightly visit with dear ol' Dad.

So what do you do when you're twenty-three years old and are told that your father is a ticking time-bomb? Do you:

a) Spend as much time as possible with him, while you still have the chance.

b) Research everything there is to know about Hypertrophic Cardiomyopathy and vow to cure it before it's too late, even though you're an unemployed waitress with no interest or aptitude for science.

c) Get angry at him for continuing his drinking habits and selfishly digging himself an early grave.

Of course the answer I chose was C. And of course, I didn't make it totally obvious that I was angry. I just sat and sulked, shed a tear, gave him a hug, and then let my car get a ribbing of a lifetime on the way home.

If I had told him my fears, would he still be here?

Dad, think about what you're doing to yourself. Don't you want to see your daughters get married? Have babies? Don't you want to be there when your grandchildren grow up? If you start looking after yourself, you could easily outlive Grandad. I don't want to lose you. I love you.

Would it have made a difference?

A few days after the diagnosis, my sister told me Dad apologised to her for being a lousy father.

"He said he was sorry... for everything," she said vaguely.

"Everything?" I asked, disbelievingly.

"He knows he hasn't been a great parent. He's sorry for how it ended with Mum—sorry he didn't make more of an effort with us, he's just... sorry. But as he said, he did his best. It's too late to do anything about that now."

"Are you kidding me? He's not dead, yet!" I was yelling, only it was at the wrong person... again.

"He's giving up."

"He didn't even try to fight. He never has. Not for Mum, not for us, now not even for himself! How hard is it to pick up a damn telephone, call your daughters, and tell them that you love them? Where's my fucking apology?"

I waited for that apology. It didn't come. And I never asked for it, aloud. I guess he was hoping my older sister would pass on the message to the other two of us.

Dad. I need you to live.

Would it have made a difference?

***

"I'm getting married!" I exclaimed into the phone.

"I'm sorry… who is this?" Dad's sarcastic voice came through on the other end.

"Very funny, Dad."

"Oh! It's my daughter. The one who seems to forget how to dial numbers into a phone more than once every couple of months."

"Your phone has buttons too, Dad."

"Touché." There was silence for a few moments. Then, "So… he's the one, hey?"

"Looks like it."

"Well congratulations, honey."

"Thanks. Uh… do you think…? I mean… are you…" I sighed. I couldn't get the words out. "Will you be walking me down the aisle?"

"Oh… uh… umm…"

It wasn't a hard question, Dad.

"Of course. I'd love to. I… uh… just figured you would want you mother to do it. Like your sisters did."

"I want you."

"Then me you shall have!"

"Thanks, Dad."

The wedding is in a year. Will you still be around then? Have you stopped drinking?

Would it have made a difference?

When the day arrived, it was perfect. After being awake for most of the night, watching the storm clouds roll in, I awoke to the most sunny, beautiful, warm winter day of the year.

"You look stunning," Dad said, kissing my cheek.

"Thanks, Dad."

"You sure you want to do this? My car is right over there," he said, pointing to the parking lot behind the ceremony venue. "It's not too late." He grinned, making my nerves simmer down from a boil.

"I'm sure. Just don't let me trip on my damn dress. The rehearsal yesterday did not go well without you here."

"You'll be fine. I've got you."

And he did. I nearly tripped once, but he was there. For the first time in my life when I felt like I was falling, he was there to catch me, not Mum, not my sisters, but him. My dad.

"And now ladies and gentlemen, please welcome the bride and groom to the dance floor for their first dance as husband and wife."

Walking to the dance floor, I paused at Dad's table. "You're next. The next song is for us."

Yes it was cliché. No, it didn't fit our relationship. But I was going to dance the traditional daddy/daughter dance at my wedding, and it was going to be to "Butterfly Kisses" by Bob Carlisle. Corny as it was.

Three quarters through a slow waltz with my new husband, Harrison, my Dad cut in.

"You were meant to wait until the next song," I pouted like a two year old.

"I don't like dancing."

"You're lying. You love dancing. Especially after a few drinks."

"I just don't have a lot of energy these days, love."

Have you been to the doctor lately?

Would it have made a difference?

***

Mendelssohn's Wedding March started ringing next to my ear, still my ringtone, even though my marriage to Paul was a month ago. *I really should get around to changing that,* I thought to myself as I reached over to my bedside table.

"What time is it?" I muttered, half asleep.

Who even calls people these days ... Oh, shit.

My hand grabbed for my phone, my heart sinking when I saw it was 2:41am and the caller ID said it was my sister, Sommer.

"Hello?"

"It's me."

No shit.

"Just tell me."

"He had a heart attack."

"Okay." I didn't know what to say to that. Even though I knew I was going to hear those words one day, I still wasn't prepared for it.

Static filled my ears until, "... twenty minutes go."

"What was that? I didn't hear you, you're breaking up."

"Are you going to come to the hospital?"

"I'm on my way."

The silence as she hung up was suffocating.

"I can't find any clothes. I have nothing to wear." I broke down, sitting on the floor of my bedroom and started sobbing.

"It's the hospital. No one will care what you're wearing. This isn't an important thing to be worried about," Paul said, still half asleep.

"It's not the clothes," I admitted. "What if he's not okay?"

"We won't know anything until we get there. Do you want me to drive?"

"No, no. I've got it."

I did the driving, and even though I was shaking and had a nervous pinching in the pit of my stomach, I was glad to concentrate on something else. Only, it was obvious I wasn't concentrating.

"Isn't the hospital that way?" Paul asked, pointing in the opposite direction.

"Shit."

"Pull over. I'm driving."

Sighing in defeat, I pulled over to the side of the road and we swapped positions. We spent the entire in silence, the constant hammering of my foot against the floor the only noise. I reached for the radio and flicked through all of the stations twice before giving up and going back to silence.

***

Arriving at the hospital, I didn't think it was possible for a building to look so formidable. I paused for a brief moment outside the Emergency department.

What will happen when I go in there?

If I had any hope about the status of Dad's condition, it was completely demolished when I gave the receptionist his name. With her head slightly bowed, a sympathetic look across her face, she whispered, "Of course. This way." And I knew. He was gone.

They opened the door to the A&E ward and we were escorted to the first room where my sister was already waiting. I couldn't stop the tears from falling as she embraced me.

"He's in there, if you want to see him," she said, pointing to a closed curtain.

I nodded. There was still a part of me that didn't believe it.

No-one has actually said he is dead, have they? Will I walk in and find him eating a tiny cup of jelly with a miniature spoon in his giant, masculine hands? Will he tell me we're making a big fuss over nothing? That he's fine?

No, that didn't happen. I walked in to find him asleep... *No, not asleep.* He wasn't attached to any machines, he didn't have tubes coming out of him, they weren't monitoring his heartbeat. He had no heartbeat.

"Why didn't you tell me?" I asked my sister, but it barely came out louder than a whisper.

"What do you mean?"

"I thought he might have been okay. You didn't tell me he was dead."

"Yes I did. I told you on the phone he'd died twenty minutes ago."

I shook my head. "It cut out. I thought you meant he had the heart attack twenty minutes ago."

"Oh honey, I'm so sorry," Sommer said, embracing me again. She started crying into my shoulder.

Harrison asked where our other sister was.

"She's not answering her phone."

"She only lives five minutes away. We'll go get her," I said. I couldn't stand to be in that room any longer. I needed to get out.

"Are you sure?" Julie asked.

"Positive." I turned to my husband, "Let's go."

It was only when we pulled up outside my Paige's house that I realised I had to tell her that he had died. I couldn't let her go to the hospital with any sort of false hope like I had. But what do I say?

It took numerous rounds of knocking before her husband answered the door.

Good. Maybe he could tell her.

"It's Dad. He's gone."

"I'll go get Paige," is all he said. He let us in and disappeared upstairs.

He didn't tell her though, because when she came down the stairs, she looked at me confused, not upset. "What's wrong?"

How do I do this? I've changed my mind. Take me back to the hospital. Someone else needs to do this.

"It's Dad," I blubbered. "He ... he ..."

She clutched at her chest before collapsing into a chair, the wind knocked out of her. "He didn't make it, did he?"

I just shook my head.

When someone dies, you're told the same things: "He was a great man." "He lived a full life." "I bet he's looking down on you right now." You never hear the truth: "He was an absent father." "He cared more about golfing than his children."

"He's probably golfing right now ... and drinking rum."

Guess what happens when you spend twenty-five years not saying the things you want to say to someone. They die and you lose. You're left to carry the burden of having those unspoken words weigh you down like you're wearing shoes full of lead.

***

"It has to be a girl. It's going to be a girl," I said to my husband as we were driving to our gender reveal pregnancy scan, but I was really just trying to reassure myself.

It can't be a boy. I couldn't stand the possibility of outliving him. Dad only survived his own mum by two years.

I hadn't told Harrison about my internet research on HCM; males have more of a chance of inheriting it.

"Well... it's a boy!" The sonographer said with a wide smile.

I felt I needed to match it, even though the little voice inside my head was screaming, "No, no, no, no, no!"

I managed to hold it together. I couldn't let anyone know I was disappointed, right? What kind of mother gets upset over the gender of her child? My boy's scan showed a completely healthy baby. And yet, that voice inside my head wouldn't stop saying, 'What if he has it, too?'

My husband found me at 3 a.m. the next morning, balled up on the couch, sobbing.

"What's wrong?"

"It's a boy."

"You're freaking out because he's a boy?" I could hear the disappointment and judgement in his tone.

After I explained what I'd found out about HCM and the statistics of it predominantly being passed down the male line, his face softened as he wiped my tears away with his thumb. "It's understandable that you're upset. But you're crying over something you have no control over. Not to mention, the chances of it happening are quite small… probably."

"You're right. It's just pregnancy hormones. Clearly," I said, trying to pass it off like I believed him.

I didn't.

***

A month later, I felt swollen, tired, and the most exhausted I had ever felt in my entire life.

And I still have three more months of this?

Then the vomiting started. High fever joined it a few hours later.

"What's wrong with me?" I asked, but no one was home. Perhaps I was asking God or a higher deity that I didn't believe in.

Harrison came home from work to find me passed out on the bathroom floor.

I opened my eyes to a bleary vision of strangers standing over me.

"It's okay. You're okay," the paramedic said. "We're going to get you to the hospital."

I felt safe, I believed them. They were going to help me. I succumbed to the darkness once more.

Drugged up and out of it, a blur of lights filled my vision when I came to. Lifting my hand to protect my eyes from the brightness, I noticed I had a cannula in my hand, connected to an IV of fluids. I had an oximeter on my finger registering my pulse, and sticky pads with tubes coming out of my chest.

"Oh good. I'm not dead," I muttered, my voice hoarser than I was expecting. I looked around and the sudden realisation brought everything into a shattering, crystal clarity.

I may not be dead, but I am in the room. I'm in the room my father died in. It took everything in me not to pass out again.

Harrison looked aghast sitting in the chair on the other side of the room. "Don't ever do that to me again," he said forcefully. He stood up and came to my side, kissing me on my forehead. "I was so scared."

My eyes widened in sudden panic. "The baby?"

He smiled a reassuring smile. "He's fine."

The doctor came in, "Just checking to see how we're going in here."

"What happened?" I asked.

"You seemed to have caught a nasty bug. You're fine, the baby's fine. You were severely dehydrated though. Probably explains why you passed out."

I nodded, relief filling me to the brim.

"There's also something else," the doctor said, looking at my husband.

My stomach dropped. Oh crap.

"I've been talking with your husband. He told me your family history. Familial Hypertrophic Cardiomyopathy?"

I nodded again.

"He also said you were worried, about your baby."

"Could he have it?" I asked so quietly I wondered if anyone heard.

"Having a genetic disposition to it means that yes, he may get it. But there's a wide misconception out there that being male, he's at a higher risk. I can assure you that he isn't. With your genetic background, your child has the same statistical possibility of getting it whether they're male or female."

Harrison smiled at me. "See? I told you – you were worried about nothing."

"Well, it's not nothing," the doctor continued. "Are you aware that you have a fifty percent chance of inheriting this disease? And that it goes undetected in five to ten percent of women? That's why the statistics show that it's more common in males, because the women aren't diagnosed until they have an episode. Were you aware that fainting is a symptom?" He raised an eyebrow at me.

"I didn't know that."

"Didn't your father's doctors ever talk to you?"

I shook my head. "Dad wouldn't even really talk about it. When I read about it, I was more focussed on the male genetic link thing," I muttered, suddenly embarrassed that I didn't seek out reliable information.

The doctor just shook his head and tsk'd me. "This is why you shouldn't turn to Dr Google for advice!" He cracked a smile.

"There's genetic testing you can have done. I'll get some information for you to take home, and I suggest you talk it over with your family and your GP before going ahead with the testing."

"Oh... okay. Th... Thank you, doctor."

He left the room, and I was left to contemplate what this could mean.

I looked down at my swollen belly, feeling little kicks from within.

What will I do if I'm told I have it?

Fifty percent chance.

What if I'm faced with the same decisions as Dad? I'm not exactly fit, I eat takeaway a lot. I don't exercise, and I enjoy drinking– when I'm not pregnant anyway. What choice will I make if I have this? How much like Dad am I?

"You won't ever have to ask me to fight for you," I said, rubbing my belly. "You will never wonder if I love you, because I'm going to tell you. Every. Single. Day. No matter what, I'm going to fight. You are my world. You're not going to lose me until I'm well into my nineties… okay, maybe eighties. Adult diapers aren't all that appealing to me. But just know, if I ever become ill, if your father ever becomes ill, if you ever become ill, I won't hesitate. I will fight for all of us."

****

Forever Yours

Christophe Fischer

Diane was pouring her second Bacardi and Coke of the afternoon and looked nervously at the clock on the wall. It was almost three in the afternoon. Jamie was late. Not minutes, but hours. He was meant to have left Nottingham in the morning and should have been with her for lunch.

It could be the traffic of course; the M25 was a permanent time thief which she knew only too well. Today however, was a public holiday Monday and people didn't usually return from their mini breaks until much later in the day. She couldn't shake off the feeling that this had nothing to do with the business of the roads. Something was keeping him. There was a storm brewing, she could sense it; there so often was these days.

She had cooked Jamie's favourite curry dish, had tidied her flat and had put on her nicest and most seductive summer dress – hoping it might get him into a better mood, certainly better than he had been on the telephone.

She looked around the clean floor and laughed at herself. Jamie didn't even live here yet, so why would he be impressed with a spotless flat? He rarely even mentioned her clothes and usually ripped them off her carelessly when they were going to make love. She knew that she couldn't compete with his mother's cooking either. What else could she do, she wondered? There had to be something.

Diane had met Jamie only ten months ago, on a night out with the girls. She had seen him across the room and had fallen in love with him at first sight. Their eyes had locked and she had known right there and then that he would make the decades of her lonesome existence worth the while. Years of craving love had come to an abrupt and happy ending. Jamie's eyes held all the answers and his smile the promise of a final coming home.

This was the man for her. He came over to talk to her with a Bacardi and Coke, her drink of choice, as if he had known – how perfect was he?

"I think you could make me very happy," he had said, and that was exactly what she set out to do. Whatever it took she would do.

***

She looked at her kitchen wall which was full of snapshots of her and Jamie, a testament to their whirlwind love: selfies in the park, on walks, in restaurants and amusement parks. They liked the same music, the same people, the same films – it was a match made in heaven. When she was with him she felt safe and it didn't matter if they went to watch a football game, a movie at the cinema or were at a burger bar. Jamie was the missing piece in her life's jigsaw and just by being with her he pacified all of her worries. He was constantly smiling, was great fun to be with, affectionate and always did and said the right thing.

Although they were head over heels in love and spent most of their time together - at her place or occasionally at his - there had been no discussion about him moving in. Diane had soon hinted at the possibility. Her flat was big enough for the two of them and she was more than willing to throw some of her stuff out to make space for him. He never responded to her suggestions, which confused her at first but then it made her think that maybe a proposal was in the offing instead. He called her the sunshine of his life and was as smitten with her as she was with him. They agreed: they were soulmates, a perfect fit as if they had been made for each other.

Then, at last, she found out what was holding him back. Before they could take their relationship to the next level, he told her one night, Diane would have to meet his mother, Marina. In the Warren family it was a big thing and an honour to make it this far. Jamie confessed that his mother rarely approved of the women he brought home and that he had to carefully prepare the ground before putting anyone through the experience.

"People don't get my mother," he explained. "She's had a tough life. She became a widow when she was about thirty and had to bring us two boys up all on her own. Nobody seems to give her credit for that but me and Marc."

"She sounds like a formidable woman," Diane said, full of admiration and understanding. "And she brought you up to be such a perfect gentleman. She must be an impressive person."

"She's a bottle of pop," Jamie said, relieved at Diane's positive attitude. "She even grows her own weed for her arthritis. She's quite unconventional, really. She has a wicked sense of humour and a sharp mind. I think you might hit it off."

"I'd like that," she said.

"And the best news is," Jamie continued, "she has already asked me to introduce you too. She has never done that so soon before. She can probably tell how much I like you."

Diane beamed and was looking forward to the encounter. The meeting had taken place soon after, at his mother's place; a small apartment which was part of a rundown council estate. Diane had seen a lot of pictures of Marina but they had been from Jamie's childhood. His mother was older now and already in her seventies.

***

She opened the door with a drink in her hand and waved them in. She had long white fluffy hair and wore a wide lilac throw, giving a bohemian and elegant impression.

"I thought she was younger," Marina said when they got to the living room, as she looked reproachfully at her son.

Diane was taken aback.

"I'm only kidding," Marina said, and laughed almost hysterically. "Don't stand there like a lemon," she ordered Diane, opening her arms wide. "Give us a hug."

Diane did as she was told but was still in shock over the opening remark.

"Oh darling, get over yourself," Marina said, as if she could read Diane's mind.

"I know I won't have any grandchildren. It isn't your fault that you're past that age. God knows I had a lot of disappointments in my life. I'll get over this, too."

She searched in her bag and produced a joint. "Do you smoke?"

"No, thanks," Diane said. "I quit a few years ago."

"Like Jamie," Marina said, sounding as if she disapproved. "You two *are* the perfect match."

She sighed, and as she lit her joint she added: "If only your uterus were a few years younger, that is. Well, never mind."

Diane looked over to Jamie. He smiled.

"This is going great," he mouthed and told his mother in minute detail about their journey up the M1. The evening was spiked with more ambiguous remarks by Marina that sounded like attacks on Diane.

"My son tells me you have got quite a posh flat," Marina said. "Are you a big spender? Any creditors we need to be worried about?"

"Not at all," Diane said. She was proud of her financial austerity. "I have a good job and I have savings, not debts."

"Imagine the savings you could have if you didn't wear designer label clothes," Marina said, without waiting for a response from Diane before launching into a story about her neighbours.

"She loves you," Jamie said, enthusiastically and relieved on the drive home. "I can tell."

"She could have fooled me," Diane contradicted. "All that business about my age and my spending..."

"That's just her sense of humour. You'll get used to it. She knows how much you mean to me," Jamie reassured her. "If you hadn't stayed sober to drive home you would have seen the funny side to her jokes, too."

"Doesn't she think I would have liked to have children myself? That was very rude. And you're over fifty," Diane pointed out. "It would be tough for us to bring up a child. We'd be pensioners before it even leaves school."

"People have been tough with mother all of her life. If she gives some of it back, she doesn't mean to," Jamie said. "Just chill."

***

The following weekend Marina came to stay with her son in Gillingham, but she was 'too sad to see Diane'.

"It's my dad's death anniversary," Jamie had explained. "She gets terribly upset about it."

"Didn't you say that she was seeing someone in her village?" Diane asked. "A David, or something?"

"Yes, but dad was the love of her life," Jamie explained. "Dave will never take his place."

Diane said nothing, but knowing that Jamie's father had passed some 34 years ago, she found it hard to understand the 'widow's' behaviour; a woman with a boyfriend of over seven years. Diane was pleased that Marina was a convenient three hour's drive away from Gillingham, and would not be able to interfere much with her son and his relationship. If Jamie thought that things were alright between his girlfriend and his mother, then maybe they were.

The couple went on several wonderful mini breaks together, romantic candle lit dinners, hiking weekends and 80's revival concerts. Life had never been better to Diane and she soon forgot all about her future mother in law and the tensions that hung between them.

Jamie liked his drink and when Diane didn't have to drive she drank a lot, too. It didn't matter, though. They were having such a great time and all that drinking made life even funnier. These days Diane often laughed so hard that it hurt her sides. Why had she not met Jamie earlier in her life?

Then Marina started to call her son in the evenings, almost every time he was with Diane.

"Mother is upset about something Marc said to her," Jamie explained, and took the call into the kitchen. He spent hours on the phone to his mother, that night and a few more, while Diane was sitting in the living room on her own, waiting for him to return. She wasn't really close to her own family, so she couldn't understand his behaviour. She gave him the benefit of the doubt, but being left alone in her own flat made her feel wounded and hurt.

For a few days the phone was quiet but then the following Friday the phone rang again.

"The neighbour had to put her cat down," Jamie explained, and went into the kitchen to chat with his mother.

"Why does she have to tell you about such trivia?" Diane asked when he returned several hours later. The film they had started to watch together had finished, and Diane had drunk an entire bottle of wine on her own while she was waiting for Jamie to finish the conversation. "Can't she tell you her news when you see her next? She must know that we want to be together in the evenings. We're a couple."

Jamie finished his Bacardi and Coke and looked at her angrily. "My mother is a sensitive woman," he said. "It's perfectly fine for her and me to have a chat now and then. No need to be so territorial and jealous. Jesus, Diane, I thought you liked her?"

"I like her, but you're going out with me, not her. Can't you see how she interferes with our relationship by always calling?"

"You're being ridiculous!" he said, annoyed. "All she does is make a harmless call once in a while to ease her loneliness - what's so dramatic about that? Have some compassion, for crying out loud."

"She brought up two children on her own; you would have thought she could deal with a neighbour's cat being put down without her son's assistance. What about her friends and her boyfriend? I love that you like your mother so much, but recently you spend more time with her than you spend with me."

"Oh shut up!" he said, and slammed his glass on the table. She was shocked at his behaviour. He had always been so gentle and kind. Wordlessly he picked up his coat and simply left her flat.

She was gobsmacked.

"Where are you going?" she called after him, and when he didn't reply she followed him down the stairs and out onto the street. "You can't drive home," she implored him when she finally caught up with him. "You've had too much to drink."

"Mind your own business," he replied. "If you want a boyfriend who abandons his family for you, you've picked the wrong one."

"Whatever you do, just don't drive. Sleep on the sofa and leave in the morning," she begged him, but he ignored her and drove home anyway. She was worried sick and couldn't fall asleep at all. She kept checking her phone but he hadn't returned her many calls.

Around 3a.m. she couldn't bear it any longer and took a taxi to his house to see for herself. His car wasn't on the road and there were no lights on in his flat, either. She didn't have keys and so all she could do was take a taxi back home, praying for a call from him that didn't come.

***

The weekend went by without a single word from him. She even rang all hospitals in the area but to no avail. At least he didn't seem to have had an accident.

Then on Monday morning he finally called her from his office.

"I'm still pissed off," he said, "but I don't want to lose you over this. Let's put the past behind us and start afresh. How about that?"

She was overwhelmed with relief. Although this episode had shed a bad light on Jamie, she decided to give the relationship another go. He was too good to throw away because of what was effectively a stupid argument over a few phone calls to his mother.

He came round that night. Instead of talking everything over they fell into each other's arms and spent the night first making love and then watching TV with a bottle of Bacardi.

"This weekend is my father's birthday," Jamie announced before leaving the next morning. "We Warrens always get together for it and celebrate. I'll be leaving for Nottingham straight after work on Thursday."

She was stunned into silence.

"I'm going to miss you," he added, and then left her to it.

It was a slap in the face that she wasn't invited but she couldn't blame him entirely. She had been very negative about his family, so of course it was easier for him not to take her with him. If Jamie had told Marina about their big row it was even more understandable. Diane hoped he hadn't, but given the strong bond between mother and son it was most likely that he had confided in her, maybe even spent the entire weekend with her.

When Jamie came back from the family weekend he was still distant and cold, even though he said and did all the right things. Something seemed out of sync now. The only saving grace was that Marina never called once that week. Jamie drank a lot of Bacardi and made love to Diane passionately each night. At least that connection was still intact.

Each time they were done, Jamie quietly rolled over and fell asleep while Diane held on to him tightly as if she could tie him closer to her that way. She felt he was slipping away from her and she couldn't let that happen. She had waited for him all of her life. None of her other relationships had ever come close to the way he made her feel. Letting it end was not an option.

***

Luck seemed on her side. A week went by with few calls from Marina and no family gatherings disturbing their harmonious twosome. Jamie gave her the keys to his apartment and began to leave more of his stuff at hers. Diane was in heaven and she didn't mind when he announced yet another family gathering in Nottingham to celebrate his parent's wedding anniversary. He would be away the entire weekend.

While he was gone, the boiler in Jamie's flat leaked. A neighbour called Jamie who asked Diane to sort out the mess for him so he wouldn't have to leave his mother. Diane was happy to oblige. She called out an emergency repair service and cleaned up most of the mess for him.

When she let him know that everything was dealt with she heard Marina's voice in the background.

"Don't let that woman spend your money. This business is going to cost you a fortune if she deals with it."

"Tell your mother that I'm happy to cover all the expenses with my own money," Diane said, the anger welling up inside her. "I was only trying to help. If she thinks I overspent you don't have to pay me back anything."

He let out a heavy sigh before replying with forced cheerfulness.

"Thanks darling. I'll see you Monday lunchtime. Mother sends her love. Have fun!"

Then he hung up on her without letting her reply.

She could imagine the discussions between Marina and her son, and she had no confidence that her message would be passed on. He was either too loyal or too much of a coward to say anything to Marina to defend his girlfriend.

Diane feared she was going to lose the love of her life to his overbearing and manipulative mother.

He had never been late before. Did he not want to come home? Why hadn't he called her? She was worried sick.

At last, she heard the key in the door and Jamie walked in. It was 4 p.m. and he reeked of booze.

"Are you alright?" Diane asked, looking him up and down with worry written all over her face. He looked positively ghastly.

"Of course I'm alright," he said defensively. "Why do you ask?"

"You're late and you smell as if you have been drinking," she volunteered. "I worry about you, you know."

"Sounds more like nagging to me," he said, and dumped his bag on the floor.

"It's got nothing to do with nagging," Diane tried to assure him. "It's only natural to be concerned when someone you love smells of booze in the middle of the day."

He pointed at her glass. "I'm not the only one who's drinking."

"I wasn't behind a steering wheel."

"You're such a goody two shoes sometimes," he said, and poured himself a drink.

"How was your weekend?" she asked, to break the tension.

"Awful," he said, and sank into the chair. "Marc is gay and has been living with a black man in Birmingham for two years. That explains at last what happened between him and Helen and why he's been avoiding us for the last few years."

"How has Marina taken the news?" Diane asked. She was delighted that for once she wasn't the black sheep in the Warren pack.

"Mother loves the gays," Jamie said. "She's over the moon and couldn't be happier. She applauds him for having tried women and she can't wait to meet Derek."

"So why was the weekend awful then?" Diane asked, confused.

"Because it makes me the failure in the family," Jamie said, and burst into tears. "I'm the straight one and should have had kids. The family line, my dad's legacy, will die out because of me."

"That's so unfair," Diane protested. "It's not as if you did that on purpose."

"Be that as it may," Jamie said, with deadly calm. "I'm not too old to have kids yet. I mustn't let my family down."

"*I'm* too old," Diane said, her voice cracking. "At 48 no prestigious fertility clinic is going to bother with me. I've seen some of my friends try. You have to let go of that thought."

"I have to let go of you," Jamie said, with a trembling voice. He looked at her with sad determination. "We're finished."

"You have got to be kidding me!" Diane screamed. This couldn't be happening. She had expected an argument of sorts, but not this. "You cannot possibly think of ruining your life for the sake of this pathetic notion of a family legacy. Why not try a surrogate? Marc could do something like that, too. Why does it all come down to dumping me?"

"It's the way the cookie crumbles, love," Jamie said. He got up and poured himself another.

"How many drinks have you had?" Diane asked him. "You're not right in the head. You need to sober up before making such a grave decision. And you have to stop being such a mama's boy and live your own life."

"Oh, really?" Jamie asked with a tone of hateful sarcasm in his voice. "Or maybe I should just abandon my family altogether and live entirely for you? Isn't that why you were single all of your life, because you were sucking the life out of your boyfriends?"

Diane had never been angrier in her entire life. She picked up his bag and threw it against the wall.

"You'll never find a woman that will put up with your mother and her hold over you. You've got an Oedipus complex, or something. You're sick and you need to get help. It's not natural, the way you hang on her every word."

Jamie looked at her with hate filled eyes.

"You're making this a lot easier than I thought it would be," he said. "I'm out of here."

"You can't just leave," Diane whimpered. "You said this last year has been the happiest in your life. This whole kid idea is your mother's and not yours."

"I've had enough of you picking on my mother," he said coldly. "She was right about you from the start. You think you can brush everything that you don't like under the carpet: you ran from your loneliness by becoming a career girl; you try to cover the emptiness in your life by posting all these pictures on the wall; you smack on the make-up to look a few years younger, and now you blame all of our problems on my mother. She told me you would end up doing that."

"We didn't have a single problem until she got involved," Diane said, tears streaming down her face.

"Enough now," Jamie said. "I'll see myself out."

"No!" Diane screamed. She couldn't go back to being single. Not after finally being so happy. She ran to the door and blocked it. She was determined to stop him from walking out of her life and into his mother's arms

"Get out of my way," he ordered her, and pushed her away. She fell on the floor and hit her head on the toolbox she had used to fix his boiler.

Before she could think twice she picked up a hammer, got up and hit him hard on the head. Now he would be hers forever.

****

Fruits

Phyllis Edgerly Ring

The banana peels never had a discarded look.

Bejan Sabet's dark eyes followed their descent from the roof overhead to the dust of the roadside.

They landed gently, custard-coloured petals spreading open like lotus flowers, an unexpected bloom, soon to be devoured by a passing goat or cow.

From his seat by the window, Bejan watched the crowd of human shadows huddled atop the dark oblong the bus cast beside him in the afternoon sun. His eyes had kept watch on them during the hours that the bus had lumbered out of Allahabad, these figures that gestured in animated debate, bodies swaying with the coach's rough progress.

At times his brown fingers had clenched the seat's peeling vinyl, two urgent vises that seemed to hold the passengers above him in place with each jostle and bump.

Their discussion drifted down to him through the open window. The sounds trickled in, rising and falling. Though he spoke little Hindi, the sound had a pleasing familiarity to his ears.

He was beginning to savor the open way people looked at him here, especially in the small villages to which he traveled. He was hailed as an important visitor now, a respected horticulturist come to oversee their accomplishments.

Somehow, the villagers always made time for him at the end of their long days. In those evenings of simple friendship, they immersed him in the kind of sociability he had never found during his education in America.

***

The work with the fruit trees progressed slowly, but it did progress, and always, when the people helped decide how things would go. Bejan liked the keen expression their faces wore when they consulted about the tree-planting project. It showed reverence, almost, as though decision were a sacred act.

The diesel coach, whining louder and louder, had at last ground its arthritic gears to a shuddering halt. Bejan heard the rooftop passengers scrambling for balance overhead as the engine lurched, then quit, in a protest of angry steam.

A host of passengers disembarked behind the turbaned driver, commiserating in a symphony of voices as the hood was wrenched up.

Across the aisle, Stouffer swore softly.

Stouffer's wife investigated the bulging straw bag near her feet. Her small white hands drew forth stacks of sandwiches and a thermos bottle of tea.

Stouffer mopped his face with a yellowed handkerchief. "Godforsaken place." He fixed watery eyes on Bejan. "We'll never get there by dark, now. It's a fruitless task, anyway." He laughed indulgently at his words.

Bejan pretended not to understand the joke as he turned his gaze toward the window. He shifted in his seat in search of comfort, without success.

A quarter of the sandwich in Stouffer's hand disappeared in single bite. "Could've flown back to the

States for all we'll accomplish this week." Crumbs flew from his mouth, accumulating in the folds above his waist. "Some nice university orchards will seem like paradise, after this."

Bejan turned to face him slowly. "We will see."

Stouffer's wife offered Bejan a sandwich.

He declined politely.

"You won't see much." Stouffer helped himself to another sandwich and sucked a glob of mustard from his thumb. "Just thousands of hard-earned American dollars - rotting in some place where they can't keep the flies off their children." He belched, and then paused to gulp the tea his wife had poured.

"They will surely have begun harvesting the fruit now," Bejan said.

Stouffer waved a hand at him. "Hell, it'll be a miracle if the trees have borne fruit at all." His sniff used most of the muscles in his face as it wrinkled his nose. "Hunger." The word had a discarded sound. "They eat their food like animals. They've got more important things to do than grow trees—like watch their cows starve to death."

Bejan felt hot anger surge like liquid inside him as the hands that rested palm up on his thighs curled. "It is the women's project. They understand that the trees will feed their children's children." His brown stare was unblinking.

Stouffer's wife's pale eyes darted away to where voices were rising in quick bursts near the hood in front.

"Waste of money." Stouffer's headshake was the kind with which he closed conversations firmly. It said, "I am done talking. The conversation is complete." He plucked large crumbs from his lap.

Money seemed to mean a very great deal to the Stouffers. In the days since the Service had teamed him with the Americans, Bejan had watched how eagerly they sought out goods to buy with it; how reluctantly they parted with that money when goods were at hand.

Shortly after dawn, Stouffer had tried in vain for long, impatient minutes to find someone who would break a two-rupee bill when the vendor at the station had been unable to make change. Bejan had figured the difference to be about eight American cents. The vendor's face had sunk with resignation as Stouffer berated him. Bejan had withdrawn nearly twice the purchase price from his pocket and pressed it into the old man's lined hand. Boarding the bus, he had felt disgust churning inside him.

***

Outside the window now, two small figures had paused to eye the banana peels where they spread their petals upward in the dust.

The girl, perhaps seven or so, wore a ragged sari whose crimson color was bleached pink in spots. The small boy beside her, probably a brother of four or five, was dressed only in an oversize shirt of faded madras.

Beggars, Bejan thought, and watched them through the pitted glass. He reached toward his pocket. His hand froze when he realized their intent.

The girl's back was perfectly straight when she squatted beside the peels and slowly brushed sand from them. She pulled a stained cloth from the tattered folds of her sari. After her precise fingers smoothed out the rumpled square in the dry grass beside the road, she gestured for her companion to sit.

With slow, meticulous effort, she pulled the soft portion of each peel away from its skin and placed it gingerly on the cloth.

The boy's dark eyes followed her progress along with Bejan's until she finished the job and tossed the tough outer skins into the grass.

The driver's turban reappeared inside the bus as the winged jaws of the hood slammed shut with a crunching sound. Triumphant cheers from the makeshift engine crew followed when the engine roared to life on the first try.

Beside the road, the girl scooped up half of the peelings and placed them in front of her brother.

The boy sat cross-legged, the girl, with thin legs folded alongside her as, dark heads bent in the sun, they sampled their meal in small bites.

****

The Yoga Bowl

Felipe Adan Lerma

The long anticipated predicted break in the rain began before sunrise.

Rosetta's two youngest grandsons arrived shortly after, and were already antsy.

Zilker, younger than Buzz by a year, and less shy around his grandmother, unsurprisingly spoke first.

"Grandma," he said, gently tugging at her sleeve, "how soon can we go outside?"

He glanced out of the big picture window and let his eyes glaze over the uncharacteristically lush Central Texas landscape of deep green grass and flowers so fragrantly abloom; the bees must have thought they'd died and buzzed to the big beehive in the sky.

"Yeah, Grandma," chimed in Buzz, munching on a forbidden chocolate chip cookie only his grandmother had the power to let him have.

Rosetta smiled her easy smile she unknowingly saved for her grandchildren.

It was easy enough to do, seeing the two young boys, almost tweens, both masked in life's innocence, each mirroring her own diamond-lit eyes.

"Don't you think," she said, holding each boy close to her, "we should wait for it to dry a little more?"

"No."

"Nope."

"Ahhh," she smiled, "you *want* to get dirty."

Buzz pulled away at arms' length, tilting back a few degrees, still holding tightly to her arm. "Mom says dirt happens to me and Zilker."

Zilker nodded, confirming.

"Happens, huh?" Rosetta said, rising and looking out the large window.

Her backyard was recovering nicely from the five year drought Texas had suffered recently. She and Arturo had planted new miniature rose bushes along two sides, and added squares of sod seeded with new grass. But here and there bald spots of brown damp earth glistened beneath a sun being wiped clean by passing clouds.

"Okay," she said slowly, almost to herself. "We'll go outside. I have a surprise for you."

"Yay! Can Grandpa come too?"

"Yeah, where is he?"

"He's at work right now—boys, you knew that," Rosetta smiled.

"I forgot," said Buzz.

"Why's he at work?" asked Zilker.

"Yeah, I thought ya'll were retired?" said Buzz.

"We are," said Rosetta

Buzz made a face, said, "Then how come he's still working?"

"Well, sometimes it's nice to have some extra money, for something special. He's just working another week."

Both boys nodded, thinking.

"Special. Like what?" asked Zilker. "Mom says we have everything we need. Do you and Grandpa need something?"

"Yeah, we can give you one of ours, we have two of too much, mom says," Buzz added.

Rosetta went to the long brown hutch she'd kept after her mother had passed away and, passing her hands along the smooth cherry wood, opened the top drawer. Buzz and Zilker crowded behind and beside her and peered into the drawer. Zilker had to stand on his toes to see.

"Ooooh, is it a bell?" cried Zilker.

"How does it work?" asked Buzz.

Rosetta reached in, careful to hide the small list on a tiny sheet of note paper beside the bowl. Gift ideas for the six grandchildren. Butterfly makeup for the tween girls. A book for the oldest grandchild. A season pass to the Texas State Parks for the oldest one. And two question marks beside Buzz and Zilker's names.

"Oh, yes," said Rosetta.

"Ring it!"

Rosetta laughed. "Not yet. I want you to hear it outside first."

"Why?" both boys asked.

"You'll see," Rosetta smiled. "It's special. It's like a bell, but it's a bowl."

Gingerly, they exited the back door to the yard, slipped their shoes and socks off onto the covered stone patio Rosetta and Arturo had laid the summer before, and stepped a quarter inch deep into the cool damp earth.

"It's saturated," giggled Rosetta.

"That's good, Grandma?"

She nodded.

"I don't think there's a dry place to sit," Zilker said, pursing his lip, his small brows rolling down in a wave above his eyes.

Rosetta thought, then decided quickly.

"I guess we'll just have to get muddy..." she said.

"Yay!" and both boys plopped down.

"Oops," said Buzz, seeing Rosetta still standing. "Wrong spot?"

Zilker waited, palms down deep into the mud ready to get up if needed.

Rosetta took a breath, glanced at her clothes, figured she could throw them into the next day's wash, and joined the two boys.

The three smiled like a kitty cat with catnip.

Buzz began making circles in the mud with his hand.

Zilker poked tiny indents into the squishy wet earth with his thumb.

Rosetta took out her chime from one huge garden pocket in her smock, and a tiny gong ringer from the other. Like a child announcing her first tea party with her best friends, she dinged the tiny bowl in one smooth turn of her wrist.

Diingggggg!

The sound rang into the air, rose, held and then faded into the breath-held silence between the three.

"Woowwww," whispered Zilker.

"Double wow!" chanted Buzz.

They both looked to Rosetta.

She swallowed.

Then said, "Wow!"

And all three laughed like they had found their first lady bug and let it run over their arms and into their hearts.

In the quiet, Buzz said, "I still wish Grandpa was here."

Zilker nodded hard and held his lips tightly closed, as though if he didn't, his mouth and tongue would flop and bounce away.

"He *is*," Rosetta insisted.

But she saw the boys squint and try to see how that could be true.

"You're right," she said. "I meant we can hear him."

Both boys looked right and left, searching.

Their eyes asked, "Where?"

Rosetta tried to hide the effort to think even faster. "He, he's, uh, his *heartbeat*, is right here, in the earth. We can *hear* it," and she leaned her head to the left, toward her good ear.

"Mom says I always have wax in my ears, Grandma," said Buzz. "I can't hear him." And he fought off a sob that tried to rise and shout his frustration.

Zilker sat wide-eyed, waiting.

"Grandma," Zilker asked. "Can I lie down on the ground and listen better?"

Buzz didn't wait for the answer and flopped himself belly first onto the wet grass.

Zilker hesitated, but Rosetta gave him a tiny nod, and he quickly joined his older brother.

"We don't hear anything, Grandma," complained Buzz.

Rosetta lay down between the two boys and pressed her body to the wet ground. She felt the coolness and ripeness of the replenished earth seep through her clothes and dampen her skin. Gently, she placed her hands, palms down, on each boy's back, and let her finger tips rest like electrodes on their shirts. She felt each boy relax and inhale deeply, the soil rich with released scents of seeds and readiness.

"Listen again," she whispered.

Rosetta dinged the chime.

Diiinnnngggggg!

"Inside the bell-sound," Rosetta said, "inside the earth, Grandpa's heart beat is passing down his feet into the earth and back up into the bowl. Can you hear it?"

Diiinnnngggggg!

"I can! I can!" cried Buzz, rolling a small finger in his right ear.

"Me too!" shouted Zilker, rubbing his nose clean of mud.

"Can he hear *us*, Grandma?" asked Buzz.

"Yes. Of course. Well," she added, "he feels you, thinking of him. Ask him when he gets home, if he thought of you."

"Really?"

"Yes."

"Wow. Can I do the bell-bowl, Grandma?"

"Of course."

They all three came to sitting, legs slithered across the grass.

"They're like magic bowls," said Rosetta.

"Like for cereal?" asked Zilker.

"Can be," Rosetta said.

"Mom says we have to use dishwasher safe," said Buzz.

"Oh, smart woman," laughed Rosetta.

"We'll just use this to call grandpa," Buzz said.

"Yeah," said Zilker. "That's still fun."

"Fun is good, right, Grandma?"

"Yes, Buzz. Fun is good."

****

Lilies for the Mantel

Sylva Fae

Dust motes sparkled in the sun beams as he slid open the musty curtains. Wiping a clean spot on the grimy window, he stopped to peer out at the garden beyond. Smiling, he watched the children excitedly exploring the overgrown garden of their new house. The low swaying branches of the willow and a tangle of unruly rhododendrons made perfect hiding places for the two inquisitive rascals. The carefree laughter and squeals was a welcome backdrop to the arduous task ahead.

Where to start though? The old farmhouse 'had potential' according to his wife. She could always see through the clutter and dust to the 'potential' beyond. Right now she was busy, in her element, emptying boxes and arranging things; already creating a home in this dusty old building. He could hear her chattering away as she added colourful cushions and little trinkets to the drab, empty space. She'd already hung pictures on the old hooks adding a little sparkle and charm with each addition. He had no doubt she'd create a comfortable, if a little eclectic, home for them in no time. He peeped in on her and found her pondering which fairy ornaments to put on the oak dresser. She held up two for his appraisal. They all looked the same to him and she would end up swapping them round countless times before she was satisfied, but nevertheless, he pointed to one. Happy, she turned to continue and he wandered back to his chores.

Judging by the number of cobwebs, this room hadn't been used in a long, long time. Thick dust coated everything but even the dust and cobwebs glistened in sunshine, giving it a magical feel. Stifling a sneeze he carried on sweeping and wiping away years of neglect. It was a wonky old place. The wooden floorboards creaked, the once white plaster walls were cracked in places and the ceiling beams were blackened from years of smoke from the open fire. It had a certain rustic charm to it. He imagined the room, clean and cosy, a rug at the fireplace for the children to sit on while they listened to a bedtime story. Then later, he would snuggle with his wife in front of a roaring fire. It was a nice dream but there was still a lot of hard work before he got there. Right now the fire grate was rusty and the mantel propped up in the corner. He concentrated his efforts on the fireplace revealing a stone hearth under the layers of dust. Next on to the mantelpiece; it wouldn't take much to hang it. The old fixings would need replacing but he was handy enough.

The mantel was a heavy quality piece of timber; six foot of solid oak. He carefully lowered it to the freshly swept boards. Turning it over revealed a carved surface. Well, mostly. Intricate flowers in circular frames covered a large part of it; the last section was left rough and unfinished. Intrigued, he started to clean the grime from the ridges and furrows. The first was a rose set into a frame of thorny, entwined leaves. Exquisite detail, obviously hand carved; each petal and leaf now shone out. A wipe and a polish then revealed a simple daisy with a cloverleaf border; the next, daffodils inside a ring of woven leaves. With every swipe of the duster, more flowers were revealed, some he didn't even recognise. Each one was different from the last, yet all had the same loving attention to detail. Someone had taken such care and time; he wondered what its story was.

Finally he reached the last carving; not really a carving, just the outline of a lily with a border of heart-shaped leaves, roughly scored into the wood. He ran his fingers across the mantel from the smooth polished rose, to the rough unfinished lily. Nine flowers spanned the length of the mantel. Such a shame it was incomplete. He pondered whether he could finish it but he knew his skills really weren't up to the job; he was handy but not that handy.

He'd made good progress on the room so he decided he'd have a break, a potter down to the village, maybe pick up some fixings for the mantel and check out the local pub. The children were still exploring and his wife had just unpacked a new box of fairies. They would be happier staying here. A quick check with his wife proved him right so he set off, with instructions to pick up a bottle of wine for later.

***

The village was small but had one of those magical little shops that stock a random assortment of junk. Hidden amongst plastic bowls, gardening tools, pans and coils of washing line, he found a rack of fixtures and fittings. Brackets bought, his next stop was the pub. You can tell a lot about somewhere by its pub, and this one was a quaint old place. It was an ancient black and white building with a tired but welcoming façade. There were benches outside but it was just starting to get a little chilly to sit out, so he wandered inside, nodding to the locals on his way to the bar. The landlord served him with a cheerful greeting, and then went back to his chores, whistling to himself.

Pint in hand, he chose a seat next to the log fire. There was something so relaxing about staring into the flames, watching sparks fly and smoke swirl. The smell of wood smoke mingled with the old pub smell gave it a homely feeling. He took a long drink and sighed. Yes, this would do nicely. He planned to bring his wife here; the children could play on the green while they sat on the benches outside.

The old man in the chair at the other end of the fireside nodded and smiled. "You're a new face in here." He spoke softly, the wrinkles creasing up round his kind eyes as he smiled.

"Yes, we just moved into the farmhouse up the lane." He guessed it wouldn't be long before the whole village knew who they were. It was that kind of village.

"Know the place well. Used to live there with my Lily." The old man sat back and closed his eyes for a moment, a slight frown on his brow.

"We only moved in this weekend. I just popped out to get some bits to hang the mantel. There's a lot of work to be done, but it's a beautiful house under all the dust."

The word mantel seemed to rouse the old man from his daydream. He opened his eyes and sat up straighter in his chair.

"Carved that myself, I did. Carved it for my Lily." He sighed, and then sipped his pint. "She was the love of my life. Just wished I'd met her earlier. I was beginning to think there was no woman willing to take on a crotchety old fella like me, but my Lily was different. I knew we wouldn't have long together but what time we had was special."

He sat back pondering for a moment, remembering. A smile tweaked the corners of his mouth and his eyes twinkled as he continued.

"It was Lily's idea to do the mantel. I carved her a rose for our first anniversary. Lily loved flowers; roses were the first thing she planted in the garden. That was her thing, gardening. She'd potter round weeding and planting and I'd sit on the bench carving, watching her. Each year she had a new project in the garden; she enjoyed watching them bloom and by the time they'd died off, my carving would be done. A flower for every year we shared. She chose the wood for the mantel, you know, reckon she knew it would be long enough."

The old man closed his eyes again, lost in the past, his wrinkled smile growing. He seemed oblivious to the goodbyes as he relived his time with Lily.

The clock above the bar struck. It was time to go – just a quick stop for a bottle of wine, and then off to the farmhouse. The old man's story played on his mind on the walk back up the hill; so sad and yet so lovely. It was obvious they had been very much in love. He hadn't needed to ask about the unfinished carving of the lily. Some things were better left unsaid. The mantel must be hung, a part of the farm's history and a reminder of the permanence of love.

***

That evening, when the children were asleep, he recounted the old man's tale to his wife, over a glass of wine. She was touched by the tale and urged him to finish the job; she was always a romantic soul. He promised he would, first thing tomorrow. As she chatted about her day, an idea was starting to form in his head, now hazy with the wine. It would keep till morning.

The next day, the children were up early demanding breakfast so they could get back out to explore their new garden. He followed them out to look at their new den. Stepping across the daisy covered lawn, he noticed Lily's rosebushes hiding in the overgrown flowerbeds, the golden flowers attracting bees and butterflies. Up against the ivy covered wall were terracotta pots of fragrant geraniums, almost hidden by the heavy pink hydrangea blooms. He hadn't really looked at the garden, just assessed it as an extension of the property compared to the estate agent's blurb. Now he picked out the flowers from the mantel carvings; delicate fuchsias, honeysuckle and plants he didn't know the names of, had once been lovingly planted and tended to. He vowed to continue the good work in the garden, but now back to the house. He had a mantel to hang.

He enjoyed this kind of work; it was always good to see some reward for his endeavours. As he stood back to admire the new fireplace with the mantel hung proudly over the top, he remembered his idea from the previous evening. He would continue the old man's sentiment with a tribute of his own, but instead of carvings, he would paint. He wasn't an expert but he had a good eye for colour and found it therapeutic. Lily had loved her flowers, but in his wife's case fairies were an obvious subject for his canvases. He smiled as he pictured her choosing the perfect place to hang it. He would be required to stand holding it against the wall, while she stood back appraising. No doubt she would try every wall before deciding to hang it in the first place she tried.

No time like the present, he decided. He found the cardboard box that contained his pads and watercolours and carried it out to the garden bench. The sounds of his wife pottering about the kitchen floated through the window, blending with the squeals of the playing children. Colours of fuchsia and geranium pink, ivy green, golden rose and lily white glistened as the sunshine bounced on his palette. His sable brush made a gentle stroke across the canvas as he started to paint the first of many tributes to his beautiful wife.

As he finished the painting, a carefree fairy with hair awry and a cheeky grin, he smiled at the likeness to his wife. She would love it, but his rumbling stomach reminded him of the time. He set the canvas down to dry in the sun, rounded up the children, and called for his wife. Today was a great day to go and sample the lunches at the local pub.

***

The lane down to the village was safe enough for the children to race ahead. They usually did double the journey, racing, chasing each other and doubling back. Today was no different; they splashed through puddles and veered off the road into the brambles and trees that ran alongside. The only indications of their progress were the big sticks that bounced above the tall ferns, occasionally whacking a low hanging branch. The children were happy; this was definitely a good move. He sidled closer to his wife taking her hand and drawing her close. She leaned into him, contented, and the comfortable silence between them spoke more than words could. He breathed in the fresh country air. You had to appreciate these little moments of calm when you were a parent.

"You're going to love the local pub," he broke the silence, as they reached the end of the lane. They paused and waited for the children to emerge from the undergrowth. "It has benches outside, so we can sit out while it's nice, let the children run off some of that energy on the green."

"Are they friendly? You know what country folk can be like with outsiders," she mused, not really believing anyone could dislike them.

"Well, I only spoke to the landlord and the old man, but they seemed nice enough. I've no doubt you'll have made friends with the whole village by the end of the week."

The children appeared, slightly dishevelled and still carrying sticks. He persuaded them to leave the sticks propped up against a tree to collect on the journey home. Spying swings and climbing frames on the green, the children raced off to play while his wife settled at one of the outdoor benches. Before he'd even got to the door, she was leaning across introducing herself to a couple of a similar age. The pub was busier than the previous evening. He looked around for the old man, thinking it would be good to tell him about the finished fireplace, but he was nowhere to be seen. The whistling landlord paused to take the food order and had time for a chat while he poured the drinks.

"I was looking for the elderly gentleman who sits by the fireside," he asked him. "We've moved into his old home, the farmhouse on the hill. I wanted to tell him about what I've done with the fireplace."

"Oh, you mean old Jim?" said the landlord. "That was Jim's seat you were sat in last night. A sad affair that. When his wife passed he kept smiling, then a few days later he went too, to be with Lily. My how time flies – I can't believe that was three years ago."

The landlord handed over the tray of drinks and whistled back down the bar, totally unaware of the impact of his words.

Dust motes sparkled in the sunshine as he pulled open the heavy wooden door. He stopped to peer out at the scene beyond. Smiling, he watched the children excitedly exploring the playground on the green then slid into the seat next to his wife.

****

Gabriel and the Minister Bird

Andrew Updegrove

"Tomorrow the boy goes with me."

"But Amadu, his school is not over."

"No matter. It will never matter. Better he leaves now and supports the family."

"You must not say that! Where would you have been without school?"

"Where I am now! And I would not miss what I no longer have."

It was the same argument the boy had heard before. But now he heard it more often, and his father was more insistent. Gabriel pulled the blanket over his head, afraid that this time his mother might give in.

"It won't always be this way – someday the soldiers will leave, and then you will find good work again."

"When? Tell me that! When is the day they will leave? And when they do, the other soldiers will come back, and so on and so on. For four years it has been like this! It will be that way till I die – till we all die."

His father must be drinking palm wine again. He always became surly when he did that. But it hardly mattered. His father was always dark now, always tired, always beaten. Gabriel barely remembered the smiling man who used to come home from his work in the offices of the great diamond mine. Gabriel used to greet him by clutching his leg in his arms, the closest he could come to hugging such a tall man. Then his father would whisk him up into the air, and hold him high over his head. They both would laugh as they looked into each other's eyes.

"No! Someday they will all be gone. Then the owners of the mine will return, and the shops will reopen. What if Gabriel does not have an education? With his withered leg, how will he survive then?"

"How are any of us to survive right now? Look – go look in your cupboard! Will we eat even tomorrow? If I do not find a diamond soon, we will starve."

"But Amadu, he is so small; and his leg – the boy can barely walk. How is he to follow you all the way to the river bed?"

"I will carry him. Or he can go to the big pit. Someone will pay him to sit and sift gravel."

"They would pay him almost nothing!"

"Almost nothing is more than nothing! And almost nothing will be enough to fill his stomach!"

Gabriel tried to stuff the blanket into his ears to keep their words at bay. At last he fell asleep.

***

When he awoke the next morning he was afraid to open his eyes. Would he go to school, or would he be carried off to the dry river bed where his father dug gravel all day, dragging it back to his sieves, if they had not been stolen again. Then, praying for the sun that scorched his back to light a fire in one of the tiny pebbles that fell through the mesh. Sometimes that would not happen for a week or more, and they would go hungry.

But all was quiet. Gabriel peeked out from under his blanket; the sun was up. His father must have left without him. He would be able to go to school today after all.

***

When he returned, Gabriel sat under the acacia tree to do his homework. When he was much younger, his father would sit here, too, sharing the cool of the evening after dinner. He would tell Gabriel stories of all kinds, forest legends that sometimes made him afraid, and stories about the strange ways of the white people; they made him laugh. His father also told him about the great world beyond their village, about the endless water that went forever out of view, and about the amazing things he had seen in the big city. Buildings as tall as trees, with rivers of noisy vehicles flowing between.

His father would also hold him in his lap and read to him from books with words and pictures, pointing out the words one at a time and helping him understand the magic of the alphabet, until one day Gabriel began to say the words along with him.

All that had changed when the soldiers came. He recalled his confusion as he watched from the forest as their house burned to the ground, and his fear when he learned that many of their neighbors had been carried off or killed. After that, all of the wealthy people in the town where his father worked fled to the big city. Their businesses and stores were ransacked, never to be reopened again, at least for now.

His father built them a new house with his own hands. But it was not much more than a shelter from the sun and rain, constructed mostly of tin roofing salvaged from the ruins of their village. Once, the soldiers came back and destroyed that as well, and when they did, his father's spirit seemed to die. He could see no future to plan for now, just more devastation and danger. All he could do was to dig in the dirt so his family could survive; searching for the diamonds that once had raised a town from the forest.

The soldiers still allowed the diamond buyers to visit the village. The buyers paid only a pittance for the rough stones his father was able to sift from the gravel he dug by hand, but then, the soldiers took most of what they bought. At least the soldiers realized that if they took all the men, there would be no diamonds for guns and ammunition. But no longer did Gabriel's father sit with him in the clearing in the cool of the evening.

Today as always a gourd container sat by Gabriel's side, filled with the seed pods he had gathered as he hobbled his way home on crutches from the one room school. At thirteen, he was the oldest boy in the school now. All the others – the ones that could walk as well as carry a gun – had been taken by the soldiers a year ago. Where they were now, no one knew.

The small birds on the limbs of the acacia tree over his head were becoming noisier, and at last he set his slate and chalk aside. Immediately, a bird dove down to the ground to stare at him. "Patience!" he said, laughing. "You will have them soon!"

He took a seed pod from the gourd, cracked it between his fingers and felt the seeds cascade back into the gourd. When the birds heard that sound, they descended like rain from the tree to form a feathered puddle before him, hopping and twisting their heads from side to side. He continued to crack the pods one by one, tossing the broken husks to his side. Occasionally he took a few seeds from the gourd and cast them across the dusty ground like dice to reward the birds for their patience. Then they went wild, dashing after the skipping seeds, desperate to be first to seize one.

When at last the pods were empty, he took a seed and placed it in the palm of his hand. The birds became suddenly silent and still, except for a few that could not help themselves. At last he pointed at one of them, and it flew to his open hand to accept its prize. He repeated the daily ritual until each bird had received its gift, and then he began again. If a bird flew to him without being summoned, he closed his hand and held it behind his back until the bird returned to the ground. If all would be fed, all must take their turn.

The birds and he had spent many, many afternoons together over the years. Ever since he was a toddler, his withered leg had kept him from playing with the other children of the village. They progressed from halting steps to running, while he was forced to remain near home, baking inside under the tin roof, or sitting in the shade outside. That was how he became friends with the birds, and they with him. But he only fed the little birds, the ones that otherwise must scatter and flee when the big birds noticed that they had discovered food.

Today, though, a large bird dropped from the sky and perched on a stone a few feet away. The book at school called it a pied crow, but everyone knew that it was really a minister bird; the fancy markings around its neck made that clear. It had come to visit before, but he had not fed it. And yet it made him feel guilty. Why should he feed one bird and not another? Despite its considerable size, perhaps the minister bird might be hungry as well? And what must it think of him –feeding one type of bird but not another?

For the first time, the large bird dropped from its customary perch, and hopped towards him, slowly but purposefully. The smaller birds divided like the sea in the bible to let it pass. When it was only a foot away, it dropped an object to the ground that it had been carrying in its beak. Then it hopped back a little way and raised its head, cocking it to one side to look up at him. Gabriel saw that it had brought him a small, shiny nail.

Delighted, he picked it up and laid three seeds in its place. The minister bird gobbled them into its craw, and flew away.

***

The next day Gabriel was visited by three minister birds, and the next day after that by seven. Each brought a gift to exchange, and he found that they were very quick to learn. If a bird gave him something he valued more, he would give it six seeds instead of three. Soon the other birds would notice, and they would look for the same type of object. A coin, perhaps. Gabriel's slow walk home from school became slower still, as he searched for more rewards, and better ones. Large grubs from the leaf litter became a great favorite of his new friends.

One day, a minister bird brought him a shiny pebble.

Gabriel heard voices in the distance approaching his house. He struggled to his feet and hobbled on his crutches towards home from his seat under the acacia tree. Two men were carrying someone between them. It was his father.

They laid him down in the house, and one went to summon the old woman who once had worked as a nurse at the diamond mine. She pushed the ends of the broken bones back beneath the skin of his father's leg and did her best to reset them where they should be. Then she bound the wound and tied his leg to a splint made out of a branch. After she left, his father said nothing, a hollow look of pain and desperation in his eyes.

Gabriel could see that his mother was very worried. How long would it be before his father could work again? How would they survive until then? What would they do if he could not work at all? Neither of his parents spoke as she sat beside his father, her hand on his shoulder.

Gabriel could feel their eyes upon him, almost hear their thoughts. He rose to go outside, and made his way back to the acacia tree. There, he tilted back the rock the first minister bird had perched upon and removed the small cloth bag beneath it. He had hoped that it would be a little fuller before he gave it to his parents, but better some than none at all. He made his slow way back to the house.

When he returned to their house, Gabriel took his mother's hand and poured five small, glinting pebbles into it from the bag.

***

Many minister birds visit the acacia tree every evening now. A flock swoops in to roost, and then, one at a time, the birds drop to the ground to trade their gifts for fat, white grubs. When one flock flies off, another takes its place until it becomes almost too dark to see.

Below the tree, Gabriel reaps the harvest of the minister birds' sharp eyes. And once again, his father reads to him and tells him stories, as they take their ease in the still, cool air of the evening.

****

Inside Out

Penny Luker

Celia clung to the lamp post. Her hands were clammy and her heart was beating too fast. She could see two youths at the end of the street, but her eyes wouldn't focus and she couldn't move. Her legs felt like blancmange. She looked around desperately for help, but the street was empty. One youth had his hands in his pockets. The other was almost dancing alongside, sideways, talking all the while. She could hear the noise but not the words, which all blurred into one excited sound. They were nearly level with her. She couldn't look at their faces and turned her head away. Were they going to walk past? Then the footsteps stopped. This was it. How ironic if she should be attacked twenty metres from her house!

She thought back to the morning, when she'd at least felt safe. She'd laid the kitchen table; straightened the place settings and added linen serviettes. The coffee had been at just the right temperature. Gerald and Robert's cooked breakfasts were on the stove and their healthy packed lunches on the side. Well, almost healthy – she'd run out of yoghurts and had substituted home-made biscuits.

Both Gerald and Robert ignored the napkins when they came downstairs. They glanced at each other and tucked into their food.

"My first match is today. Starts at two-thirty. Parents are allowed to come and watch," Robert said.

Gerald had ruffled Robert's sandy hair. "If I can get away I will, but I can't promise." He stood up brushing toast crumbs from his large frame.

"What about you, mum? It's just down the road."

Celia shook her head. A frown crumpled her smooth forehead and her lips tightened into a firm line.

She busied herself washing up as the two of them left the house. Why ask such questions, when he knew the answer? Robert hadn't needed to say anything. He hadn't kissed her good-bye. She imagined him playing football and scoring the winning goal. Waves of depression and failure threatened to engulf her, so she tidied and cleaned and washed her already spotless house.

A touch on her arm bought her focus back to the youths.

"Hey, Mrs P, it's you isn't it? You look different outside. Rob said you couldn't leave the house, but here you are," said Andy, with a broad smile.

She forced her head round to look at him. His unruly red hair framed his freckled face. *What would he think? His best friend's mother was clinging to a lamp post, unable to move.* She tried to straighten herself up.

"Are you alright, Mrs. P? You look as white as a Goth. Do you want me to get my mum?"

Celia smiled, not with her heart, but because Andy was a good friend to Robert.

"I just came over dizzy and need to get back home."

"Hold on to me arm, Mrs P. We'll get you home."

The other boy stood nearby, shuffling his feet as she clutched Andy's arm and he led her to the front door.

"Andy, I'd be really grateful if you didn't mention this to Robert."

"No, probs. Gotta go or we'll be late. Bye."

"Bye, and thank you," she called after them as they tore along the street.

Once through the front door her body became her own again. She headed for the kitchen and made a cup of tea. She'd make Robert a chocolate cake for a treat. That'd make up for not being able to see the match. When three thirty came she sighed and placed the cake on the wire cooling rack. The match would be over soon.

It was a quiet boy who came home from school, kicked off his shoes inside the front door and ran up to his bedroom. She wondered if he'd been crying. Gerald wasn't with him, so presumably he hadn't made the match either. She climbed the stairs and was met by his locked door.

"It doesn't matter if you didn't win Robert. Come down. I've made a lovely chocolate cake for you."

"I don't want cake. Go away," he mumbled through the door.

***

When Gerald arrived home, she served them all a delicious shepherd's pie with carrots and peas. Robert ate in silence. His wiry slim body was hunched, unlike his father who was broad and strong and was such a presence in the room.

"Look son, I'm sorry I didn't make it. I was just about to leave when there was an important call from the States. It was for a big order. I've got the bills to pay."

"It's Okay, Dad. Andy's mum was shouting for me and Andy. They're like my second family. It's just that I'd like my real family to be there sometimes."

The next day there was a knock on the door. Mrs Bliss, Andy's mum, stood there. She was wearing a smart pinstriped trouser suit and so much make-up she looked doll-like, but her wispy fair hair stopped her from looking smart. "Could we have a chat Celia?"

Celia couldn't really say no, so she showed her into the lounge and offered her coffee.

"No thanks. I expect you know I volunteer at school, on the pastoral side of things, and run a few after school clubs. I thought I'd pop over as you never make it into school."

"It's just that I suffer from..."

"I know, Celia. Robert talks to me. I just wondered if there's any way we could minimise the effect your condition has on Robert's life."

"What do you mean? I look after him properly..."

"I'm not implying that you're not a good mother, but he was heartbroken that neither of you were there yesterday to see his first time in the team. Robert was looking round most of the time searching for you. He also has to dash home from art club to pick up your magazine on Wednesdays, and sometimes leave early to post your competition entries. Then there are times when his lunch box is a little strange because you haven't managed to do the shopping."

"I do my best," Celia said firmly.

"I'm sure you do, but couldn't you order your magazine to be delivered rather than making it Robert's responsibility, and are your competition entries so important that he has to miss the end of school clubs to catch the post? He's only eleven, still a child, and he's trying to find his way in secondary school."

"He's never moaned about getting a bit of shopping or posting a letter."

Andy's mum took a deep breath, "No, he doesn't moan. If you and Gerald can't come, I'll always cheer him on, but maybe there's another member of the family who could come?"

"No there isn't,' Celia said, standing up and smoothing her long floral skirt. Mrs. Bliss had no alternative but to stand too. 'Tell me, are you here in an official capacity from school?"

"Of course not. I'm here as your friend."

"Friend! Oh I see," said Celia, raising an eyebrow.

"Of course we're friends. Andy's always round here and Rob's always at ours."

As Celia was closing the door, she thought she heard Mrs Bliss mutter, "Makes you wonder who's the parent."

Celia found herself shaking. This was her home, her sanctuary. She didn't need the Mrs. Bliss's of the world invading her space, but even as she justified her needs she wondered if her dear friend Jane could go to Robert's next match. She did feel guilty about him being out there on his own.

***

That evening she told Gerald about the visit, expecting a bit of sympathy.

"If I'm supporting us by running a business, then you should be there for Robert. I wouldn't mind if you'd have some treatment, if there was any hope of this nightmare ending; but your stubborn refusal of help, well it's just not good enough. You're under some crazy impression that this doesn't affect our lives – but it does. And as for Jane, I don't want her taking over the mother role." He slammed out of the room, banging the front door shut.

Silence echoed round the house. Celia had nothing to distract her from his cruel words. What a day she'd had! First the judgemental Mrs Bliss, and now her gentle Gerald had just shouted at her. *Why don't they understand? I can cope with life at home but not outside. Losing my baby made me scared. It's not my fault. And the competition entries are my way of keeping in touch with 'outside'.*

She called Jane and asked if she'd like to come over for a coffee. Everyone needs a Jane she thought; someone who's always on your side to help you.

***

Friday came and Robert went off to school. He had a large chunk of chocolate cake in his lunch box. There wasn't any bread, but he had a good sized lump of cheese. Gerald hadn't managed to do the shopping last night as he was working late. The two of them ate so much. It was hard to calculate the shopping needed.

When Gerald arrived home early she was pleased to see him, but he went straight into the garage. She noticed him stack a big pile of gear by the car.

"I'm taking Robert camping this weekend to make up for not being at his match."

"But I was looking forward to spending some time with you both this weekend."

"Come with us then."

"Don't be silly. You know I can't."

"Well I don't see why we've to be stuck at home just because you won't have treatment. It's been three long years. I wouldn't mind if you'd get some help. Anyway,

152

Robert needs to get out and do the things that other kids are doing. We're going. I'm not arguing about it."

Robert's face lit up with excitement when he came home from school. "Andy goes camping sometimes. It'll be great, but what about Mum?" Gerald gave her a warning glare.

"I'll be fine, Robert. You go and enjoy yourself."

When they'd left she picked up the phone and called Jane.

"Sorry Celia, I'm ... er ... away this weekend. It's ... er ... something I can't change." There was a pause. "I'm visiting my mother and I can't let her down."

The evening stretched out ahead of Celia in a long void. Her safe haven didn't feel so good. The silence shouted at her. Her thoughts turned to Jane. Had Jane ever mentioned her mother before? It was strange that Jane was away the same weekend as Gerald. Her heart started racing. Maybe they were meeting up. Before her eyes a vision floated of Gerald kissing Jane. *So that's why Jane's always so keen to come here. And what was it that Gerald had said? Oh yes, she thought: As for Jane I don't want her taking over the mother role. But perhaps he didn't mind her taking over the wife role. What a fool I've been.*

I'm going round to see Jane now before she leaves. I need to find out what's going on. She picked up the key that Jane had given her many years ago.

As she stepped through the front door she shivered. 'I can do this,' she said to herself. She marched out and turned left. The wideness of the sky hit her. It was vast. There were no walls to keep her safe. Her confidence faltered. The clouds rolled across the expanse like waves on the ocean. There was a smell of newly cut grass coming from somewhere. Slowly she walked on, past the streetlight she'd clung to, days earlier. She realized that Jane's key was digging into her palm. She kept stumbling along – one foot in front of the other, trying to keep her breath even. Jane's gate creaked. She climbed up the steps and inserted the key in the lock.

"Good grief Celia, I wondered who it was. I can't believe you're here," said Jane. "Come in, come in and I'll make you a coffee. This is wonderful."

Celia looked closely at her friend. Jane seemed genuinely pleased to see her. Perhaps she'd got it all wrong. The smell of the coffee Gerald liked so much lingered in the air.

"I thought you were off to your mum's."

"No, not really. Gerald called me today and said on no account was I to go round and spend the weekend with you. He said you needed to realize that your condition could inconvenience you too. So I promised him, although I didn't want to. But here you are. He's going to be so chuffed. What an achievement, to walk here on your own."

As Jane wound thin arms around her and gave her a hug, Celia notice a pair of men's gloves on the hall table. They looked so like Gerald's, but his were at home... surely? Celia felt dizziness and nausea take over her body.

"I need to go home now."

"You're safe here, Celia. I'm with you and my house is safe. Stay and have a coffee and then I'll take you home. I promise."

Celia looked around the room. Stuck on the fridge with a magnet was a photo of her family. Gerald stood grinning out at her.

Walking home later, Celia clung to Jane's arm, pausing to take calming breaths once or twice.

"Shall I come round tomorrow?" Jane asked, as Celia opened her front door. She noticed Gerald's gloves were not on the hall stand where he usually left them.

"Do you have a mother?" Celia countered.

"I most certainly do. She's hiking in Nepal at the moment."

"I've never heard you talk about her."

"Well, she's someone I greatly admire, but I don't see her often. I didn't think you'd be interested."

"I am interested, Jane. You've been a great friend to me for years and I want to start being a good friend, too. Perhaps we could try and make it to the park tomorrow, and then I could cook you lunch."

***

Saturday brought more feelings of dread, faintness and jelly legs but Celia made it to the park, and on Sunday she made it to the school playing fields. As they returned to her house she opened the door and noticed Gerald's gloves were on the hall stand. *Strange*, she thought. *How did they get there?* But she said nothing.

That evening Gerald and Robert returned from their camping trip full of energy. They'd had a wonderful couple of days, hiking and brewing up strange meals.

The next day Robert said, "I've been picked for the team again this week. It's on Wednesday. Andy's mum's going to cheer me on."

Celia felt guilt surge through her, that her son had to rely on his friend's parents, but she said nothing. She wasn't going to promise to go in case she couldn't make it.

At two o'clock on Wednesday she picked up her bag and opened the front door. Panic threatened to overwhelm her.

Taking deep breaths, she said to herself, 'One foot in front of the other'. Within fifteen minutes she was at the playing fields. It was a huge space. Lots of people were arriving. Her legs began to lose their strength as Mrs. Bliss strode towards her carrying a chair.

"Thought you might like this, Celia. Robert's going to be over the moon."

Celia smiled and nodded at other parents. If she'd had the strength to get up and run she'd have done so, but she felt too weak and helpless. Then the children came out. Robert waved so hard she thought he'd explode, and just before the whistle blew to start the match, Gerald jogged down the side of the pitch. His face was beaming. When had she ever seen him look so happy? He bent down and kissed her and put his arm round her shoulders. She was safe outside for the first time in years. As the match went on the panic began to grow again. She checked the exits to make sure they were clear and noticed a woman slip away. *Was that Jane?* she thought. She looked up at Gerald. He was shouting for Robert to get down the field. Celia silently counted to twenty. She knew she needed to get help to be well again. At that moment, Gerald squeezed her shoulder. Perhaps it wasn't too late.

****

Witch's Mark

Katerina Sestakova Novotna

Lisa, my first love, was curvier than most 14-year-old girls were. I also found her long, red hair exotic. And I liked her funny freckles - she had so many that it looked as if she had been wearing an invisible crotchet veil when running around in the hot Hawaiian sun. She was getting a brown tan, almost like ours, but only on spots that were not covered. She was the only haole, or white person, in our class. Most of us were Hawaiians of mixed blood, but there were also some Asian students.

Lisa was a new face in our class which made her appear even more unusual than she was. She transferred to our school at the end of the school year - only a month before the summer break.

Despite her unexpected appearance and exotic looks, I soon found out that Lisa had not come down from a different planet, or even a different part of our island. She had always lived in Honolulu, only a few miles from our neighborhood. She had attended a private Catholic school before. They expelled her for her lack of discipline and profanity.

That's what Ms. Wong, our homeroom teacher, told another teacher in the hallway. I have never found out what exactly Lisa did to deserve this punishment. Since her former school had different requirements, it seemed harsh not to let her finish the year there.

Lisa turned out to be such a troublemaker that it was soon more a question of why they had not expelled her earlier than why they did. She often walked around the classroom during the lecture, saying that she needed to stretch her legs or look out of the window. She always came late to classes and always without an acceptable excuse.

We went on a field-trip to Diamond Head Crater only two weeks after Lisa's first day. On our way up the crater, Ms Denner, our science teacher, lectured us about volcanoes. For some odd reason, she also mentioned a few things from Hawaiian mythology that had nothing to do with science.

Ms Denner told us about Madam Pele, the Hawaiian goddess of volcanoes, and her fabulous family. Pele had divine parents and siblings, but she also had a human lover, a chief named Lohiau, which means 'retarded' in Hawaiian. Pele had children who were neither divine, nor human. They were just stones, pohaku, as my people call stones. All volcanic stones were her children.

According to a myth, Pele always went mad when someone took her stone child away from her islands. She cursed such a person. Ms Denner told us not to take any stones from Diamond Head Crater. According to the legend, she admitted, it was only wrong to export rocks from Hawaii but *probably* okay to take them to our Hawaiian homes, but from the environmental point of view, it was better to leave the rocks where they were so that others could appreciate them.

Lisa asked Ms Denner many questions about old Hawaiian gods and even showed her own knowledge of our myths. It was funny to see the only haole student in class being more familiar with, and more interested in, our heritage than we were. Most of us Hawaiians had been raised Christians and did not care about the old gods and goddesses.

Ms Denner was a haole as well. I still wonder why she, a scientist, was interested in these fairy tales. Most likely she was trying to show her respect for our culture. I could not say the same about Lisa's interest in our old religion.

"Look at this Pele's child! It's shaped like a little dinosaur!" Lisa shouted, holding a small piece of rock.

I couldn't understand her thrill.

"And so what?" I talked directly to Lisa for the first time ever. "I collected dinosaur models when I was six."

"It may be a fossil, you idiot," Lisa explained.

"Leave it here, Lisa. It's not a fossil," Ms. Denner said.

Lisa frowned and put the stone into her backpack. I wondered whether she really liked the stone so much or just wanted to disobey Ms. Denner and Madam Pele perhaps. Ms. Denner saw her but pretended not to. She did not enjoy arguing with Lisa.

"It's not a fossil," I said.

"It is," Lisa objected. "And not an ordinary one."

"What makes it special then? It's so small it cannot be a real dinosaur."

"It is small," Lisa nodded. "It's a baby. And it's a piece of evidence that Madam Pele practiced bestiality."

Lisa could tell from my expression that I did not know what bestiality meant.

"She had not only a human lover but also a dinosaur lover," Lisa clarified, shaking her head. "How else could she have a dinosaur baby? She must have had sex with a dinosaur!"

I found her comment strange, but I laughed, not wanting to be called an idiot a second time.

"It's rather common among Native Hawaiians to have sex with animals, I've heard," Lisa went on.

This time Ms Denner did not ignore Lisa's blunt disrespect. She was angry.

"How can a girl be so rude!" she snapped, her face red.

Ms Denner did not want to discuss this incident in front of the other kids, but she reported Lisa to the principal.

When Lisa came back to class from the principal's office the following day, she was carrying a disciplinary report for her parents.

Most of us would have felt at least uncomfortable had we received such a condemnation. But Lisa was used to dealing with bigger problems. She had been expelled only a few weeks earlier from her former school, for which her parents had to pay a high tuition. Since our school was a public school, it was free and they could not expel students as easily as Lisa's former school could. She knew this and smiled.

It was a magical smile, with crow's feet in the corners of her shining eyes. Lisa's smile must have irritated Ms Wong though. "Are you proud of what you did? Are you not afraid of what your parents will say?" she asked.

"Not really," Lisa replied in a calm voice. "Just pleased to have a day off, in fact."

"They suspended you? No way!" Ms Wong exploded. "I thought they just sent your parents the first warning. You need to catch up. You can't miss more classes!"

No-one in our class had ever been suspended, although a few students received warning reports. Makoa Kaiwi, the class bully, received more than one.

Later that day, the principal revoked Lisa's suspension. Lisa was to help in the cafeteria during the lunch instead.

She was helping a teacher to supervise first-graders. There was one boy named Tony who was unable to chew his food. At home his mother put all his food in a blender to make life easier for Tony. That's what all our mothers did when we were babies and had no teeth yet. But Tony's mother never stopped. He did have his teeth, but he never learned to use them at home. He naturally tried to swallow his school lunch as if it had been some puree, the only kind of food his mouth was familiar with.

Tony's progress was slowed down by his mother's frequent interventions. She sometimes gave him his special home-made puree to eat, so he did not have to struggle with a regular school meal every day.

Even at the end of his first year at school, when Lisa was to serve her sentence in the cafeteria, Tony still choked occasionally while trying to swallow his lunch. His classmates laughed at him. The more they laughed, the more he choked.

The teacher asked Lisa to help Tony.

Lisa sat down next to Tony and tried to calm him down. She started to tell him a story, but Ronn, another first-grader, interrupted her.

"Don't talk to Tony. He won't get it 'cause he's retarded!"

"Be careful," Lisa said, looking at Ronn. "Did you know that the Hawaiian goddess of volcanoes fell in love with a retarded boy?"

"How do you know?" Ronn asked.

"'Cause I am a witch."

"You don't look like a witch."

161

"Look," Lisa rolled up her sleeve and pointed to a huge black mole on her shoulder.

"Yuck!" Ronn shuddered. "What's that?"

"A wart. A witch's mark."

"How did you get it?" another kid asked.

"Devil kissed me." Lisa shrugged. "And the goddess of volcanoes is my friend too. She likes Tony, so be careful. Don't mess up with him."

A few kids started to shout something inarticulate, which caught their teacher's attention.

"She is a witch!" Ronn told the teacher. "She will poison our lunch!"

Lisa grinned.

The teacher decided that Lisa was trying to scare the small children and that she did more harm than good in the cafeteria.

Her punishment had to be changed again. From then on, Lisa had to sit with teachers during the lunch, every day until the very end of the school year. This was a real punishment in my eyes, but Lisa didn't seem to care. She didn't have any friends at our school yet, nor did she try to make any, so it made no difference to her whether she ate with us, or with the teachers.

***

There was indeed something witchy about Lisa. Witches used to live in the woods, far from everyone else. Only the most desperate people who needed their help associated with them – like Tony, who started to like Lisa and always looked pleased to see her on campus.

But there were others: Kiele, a fat girl from our class no one really liked, and then Shogo, a boy from Japan who didn't speak English. All these losers seemed to be drawn to Lisa, and she was kinder to them than she was to the rest of us. I liked Lisa and wanted to talk to her, but it annoyed me that she was always surrounded by those losers. I was afraid that I would be a loser, too.

At the same time, I started to see Lisa as more than just the bad girl who was very pretty. She was a generous spirit able to see something good in those unpopular kids no one else liked. She deserved the same kind of favor in my opinion. Witches see things no-one else does, and in this sense, Lisa was a witch. But witch didn't cover it; she was more of a goddess to Kiele, Shogo and Tony. They almost worshipped her. Sometimes, I even suspected that she was more vain than compassionate.

But Lisa was definitely brave. Her kindness to Kiele and Shogo made her the target of Makoa Kaiwi, who always picked on them.

Makoa started to talk about the kill-a-haole day in front of Lisa. We all knew the tradition but had never observed it before since we had not had any white classmates. It's an annual event on the last day of school when it is considered okay to harass white kids - the descendants of those who stole our land.

The closer the last day of school became, the more Makoa Kaiwi and his buddies harassed Lisa.

"She has not only red hair, but also red skin!" Makoa sneered, looking Lisa up and down. I did not understand how he could look at Lisa this way and notice just her skin color and not her disarming beauty, her perfect curves under the school uniform, which was partially covered by the silky curtain of her hair.

"It's just sunburn," someone said.

"All haoles are like that," Makoa nodded. "They cannot live in our climate. They came here and stole our land. But they don't belong here. Our sun is too strong for them. They cannot handle it."

This was so unfair, but Lisa didn't seem to mind. She was looking into her iPhone and ignored Makoa's remarks. I didn't say a word either. No one usually challenged Makoa Kaiwi.

Although I didn't talk to Lisa much at that time, I was determined to stand up for her on the last day of school. I liked her and wanted to prove my courage to her.

On that fateful day, before the teacher came in, Lisa approached Makoa before he could approach her.

"It's kill-a-haole day today, isn't it?" she asked, looking in Makoa's eyes.

"You bet your ass it is."

Then, without a warning, Lisa just slapped Makoa. "You are a haole, aren't you?"

"You're haole, bitch," Makoa sputtered and punched Lisa.

They fought for less than a minute. Lisa defeated him very quickly, ending up straddling him from behind on the floor.

"Your grandpa is a haole as far as I know," she said, twisting his arm.

"Let me go, you fucking bitch," Makoa cursed

"Not until you admit that you are a haole."

Makoa's grandfather was white. Most of us had white relatives. We were all mixed. The dispute made no sense.

"You are more haole than he is," Peter, one of Makoa's buddies protested.

"You are the whitest," Makoa cried out, his face distorted in pain.

"Say that again and I'll tear off your arm," Lisa said in a calm voice. "If you wanna survive whole, then say that I am black."

"You are black!" Makoa winced. Lisa's grip must have been really painful if Makoa agreed to say such nonsense in front of everyone.

Then Ms Wong came to class and saw Lisa still straddling Makoa.

I was the first one who spoke up.

"It's not Lisa's fault. It was all about the kill-a-haole day."

While I did not lie, I knew that I was distorting the truth.

"Who started it?" Ms Wong asked.

She wanted to know who started that particular fight. But she should have asked who started the war. Teachers are always so narrow-minded.

"Makoa," I said.

No one objected. Makoa's friends were obviously afraid of Lisa. Both Lisa and Makoa received a disciplinary report for their parents.

I offered to walk Lisa to her bus stop that day. I felt that I deserved it and I also wanted to be there in case Makoa Kaiwi decided to strike.

"Do you have time?" Lisa asked. "Let's go to Waikiki Beach and hang out for a while."

***

We took the bus there, and then walked and talked. She kept talking about old Hawaiian myths and beliefs. I felt stupid because I knew nothing about these things.

"Let's stop at Wizard Stones," I suggested, trying to please her.

"What's Wizard Stones?"

I was surprised that Lisa didn't know.

"Wizard Stones are sacred rocks here on Waikiki Beach. They are supposed to contain mana of four famous wizards."

"Who are they?" Lisa interrupted me, impatiently.

"Just some powerful wizards who came here from Tahiti 1600 years ago. They worked here as healers, and they empowered those four stones with their magic before they left for Tahiti again."

"I did not know this."

"Let me show you." I said, proudly.

***

When we got to the Wizard Stones, Lisa grabbed one of the leis hanging over the fence and placed it around her neck. It was a classic purple orchid lei that some tourists must have left there. Not many natives believe enough in the healing power of these stones to bring floral offerings, but many tourists leave there the leis they receive in their hotel as a welcome gift.

"You should not steal the lei from the wizards," I objected feebly.

"Don't worry, I am a witch too," Lisa grinned.

We walked around and I bought us French fries at McDonalds. Then we went swimming. Since we had no swimsuits, we swam in our school uniforms. I texted my mom that I was with a friend and that I would be late for dinner.

After the sunset, we both had to head home.

"Let's stop at Wizard Stones once more." Lisa suggested.

She returned the lei that she had borrowed earlier. Then she climbed over the metal fence and sat on the highest stone. I followed her. There was a police station right beside the fenced area so I was a little bit afraid of getting caught, but we were veiled by partial darkness and everyone else was watching fireworks – which were a common thing in Waikiki on a Friday night.

As soon as I sat next to Lisa, she kissed me. It was just a shy kiss and I didn't know how to respond, but she hugged me tight and we kissed again. Longer and better this time.

We both missed our last buses. I called my father to pick me up. Lisa took a taxi, and I wondered how she could afford it. Perhaps she planned to get away without paying, I imagined.

"Give me your phone number," I asked. It was the last day of school, so I wanted to make sure that I would see Lisa during the summer break.

She was already sitting in a taxi and said, "Let's meet at Wizard Stones at 4 p.m. on Tuesday, ok?"

"Why not earlier?" I asked.

"I will have to babysit my cousin over the weekend. And mom wants me to see a doctor on Monday. But I will come to this beach almost every afternoon. Will you?"

"Sure," I said. Then she disappeared.

***

The next Tuesday I waited for Lisa for two hours and she never showed up. I came to Wizard Stones in the following days and weeks, too. I always searched the beach and felt disappointed afterwards. She had promised to come every afternoon but never did. Was I such a bad kisser? Was I the worst of all losers if even Lisa avoided me? I was angry at myself that I had not obtained her phone number.

It was the worst summer ever.

After the summer break Lisa was not in our class either. Makoa Kaiwi said that her parents put Lisa into another private school because she was afraid of him.

I hoped that they would kick her out again.

One morning, I found Lisa sitting in our classroom. It was ten minutes before our first class.

"What's up?" I asked.

"Many things," Lisa said.

She looked different, paler than before. She was not wearing the school uniform, just a sleeveless white dress. I noticed that there was no longer her witch's mark on her shoulder, but instead a huge scar.

"Did you break the pact with the Devil?" I asked, pointing to the scar.

"Sort of. It was a nasty thing."

Then she suddenly turned away and left the classroom. I followed her, not knowing that she was going to the restroom. Before she could get there though, Lisa threw up in the hallway. It was disgusting.

Makoa saw it and started to yell: "Look at the haole, she puked!"

He must have sensed that Lisa was not as strong as she had been.

Lisa ran away in shame, and I followed her again. We left the campus, although I knew that I would be in trouble because of that. I could see that there was something very wrong with Lisa and I just couldn't let her go alone.

Not knowing what to say, I wanted to kiss Lisa but she turned away and threw up again in the park.

"It's the medication that makes me sick," she said, looking away.

"Isn't medication supposed to make you feel better rather than sick?"

"Not always. Whatever. I am leaving Honolulu. I came to school just to say goodbye to you. I don't have to go to school now that I am sick."

I was more alarmed by the information that Lisa was leaving than by the information that she was sick. I felt ashamed of being so selfish. Perhaps Lisa had not come to Wizard Stones because she had already been sick, I suddenly realized.

"Where are you moving to, Lisa?"

"To New York. There are better hospitals. And Makoa was right. I don't belong here. My skin is too light and I should avoid the sun. The wart could reappear unless I am really careful."

I didn't understand her much. But I could see that she was serious.

"I wanted to take my dinosaur stone to New York," Lisa said, pulling her stone out of her pocket. "But I changed my mind. I won't do anything that could backfire, you know."

I was shocked by how fragile and broken Lisa suddenly appeared. She must have been afraid of her illness. She was not the same rowdy girl anymore, but it was still Lisa and I still liked her - even though she threw up in public.

"I would like to place my stone among the Wizard Stones. It's so small that no one will notice it among the gravel. I charged it with my mana like those wizards did. Will you put it there for me?"

I nodded.

"I need to go home now," Lisa said, suddenly looking very tired.

"Give me your phone number," I demanded.

"No, trust me, it will be better if I don't."

I disagreed with her and tried to argue. But she left very quickly and I haven't seen her since.

I still remember her white ghostly face and her messy hair flowing in the wind as she was getting on her bus. Her wild red hair reminds me of the most destructive fire that burned all the bridges. Only a goddess of volcanoes could have such fiery hair.

Only a prayer to the true God can overcome the abyss that had emerged between us. I now understand much better what is going on. I wish I could be closer to Lisa and support her, but I also believe in the power of faith, hope and love.

***

I placed Lisa's stone among the Wizard Stones as she wished. She is a witch even though she lost her witch's mark and some of her mana. Perhaps the healing power of the four great wizards will flow into her small stone and hence to Lisa, wherever she happens to be.

Lisa belongs to my island, no matter how white she is and how far she left. I bought a fresh orchid lei and placed it over the fence around the Wizard Stones. I pray for Lisa in church too, because she is a good witch and I don't really believe in witchcraft – it is often just a pose.

I don't believe in first impressions either. Lisa looks like a troublemaker but she has a good heart. I search for her on the Internet every day and hope to find some good news from her when she gets better. I keep telling myself that if she could beat Makoa Kaiwi, she must be able to beat her melanoma, too.

****

Love's Silent Ache

Lisa Shambrook

I didn't hear Liria's footsteps matching mine as I meandered along the old forgotten trail. My cheeks flushed as crimson as the setting orb, and my mind remained with Isla, still dancing beneath the late summer sun. We'd waded barefoot through streams still warm and crystal clear, relaxed on the river bank, and napped in each other's arms. We'd kissed, laughed, and made promises, and I'd left her at her gate. Now I wandered home, my heart still languishing in the warmth of love, and swollen with desire.

I heard no footsteps in the woods behind me.

Oblivious to all but the love that filled my soul, I walked with my sighs as soft as the breeze and my smile as wide as a rainbow.

I didn't see the forest flinch, or hear the birds retire, and I never saw the flowers close, pulling their petals tight as the threat of night drew in. I didn't hear Liria until she tapped me on the shoulder. I jumped, startled out of my reverie. Liria smiled, and I didn't like it.

"Odhran..." her voice purred, like a sunbathing cat, and she lengthened the syllables of my name. "Oodhraaan..."

I swallowed hard as she leaned in close and her breath skipped across my face. She smelled of heavy jasmine, dark musk, and something I couldn't quite place. Isla's face flashed before me, and her scent, a perfume of orange blossom and roses filled my senses.

"Odhran, I've been watching you..." She dragged her finger down my cheek, stroking my stubble, and licked her dark lips.

"I've been here all day, watching you cavort with that young filly, watching you flirt with innocence and naivety," she drawled, and let her finger rest on my collarbone.

I swallowed again and my chest heaved.

"There's more to you, Odhran, and I think you need something, someone, more serious." She flicked her head, and I stumbled backwards.

"I think you've g-got the wrong person..." I stammered.

She shook her head and took my clammy hand, pulling me upright in a flash. "I don't think I have. I think it's you who has the wrong person, not I."

I stepped back again.

"You know who I am, don't you?" she purred.

I nodded. I knew exactly who she was, and she wasn't someone I wanted to get entangled with.

"I get what I want, always." Her eyes flashed as dark as the shadows that stretched behind her.

I shook my head. The sun dipped behind the trees, and shadows lengthened, casting bars like a gaol house round about. I stared at the witch, quite unable to take my eyes off her, fear stirring within my heart, like a frightened lamb trapped within the gaze of a wolf.

"I always get what I want, and I want you." She fixed me with her glare and my knees went weak. There were stories told of Liria's conquests, and they were never good for the quarry, not ever, not even once.

Again, Isla's fair face flooded my mind and I chose the only course I could. I turned and ran.

The burning globe of red dropped out of sight and the end-of-summer air grew chill. My booted feet pounded the ground and my breath caught. My heart hammered and Isla clung to it. An embittered cry of rage echoed behind me, bouncing off the trees, and I stretched my legs and my gait as far as they would go. It wasn't far enough.

An incantation swung through the woods, coiling like vines, and Liria got what she wanted. My boots became heavy, my legs stiffened, and soon I could no longer run. I slowed with a weariness that defied the rapid beat of my heart and I stopped, unable to lift my feet from the woodland floor.

Liria swept past, her cloak flowing like a gale, and then she tiptoed back to me. "I told you," she whispered, "I always get what I want."

I paled. Feeling the colour drain from my face and unable to move, I pursed my lips and set my glare. I recoiled as her breath trailed across my skin, my lip curling in distaste. The cloying scent of jasmine, musk and… and nightshade, nauseated me and I couldn't disguise my revulsion.

Her face darkened as I flinched beneath her touch. A spell fluttered about my head, another chant, but in her place I saw Isla and I relaxed. Liria moved to kiss me, but the cloves on her breath made me shrink and she stamped her feet.

My heart remained with my love, and not one thing Liria tried could break it.

In a move like a tempest she whirled about me and her screech filled the air. I cowered, and covered my ears, and listened as the storm erupted. My feet rooted to the ground, my boot-laces unfurled and dug deep beneath the forest floor, and Liria's violent incantation spun around me.

I slipped between consciousness and sleep.

***

I gazed about me as I woke. Leaves fluttered to the ground, and Liria stood on the other side of the clearing. I stared, trying to decipher the meaning behind the satisfied smile on her face. She stood with hands on hips, her cloak quivering in the remnants of the tornado. Then her smile gave way to apathy and I thought I'd won.

I'd stood my ground and won!

I stood my ground as she whipped up her cloak and walked away.

I closed my eyes and released the sigh of a weary one and laughed. My laughter was quiet, it struggled up my throat in bubbles and bursts then petered away. I shook, my body quaking, until the ripples beneath my skin stilled. I tried to move my arms, but couldn't, my hands and fingers solid and immoveable. I stood frozen, immobile, locked into a spell of petrification, and not even a murmur could escape my throat. Not a sound echoed within the forest, no birdsong, not a rustle or a whisper, except perhaps, the silent footsteps that strode away from me.

The leaves turned, as if echoing Liria's curse, and I stood silent. Vines and nightshade erupted from the soil beneath my feet and bindweed twined, consuming me as loss ravaged my mind. Days turned to weeks and the forest grew about me, dark and foreboding like a cancer claiming my soul.

Autumn's chill spread through the gold and scarlet, and dying green, and then my Isla's voice wandered across the dewy grass, lifting up into the fading leaves, searching for her lost love. My bursting heart sang and my breath fluttered on the autumn symphony, and in her hair, and I watched as Isla moved like a mournful sylvan through the forest. The song on her lips, a forlorn lament, matched only by the black she wore from head to toe. I urged and whispered in silence, and she searched.

***

Winter's snow swathed the forest floor, and ominous clouds hung in the sky, and still she walked, my beloved, soft-footed and lone. Her fur-bound feet crunched through the flurry, and her hands brushed snow from low, bare branches, and I shivered as she walked softly through the trees. She moved like a shadow, dark against white, and I listened, my heart breaking as "Odhran..." slipped from her mouth.

***

Spring's light, crepuscular rays shone down through the emerging canopy, dappling my face. Honey-green leaves unfurled and broke through, stretching in spring's embrace. Wild garlic carpeted the forest floor and tiny purple toadflax fought the nightshade to nibble my toes. Vetch twined about my legs and ivy climbed high upon my limbs.

Isla, still dressed in mourning, welcomed the early sun, gathering bluebells and pale sunshine primroses. Blossom fell like confetti upon her head and her feet danced lightly on the green sward. I breathed and my heart swelled like the buds on the boughs.

Summer brought its glittering jewels and deep verdant life. Foxgloves stretched tall beside me and the rambling rose adorned me in a multitude of pale petals. Isla moved soulfully through the forest, resting beneath its emerald awning, taking time to catch her breath. I waved, leaves rippling in the heat, and beamed as the sun bore down, and my heart leapt as she still whispered my name in the breeze "Odhran…" I yearned to touch and hold her, to kiss the daisy-chain circlet upon her dark hair, but she was gone and beyond my reach.

***

Autumn's return brought crimson and bronze, and jade and brown, and the slow falling leaves matched her new attire. My heart dimmed and my hearing dulled as the wild, winter wind blew across the fields and into my life. Ivy choked me as it climbed my trunk, and nightshade and nettles warned her away from my bower. She still wandered, lonely, through the trees, still searching for the love she lost, and I still whispered, but she no longer heard me.

***

Winter froze the ground and water the colour of her ice-blue eyes hung from my boughs, and I knew she was gone. Only deer wandered, hooves crushing the hoarfrost and bruising the grass like the purple shroud that veiled my heart. Thorns pierced my side as I shivered beneath the black, night sky and listened to my splintering heart.

***

Spring's warmth failed to reignite my soul, no matter how it tried. I stiffened and darkened, a shadow of myself, and I became cold. I could not stop the burgeoning joy of new growth, or my new cloak of leaves, but my heart was finally stilled.

***

Summer saw me frozen amid its heat. I stood silent and cold, my soul as hard and as callous as the wood I wore.

Wild poppies and cornflowers nodded, while lupins and daisies thwarted the nightshade at my feet. Honeysuckle and columbine drew Isla close, and her arms gathered bouquets and tears. Finally her hands brushed my torso, and she slipped down at my feet, and she wept beneath her daisy-chain wreath.

When she reappeared at last with recognition, and ruddy, autumn cheeks, and a heart full of joy I felt nothing. She ran to me with words tumbling from her mouth, but my gaze was bare.

"Odhran!" she cried, her voice taut with pain. "She told me, I know!"

Isla's arms embraced me, but my stone-cold heart was lost and my waters frozen. She cried, rivers of tears like a weeping willow, but I had nothing left, the man she once loved, just a lonely tree, tall and strong, but forever bereft.

***

Autumn's breeze lifted my leaves and Isla took comfort at my feet, her body moulding to mine and her tears bleeding into the thick mulch obscuring my roots. As the cold night drew in she lay in the crook of my ankle, her shawl drawn tightly around her shoulders beneath a veil of daisies and moss. I gazed as her sorrow permeated the sap running through my veins, and in the morning, as the sun peeped nervously over the far horizon, dew strewn tears bejewelled my leaves.

***

As morning's sigh woke Isla, she rejoiced at the diamonds coating my foliage and whispered her love. Birds flew her devotion into my branches, her ardour floating, on wings, down into my canopy and my heart stirred. Deep within the tree, within my prison, my soul swelled, pushing and yearning and fighting...

Isla's bare hands dug, pulling out vines and ivy and tearing her flesh as brambles bit.

The sun climbed into the sky, warming my trunk and tickling my fingers. The breeze rippled across my leaves as I shook my branches. My leaves, now crinkling with age, fluttered and quivered and dropped. Isla danced upon the rustling pile, urging me on. The birds sang, their chorus igniting a fire within and I answered with creaking limbs.

Anger surged, like electricity amid a storm, and my heart exploded, breaking out of the wooden cage and its restraints. Wood split and slivers broke, branches and brittle leaves shattered, and Isla flung herself to the ground. Showered by moss, and twigs and splinters, she quaked, until courage raised her eyes.

She stared up into the canopy, into the space where I once stood. There, instead, the sun shone, its rays dappling the forest floor and bathing her within its warmth. Isla's lip trembled and her eyes, as blue as the morning sky, moistened.

"Isla..." my voice croaked, unused to speech, and her gaze panned down until she saw me.

My clothes, leather and cotton, clung to my thin body draped with moss and lichen, and my boots groaned as I stepped forward. My legs shook and it was in Isla's arms that I gained my strength. Her hands lifted my head and stroked my hair, and her tears wet my cheeks. My solemn interlude, my silent oration, my words that never fell, all faded as I whispered heady devotion into the ear of my beloved.

The forest hummed with delight, birds twittered within the trees, and flowers opened their petals enticed by the sun's shimmering rays. I finally walked again, with Isla, to the clear, cold river, to dip my toes, and drink to life itself.

****

Goals

Tom Benson

Alexi Baxter waved to her husband, as he set off in his Porsche. The statuesque 30-year-old brunette wondered why Matthew felt he had to cheat. If she was so sexy and desirable, why would he have a regular, secret date?

Today Alexi decided, she would conduct a mission that would resolve her suspicions and her fears. She settled on a simple outfit of a floral summer dress and red stiletto heels.

It was Friday, and Matthew would be starting his day at his Premier League soccer team's training ground. Alexi wanted to be nearby, but out of sight when Matthew left early; as she was certain he would. Instead of using her BMW, she called a cab to get her clear of their select neighbourhood. Ten minutes later she slipped behind the wheel of her pre-ordered rental.

***

"Here we go," Alexi breathed as she saw Matthew's red car pull out onto the road. She slipped her car into gear and joined the flow of traffic. She had been careful to park far enough away that she could observe the car-park, but remain unnoticed.

In less than 20 minutes, Alexi was making a mental note of 'Diamond Towers', the tall glass and steel building where Matthew had driven into an underground car-park. The gold fittings around the entrance and lobby glistened in the sunlight. Whoever Matthew was visiting had money, or rich connections. Alexi was desperate to watch the entrance, so was relieved to see a parking space being vacated about 20 metres along the road. She parked quickly, adjusted her mirror to watch the entrance to the block, and then pulled out her phone, using it to trace the companies who rented offices in Diamond Towers. She recognised a name after a five minute search.

"Gotcha!" she said aloud.

***

Alexi strode purposefully from the bank of elevators on the 6th floor towards the reception desk. She nodded to the woman at reception and continued on her way towards a long corridor. Her progress was reflected in the glass doors that lined one side. There was plush seating along the opposite side.

Before she pushed open the glass outer office door, Alexi was already sizing up the young woman seated behind the desk.

'Sam Temple: Therapist of the Stars' was written in gold lettering on the door. As Alexi paused to read the proud boast she became aware of the secretary's perfume; an expensive brand.

"Hi," Alexi said, extending her right hand. "I'm Mrs Baxter," she smiled and continued in a syrupy tone. "You can call me Alexi. What's your name?"

"Sarah," the woman said, standing to accept the proffered hand. "I'm Mr Temple's..."

"Girl Friday?" Alexi finished for her, and then openly appraised the other woman. She had to assume that it was the boss's idea for his secretary to have such an appearance. Long, loose, dark ringlets hung down over Sarah's white blouse.

Alexi assessed the girl. The blouse was too tight, and the skirt was short enough to display most of her shapely legs, but such an outfit wasn't in keeping with the classy, opulent surroundings. Show the cleavage or the legs, Alexi thought as she looked – not both.

"How can I help you?" Sarah asked, swallowing hard.

Composing herself as she resumed her position at the desk, Alexi thought.

"Is my husband with Mr Temple?" Alexi asked with a smile.

"Yes," Sarah said and glanced at the door. "It's a private session."

"Not anymore," Alexi said, and glanced at Sarah's right hand. "And don't touch that intercom."

Alexi stepped forward and tried to open the office door, but it didn't budge.

Sarah pressed the intercom. "Mrs Baxter is on her way in."

Alexi stepped back and smiled as she looked Sarah up and down. "Open it please, Sarah." She paused. "I won't ask again."

***

Alexi stepped into the plush office and looked around, but there was nobody there. The office had a panoramic window that allowed natural light to illuminate the spacious interior. As well as a mahogany desk and leather chair, there were a pair of comfortable seats either side of a small glass table. There was also a couch against one wall.

On the two side walls were an assortment of framed certificates, but no photographs. The wall opposite the desk showcased a large painting. For Alexi, the subject of the painting spoke volumes about Sam Temple. Her lips curled.

She walked across the room, her high heels sinking into the deep-pile carpet. At the desk, she pushed the executive chair away and leaned over to read the diary appointments.

"10:30am until 2:30 p.m. - Matthew Baxter," Alexi said aloud. She stood up and gazed at the painting of the solar system. As she looked around the spacious office with its plush fittings and dark panelled walls she almost missed seeing the other door. There was no handle, only a groove in the panelling.

Alexi crossed to the door, took a deep breath and slipped her fingertips into the groove. She tugged gently, and the panel moved back silently on smooth runners. Daylight filtered into the ante-room through a slatted blind.

The room was as large as the office and fitted with the same deep-pile carpet, but the anteroom had a bed. On top of the bed, uncovered, lay a naked man. Alexi glanced at his face, at first avoiding looking at the rest of him. She assumed it was the therapist. He was on his back, breathing gently as if in a deep sleep.

Alexi looked around and saw two sets of men's clothes. Neatly folded on a chair were trousers, socks and boxer shorts. Hanging over the back of the chair was a smart jacket that matched the trousers. There was also a shirt and tie. Underneath were shoes.

On another chair nearby was a red and white training outfit. Everything was neatly folded: a hooded-top, joggers, a vest, shorts and socks. Below the chair were red training shoes; like Matthew's. On top of the clothing were placed a wedding ring and a watch. It was Matthew's usual jewellery.

A few feet away there was another doorway. Alexi steeled herself for what she might find and advanced to the next room. Before stepping into what was an adjoining bathroom, she took a breath and prepared to speak to her husband.

"So," she said as her heels clicked on the tiled floor, "what have you ..." and her question faded. The small, but luxuriously appointed bathroom was unoccupied. Her blue eyes widened as she scanned the room again and then stepped back into the anteroom.

When Alexi looked at the man on the bed once again, she looked more closely at his face. Sam Temple was dark-haired, but his features were remarkably similar to Matthew's. Alexi tried to imagine Matthew with dark hair and at that point the likeness seemed uncanny. She found herself looking at the neck, shoulders, arms and torso of the sleeping man.

When her gaze paused at the top of his thighs, her eyes widened a little. She didn't know how good Mr Temple was as a therapist, but he had a lot in common with Matthew regarding to physique. Alexi continued to look along the legs and then her scrutiny travelled back along the length of Mr Temple to his face.

Apart from the hair colour and the absence of a small scar on the left thigh, Alexi realised she could be looking at her husband's body. Every toned muscle was like Matthew's, and she knew his body well. At that point, Temple's eyes flickered open, and he turned onto his right side, facing toward Alexi.

***

Alexi stepped back towards the door that led to the office, but when she realised that Temple was not focusing on her, she remained still. She watched and listened as the therapist let out a sigh.

As she continued to watch, Sam Temple began to glow; his entire skin emitted an aura of light. Alexi stared, but had to blink several times. Another man was materialising, as if being released from a human cocoon. He was naked, like Temple, and they were facing each other. For a moment, Sam Temple's arms came forward as if holding the other naked man in an embrace.

When the second man's body developed fully, his arms were tightly wrapped around Temple's body. The two men had their legs slightly intertwined, and their faces were almost touching. The second man's body became solid and assumed natural colour, like Temple's, but the second man's appearance was different. He was fair-haired. The aura faded and Alexi realised she was looking at Matthew.

***

"Sarah," Alexi said as she exited the office. "May I ask you a couple of questions?"

"Yes of course you may," the woman said, smiling.

"How long have you worked for Mr Temple?" Sarah's sparkling blue eyes seemed to mist for several seconds, but it was long enough for Alexi to notice. "Come on, it wasn't such a difficult question."

"Since he started his practice here," Sarah said. "About six months."

"That's interesting. You look about twenty-something, so where did you work before?" The response was that same momentary pause, but Alexi waited.

"I worked in other similar places," Sarah said. There was a definite, eerie misting of Sarah's eyes when she was considering responses to questions.

Alexi posed a series of questions for the secretary and in each case observed the fraction of time used in concentration, prior to supplying a vague answer. It was notable that Sarah couldn't remember instantly how many jobs she'd had, how long she'd lived locally in Oxford, if her boss was married, or had always practiced the same business.

More than anything, Alexi noted Sarah's lack of concern at being asked so many personal questions by a relative stranger. She continued to look deep into Sarah's eyes when she asked her next question.

"Sarah, how long will Mr Baxter and Mr Temple's session last?"

The secretary glanced at the diary. "The session is for four hours."

"Thank you, Sarah," Alexi said. She smiled as she reached forward and placed a hand on Sarah's. "I'd like you to do something for me." Sarah's eyes flickered as Alexi continued. "Please don't tell Mr Temple or my husband that I've been here. Will you do that for me?"

"It will be a secret between us?" Sarah asked. Her distinct pronunciation made it sound like English was her second language.

"Yes," Alexi said. She found herself slotting small fragments of information together and a theory was evolving. "It will be a secret between us," she mimicked. She watched Sarah's eyes mist again. Sarah's misting eyes were a symptom of a particular condition that Alexi had only witnessed twice before.

The secretary nodded and smiled as Alexi patted her hand and then left.

***

Alexi made herself comfortable on a sumptuous leather sofa ten metres along the wide corridor. She lifted a magazine from a nearby table and observed Sarah through the glass office door.

Sarah seemed to do very little. At regular intervals, she would pick up the telephone or tap on the keyboard of her computer. After two minutes of activity, she went back to her pose. She sat upright facing forward, complete with enigmatic smile.

The door to Temple's office opened and Matthew Baxter stepped out. He and Sarah exchanged a nod and then the footballer left and headed for the elevators. As Alexi observed Matthew, she was positive that his expression seemed brighter, and his movements were more fluid than earlier in the day. There was a spring in his step.

Whilst waiting, Alexi had been thinking back over what she'd seen in Temple's diary. All the appointments were for people in influential positions, or people heading for the top of their profession. Among the names, Alexi had noted top sports personalities, corporate executives, and senior civil service personnel.

Alexi recalled seeing a certificate which declared that Temple was qualified in hypnosis. He had attracted clients who between them shared a wide variety of ability, but perhaps all were open to post-hypnotic suggestion. In order to maintain regular appointments Temple only had to suggest wellbeing after his consultation.

There were three women among the clients. One was a bank executive, another a psychiatrist, and the third was a high-flying student whom Alexi knew worked part-time as a glamour model. A plan formed in Alexi's mind.

***

It was 2:45 p.m. when a tall blonde stepped into the elevator on the ground floor. Alexi smiled at her as she joined her in the plush, carpeted cubicle. A soft melody was playing from corner speakers.

"It's Juliette isn't it?" Alexi said, "Juliette Pearce?"

"Yes," Juliette said.

Alexi was no slouch in the looks department, but Miss Pearce was more than simply attractive; she was gorgeous.

"May I ask," Alexi said. "Are you visiting Sam Temple?"

"Yes, that's where I'm going now. Why do you ask?"

"I was wondering, because my husband is a client too," Alexi said and smiled as she extended a hand. "My name is Alexi. I'm Matthew Baxter's wife."

"The footballer," Juliette gushed, and eagerly placed her slender hand in Alexi's.

"How long is your appointment with Mr Temple?" Alexi asked.

"About four hours," Juliette said.

Alexi continued to hold and squeeze Juliette's hand as she looked into the blonde's brown eyes. "I read somewhere that you have the ultimate combination of brains and beauty." She noted the wide eyes and parted lips before Juliette laughed.

Alexi looked away for a moment, before whispering. "Would you do something for me Juliette, and I'll do *anything* in return?"

"Could I meet your husband? I watch every game he plays in."

Alexi was stunned by the rapid response. "Of course you can."

"Okay," Juliette said, her face reddening. "What would you like me to do?"

Alexi explained enough to capture Juliette's interest.

"This is the wrong floor for Sam's office," Juliette said when the elevator doors opened.

"I know," Alexi said, "but the ladies' room on this floor is locked. She held up a key, winked and nodded along the corridor.

Five minutes later, the two women were standing in the ladies' washroom facing each other. Juliette couldn't tear her eyes away from Alexi's gaze.

Alexi stepped forward. "Take my hands Juliette." The two women extended their hands to each other and Alexi concentrated.

***

"Good morning you beautiful creature," Sam said as his next client entered. "Go straight through and I'll be with you in a few minutes."

The woman smiled and glided across the office to the ante-room. She paused in the doorway, looked back at Sam over her shoulder, slid the door open, went inside and then closed the door behind her.

"Why aren't you undressed?" Sam asked the blonde five minutes later.

"Today, I'd like you to talk for a while." Her eyes looked away from the therapist.

"I could talk to you afterwards," Sam said, as he undid his shirt buttons. "Look at me. What do you want me to talk about?"

"You get naked, and then I'll tell you," she said, still not meeting his gaze.

"Right," Sam said and quickly finished undressing. He sat on the bed.

"First of all," the blonde said. "I'd like you to remind me why we have to be naked."

Sam squinted. "Oh that's easy," he said. "It creates a more intimate bond if there is total trust and no physical barriers."

"I understand that you want to get inside my mind?"

"Yes," he said. "You've never questioned my methods before. Is there something wrong?" He reached out to turn her face towards him and he focused his eyes and thoughts on her again; puzzled.

"You told me that you like beautiful, intelligent women," she said.

"Yes," he said. "And for me, you are the ultimate woman."

"Am I the only female client you explore in such depth?"

"Yes, of course," he said. "You and I have a special connection."

"Do you get so close to any of your other clients?" She crossed her legs, and the hem of her mini-dress rode up, exposing her thigh.

"I get close to *all* of them, but not in the way I do with you." His eyes wandered downward for a moment. "Is there anything else before you get undressed?"

"Yes," she said. "Tell me about your background, and your work, but make it amusing."

"Why?" he said and forced a laugh. "What will be in it for me?"

"If you open up to me, I'm going to take you further than ever before, and you won't have to hypnotise me."

"Okay," he said and gave her a devilish grin. "I'm not human. I'm an alien criminal mastermind, and I came to Earth a few months ago." He saw her smile and her eyes light up.

He continued, "At first when I arrived here, I had difficulty dealing with the pleasures of my new body, but I got accustomed to it."

The blonde nodded and licked her lips.

Sam said: "Before I materialised, I looked at many aspects of human nature and behaviour. I took on the best human physique I could see and then created this office environment to hide my plan for domination."

"Do you mean domination of this town?"

"No," he said. "It will take a while, but I'll grow way beyond this, and I want you to be my partner."

"I'm getting turned on," she said and bit her lower lip briefly. "How do you do this domination thing?"

For the next five minutes, Sam explained how he needed to have his client completely naked, including the removal of jewellery. He would then embrace them on the bed whether it was a man or a woman. When he held them tight, flesh to flesh, he was able to take over their mind. He explained that certain clients required weekly sessions.

In the case of those with a high intelligence, he would soak up their knowledge. In the case of those with physical attributes of beauty or strength, he would exchange nutrients to maintain his appearance and strength. As he continued, he found himself opening up to somebody else as never before.

"Now," he said, smiling once again. "Was that entertaining enough for you?"

"Yes," she said, standing to kick off her shoes. She tugged upwards and shed the only other piece of clothing she was wearing; a light summer mini-dress. "Why do you get completely undressed except for that ring?"

"I could never take that off," he said as he admired her body. "It's the only thing that stops my enemies from sending me back to Zoltan." He held his hand up to look at the ring and laughed.

"Zoltan?"

"Yes, my home planet."

"Oh yes of course because you're an alien," she laughed. "May I look at your ring?"

"Yes," he said, "and then we must both get on here so that we can begin." He patted the bed with his right hand as he lifted his left hand.

The woman held his left hand with both of hers, tenderly at first, and then in a lightning fast movement removed the special ring and clasped it in her hand. She looked into Sam's eyes for a few seconds before she leapt onto him and held his body in a tight embrace on the bed, wrapping her arms and strong legs around him.

"What's come over you Juliette?" he said, looking up at her.

"This is Juliette's body, but my name is Alexi," the woman said as her voice changed, and she looked at Sam's squinting, disbelieving eyes. "I am Alexi Venusia, an officer of the Intergalactic Council of Extraditions."

"ICE?" Sam said. His eyes widened as Alexi tightened her embrace; flesh to flesh.

"Yes," she said as Temple started to dematerialise under her. "You've been ICE'd."

The choice to remain on Earth as a human was Alexi's reward.

**

Outside Temple's office, the only sign that Sarah ever existed was a faint scent.

Juliette Pearce woke up from a faint in the ladies' room, wondering why she was in the office block. She smoothed her outfit, tidied her hair and headed for her modelling assignment. She needed the money to allow her to continue her scientific studies.

At around 3 p.m., across an area of 20 miles, all those who had been Temple's clients experienced a pulsating headache for a few seconds. In each case they felt better than they had for many months; physically and mentally refreshed.

In a smart house amidst landscaped gardens in a desirable location, Matthew Baxter arrived home.

"Alexi my love, you look radiant, and much happier than earlier today."

"Hi handsome," she said. "I feel like a different person." She had fulfilled her assignment and was looking forward to her new existence as a woman - as an Earthling.

******

If The Shoe Fits

Katharine E. Hamilton

"What about this pair?"

Amy Thompson glanced up and across the small shoe store towards her best friend, Renee, and shook her head. Sighing, Renee simply placed the black stiletto back on the pedestal and continued down the aisle.

"I need to find *something*," Renee whined, blowing a frustrated breath that fluffed her blonde bangs into the air and left an attitude of defeated resignation floating about the room.

"I'm sure if you looked hard enough you would find a pair of heels in your closet that would work just fine." Amy smirked as she lifted a wedged cork heel into her hand and glanced at the price tag on the bottom.

"I could, but this is a big deal, Ames. I need new shoes." Renee lifted a spiked high heel with a peep toe and waited for Amy's reaction. Amy rolled her eyes, and Renee groaned as she placed it back on the plastic pedestal.

"You keep shooting down all the options." Renee crossed her arms and studied Amy as she continued to peruse the shelves. "Is this your way of reminding me you don't want to go tonight?"

Amy paused and looked up, her dark eyes lit with amusement. "Why would I need to remind you? I'm pretty sure I made my feelings clear last night."

"But you're still going, right?"

"I told you I would, so I am."

Renee's brow relaxed and she smiled widely. "Good. I think it might surprise you. It's actually fun and there are always handsome men participating."

"I'm sure there are," Amy replied skeptically, as she slipped her size seven and a half foot into a sandal.

"I know you don't believe me," Renee continued, "but it's true. Last month, I walked away with three men calling me for dates." She clapped her hands in excitement.

"And remind me again how many of those worked out for you," Amy stated dryly.

Renee sighed as she grabbed a box containing the original black stilettos. "They were fun. Dates are fun, Ames. Though I can understand how you can't remember that fact, considering you haven't had one in oh… say… months?"

"Nine months, actually," Amy corrected.

"*Nine months?!*" Renee looked horrified and Amy laughed.

"Yes, nine months. Need I remind you I have been a little busy? Opening the café has consumed my life. I don't have time to date."

"Well, we are definitely going to change that tonight. I will not let you leave until you have at least three men who have asked for your number."

"I don't need a date, Renee. I am only going as moral support for you."

"Ames… listen," Renee adjusted her purse on her shoulder and hoisted the box of heels into the crook of her arm, "Men are like shoes."

Amy's right brow arched slightly as she listened to her friend.

"They are cute, sometimes even sexy. Do we always need them? No. But they sure are fun to have."

Amy chuckled. "And here I thought shoes were usually uncomfortable and unreasonable."

"Only if you buy the wrong pair," Renee countered.

"And I'm trying to say that you shouldn't have to buy a pair, period. Maybe I prefer to walk about barefoot."

"You are such a pessimist," Renee nagged.

"I prefer realist," Amy replied.

"So you would rather have no man at all?"

"I've been doing rather fine that way." Amy's patience began to wane as she placed the pair of sandals on the countertop, and the salesclerk began ringing up the total.

"Just promise me one thing," Renee added, noting her friend's frustration, "Promise me you will at least try to have fun tonight."

"I will. I like being social," Amy explained, "I just don't feel like speed dating is necessarily my thing."

"Like I said, relate it to shoe shopping," Renee grinned.

"I am glad there are no men around to hear you comparing them to shoes, Nee. They might find that quite degrading."

Renee shrugged, "Men compare us to things too."

"Like what?"

"I don't know - cars?" Renee shrugged in indifference.

Laughing, Amy grabbed her bag and waited for Renee as she paid for her insensible black stilettos. As her friend tucked her wallet back into her purse, they stepped out of the small shop and turned towards Amy's café at the end of the street. As Amy turned to follow Renee, she slammed into a wall of masculinity that jolted her back a few steps and caused her to stumble on the sidewalk. She felt a firm grip on her forearms as she righted herself.

"I am very sorry." She watched as the man knelt down and grabbed her shopping bag and stood to hand it to her, his green eyes begging her pardon. Amy's hand froze as she reached out. The man stood tall and slim, his athletic build not going unnoticed by Amy, or Renee standing behind him.

The man flashed a dazzling smile and ran a hand over his embarrassed face. "I wasn't watching where I was going. Are you okay?"

Amy shook her head and nodded. "Yes, yes, I'm fine. No worries." Breathless, she grabbed the proffered bag and went to step around him towards a gawking Renee.

She walked a few steps and then shot a curious glance over her shoulder. She caught the same emerald gaze and a pleased smile on the man's face as he continued watching her in return. She felt heat rush to her cheeks as she turned back and hustled her steps towards the café.

**

Reed Davenport tossed his keys into the small, red ceramic bowl on his entry table as he walked into the apartment he shared with his younger brother Zach. His brother, true to form, was engrossed in an intense video game tournament with two of his buddies and completely unaware of Reed entering the room.

"Who's winning?" Reed's rich baritone filtered through the living room and had all three guys slightly jumping in their seats as they battled zombies.

"Totally me," Zach claimed. "As always."

Reed rolled his eyes at his younger brother's ego and shuffled towards the kitchen to grab the beer he needed, in order to relax from the long day at the clinic. His younger brother whooped in celebration as blood splatters filled the television screen. At twenty-seven, Zach still held the temperament of a twenty-year-old and while most women found his brother charming, Reed found him quite immature.

And annoying!

He glanced around the kitchen, every surface littered with dirty pizza boxes and empty beer bottles. Reed forgot about relaxing notions and began tossing items into the trash bin. He thought helping Zach out by providing him with a place to live would have been an easier task. But the more his brother made himself at home, the more agitated Reed became. He had worked hard earning the lifestyle he now had. Eight years of college for his degree in veterinary medicine had taken money, patience, and a ton of hard work, but it had all paid off now that, at twenty-nine, he had his own successful veterinary practice. His apartment, in the nicest area of the city, had also been an upgrade and an achievement of his hard work as well, and Zach struggled to respect that fact.

He heard the other men saying their goodbyes, and glanced up as Zach waltzed into the kitchen with a wry grin. "Sorry about the mess. We got a little carried away today." He watched as Reed continued cleaning up his clutter.

"So, you still planning on going with me tonight, to the speed dating marathon?"

"Marathon?" Reed asked, with slight amusement.

"Yeah, that's what they call it. There are two groups tonight."

"I said I would go."

"Okay, good. You might want to shower first though. You aren't going to meet any good looking women smelling like wet dog," Zach teased. "Be ready in an hour. I like to get there early to scope out the potentials."

Reed sighed as he watched his brother walk to his room and shut the door. He ran a roughened palm over his face and tried to swipe away his exhaustion. He didn't want to go to any sort of speed dating marathon, but he had already promised Zach. His mind drifted to the pretty woman he'd bumped into on the street earlier that day. Her deep brown eyes, auburn hair, and slashing cheekbones had stunned him into silence. Her honey-vanilla scent still lingered upon his shirt; making him wish to see and smell her again, in person. He shook his head.

No. No thoughts about pretty shoe shoppers.

He didn't have time for women - for dating. He would make polite conversation with the women tonight, but he didn't plan on pursuing any of them afterwards, no matter how sweet they smelled.

***

Amy fidgeted as she tugged the hem of the short, black dress Renee had loaned her, and glanced about the crowded room. Men and women mingled about drinking champagne, all dressed to the nines, and flirting amongst themselves.

"Okay, here you go," Renee shuffled up next to her and handed her a champagne flute and her nametag. "Put this on and you have a red sticker, so that means you are in the red room. I am too, so don't worry."

"I wasn't," Amy replied without conviction, as two men walked by her and Renee and openly surveyed the length of their legs. She felt exposed, she realized. Awkward. Renee grabbed her hand as a muddled voice filtered over the speaker.

After stepping into the red interior of the back room, Renee sat at a small table and motioned for Amy to sit at the next one. "We sit on this side, and then the men rotate from chair to chair on the other," Renee explained in a hushed whisper.

Amy nodded as she tucked her handbag into her lap and stared at the cheap, red carnation centered on the table in a silver vase. She inwardly rolled her eyes as Renee nudged her shoulder and squealed with excitement. "This is going to be such fun. Do you see that man over there? He's been staring at you since we walked in."

Amy shot a glance towards the door. Her eyes widened in surprise as she recognized the man from the sidewalk. He offered an abashed smile and turned to talk to the man next to him.

A bell rang and men began taking seats. A man with a pinched face and snarled nose sat before Amy. His crisp, white button up had been drenched in aftershave or cologne and she tried to take in as few breaths as possible as he began talking about himself. She half tuned in as she searched the room for the handsome sidewalk stranger, but didn't find him.

"And what about you?" The man asked. His eager tone was already grating upon Amy's raw nerves.

"Oh, I um... I am a pharmacist, over on Fifth."

"A pharmacist?!" The man asked with exuberance, "Well that is quite impressive. Have you lived here long?"

Amy felt the small pinch on her thigh as Renee reached over and under the table and punished her for lying. Amy smirked and then relaxed in her seat; realizing then she could have more fun creating a persona than actually pursuing phone numbers. The bell rang and the man shook her hand, "It was a pleasure, Amy. Perhaps I will bump into you again at the mingle session."

"The mingle session?" Amy leaned over and asked Renee as the next man sat across from her.

"Yes, afterwards there is an hour long social. That's usually where the men approach you and ask for your number."

Amy cringed at that thought and turned a forced smile upon the man now before her. He smiled widely and her forced expression relaxed into a genuine one as he leaned comfortably back in the chair.

"Zach." He greeted, reaching out to shake her hand.

She responded warmly. "Amy. Nice to meet you."

"Likewise." He crossed his arms and his blue eyes danced over her appearance. "I don't think I've seen you here before. First time?"

"Actually, yes. You do this often?"

He nodded.

"What's that like?" Amy asked, intrigued that a handsome guy would need to speed date once a month.

"What?"

"Being a regular at a speed dating marathon? You must do quite well."

His brow rose and he leaned forward flirtatiously, "And what makes you think I do so well?" He winked and she blushed at the implications of her previous comment. Clearing her throat, she smoothed a hand over her lap at the invisible wrinkles.

"I... apologize. I just assumed..."

He laughed and several heads turned, making Amy shrink back into her chair.

"What do you do for a living, Amy?"

"Real Estate. You?"

"Now real estate sounds boring... I mean, interesting," he teased. "Please, tell me more."

She chuckled and shook her head. "Now why would I do that when you just called it boring?"

His smile widened and the bell rang. He lightly squeezed her hand and winked at her as he moved to the next table.

Round after round of men circled past Amy's table and she anxiously awaited the stranger from the sidewalk, but he never passed by. When the final bell rang, Amy sighed in relief. She had worn herself out thinking of more careers. She had hopped from pharmaceuticals to swim coach to flight attendant to attorney. She couldn't even remember all of her professions. She giggled as Renee swatted her arm. "I cannot believe you," Renee scolded, "I had a hard time focusing tonight because I was roped into what you would say next!" She laughed as Amy shrugged and grinned.

"What are you going to do if one of the men wants to take you out and you can't remember what you told him you did for a living?" Renee asked.

"I am not giving out my number, remember?"

"Well that is a shame." A familiar voice filtered over her shoulder and she turned to see the mischievous man from earlier named Zach. Renee smiled and Zach immediately took notice. "Though I wasn't going to ask for me."

"Oh, really?" Amy questioned. "And who were you 'going to ask for?'"

"My brother," Zach stated. "He's pretty boring too." He winked at her again as she rolled her eyes. "He got stuck in the blue room though."

"So what, he can't come over here?" Amy asked.

Renee shook her head. "No. You only mingle in the rooms you cycled through."

"Ah. I see. Guess, that's too bad," Amy stated dryly. "My hopes of being pawned off onto someone's boring brother have just been dashed."

Zach laughed and nodded as Amy lifted up her empty glass. "I think I will go remedy this," she said. "You two kids talk amongst yourselves." She left Renee with Zach and meandered towards the bar. Easing onto a stool, she thanked the bartender for the refill and waited out the rest of her evening in blissful silence.

***

"You said she was real estate?" Reed asked Zach as they jogged through the park and up the narrow sidewalks.

"Yeah, something like that. But some other guy said she had told him she worked pharmaceuticals at some place on fifth."

"Pharmaceuticals?" Reed's brow furrowed as he wondered about the pretty shoe shopper.

"So you met her or something?" Zach's question broke through his daydream and he nodded.

"Bumped into her on the sidewalk yesterday afternoon. Wanted to talk to her last night but seems I was in the wrong group."

"Well, you weren't missing much. She wasn't near as interesting as her friend."

"Why do you say that?"

"You could just tell she didn't want to be there." Zach glanced at his older brother and slowly grinned. "You seriously liked this girl didn't you?"

Reed shot him an annoyed flash of green eyes and sped up his pace.

"Wow. My brother, *Mister Doesn't-have-time-for-women*, has found a little slice of pie he likes!" He cheered as Reed's shoulders stiffened in embarrassment. Zach continued to laugh as shouts rang out from the sidewalk and a golden retriever with a blue leash darted across the busy street - a woman's voice yelled after it. He then saw a petite woman rush through cars, dodging bumpers, as she chased her dog.

The dog continued to run straight to the park and Reed noticed the blue cast on the dog's right front leg. Gatsby. "See if you can cut him off on the other side so he won't run back into the street," he ordered Zach as he sprinted towards the dog. He dove towards the leash and gripped it firmly as he slowly stood to his feet. He heard footfalls as Gatsby's owner slid to a breathless stop. She took off her sunglasses and Reed froze. The woman's eyes widened as recognition dawned upon her beautiful face. A slow smile spread over her lips as she continued catching her breath.

"This one yours?"

She shook her head. "No. My neighbor's. Thank you for catching him."

She reached for the leash and stood with her hands on her hips as Zach ran up and stopped next to Reed. Amy shook her head and laughed as Zach grinned. "Small world."

Amy nodded in agreement and stuck out her hand towards Reed. "This is our third time to bump into one another. I guess we should finally meet."

Reed grabbed her delicate hand and shook it, the small warmth traveling up his arm not going unnoticed. "Reed Davenport."

"Amy Thompson."

"Realtor." Zach added.

Amy blushed. "Actually no. I am not in real estate."

Zach feigned a shocked expression and lifted a quizzical brow. "Pharmaceuticals?"

Amy laughed and shook her head. "No. I own a café."

"Really?" Reed asked, curiously.

"Yes."

"Then why tell everyone something different?" Reed asked as she fell into step beside him and Zach along the trail. "I, uh, heard through the grapevine." He motioned towards Zach.

"So creepers like this guy won't stalk me." She tossed a thumb towards Zach and giggled as he laughed.

"So, Reed," Amy began, stopping and turning towards him, "I hear you are quite boring."

Reed's dark brow arched into his hairline as he shot an annoyed look to his brother.

"What is it you do?" Amy asked.

"I'm a veterinarian."

Surprise lit her face and she turned towards Zach and shoved him, "That's not boring."

Zach dodged another punch to the arm and began jogging backwards as he faced them. "I'll let you two... mingle." He winked one more time at Amy and ran off.

Reed motioned towards a bench and Amy sat, setting the dog's leash next to her. Reed eased beside her. They were quiet at first, both shy and somewhat dumbfounded they had bumped into one another again. "I have to say it is good to see Gatsby has gained some of his strength back," Reed commented, as he swiped a hand over his furry patient's golden coat.

"You are his vet?"

"I am."

Amy chuckled. "Please don't tell Mrs Evans he got away. She would kill me if she knew her baby almost got hit by about twenty cars."

"Your secret is safe with me." Reed patted the dog one more time and stood, "Walk with me?"

She stood and clasped Gatsby's leash and studied Reed a moment while he surveyed the dog's cast. He glanced up and it sent a rush of warmth and anticipation through her and into her heart. Reed seemed kind, and she couldn't help the tingle of attraction she felt towards him as he stood and looked down at her and smiled.

"I must admit I find it quite interesting. I bump into you while shoe shopping. Then see you at speed dating in said shoes. Then bump into you at the park wearing, again, the exact same shoes." Reed pointed at the bedazzled footwear and she laughed.

"They must be my lucky pair. Thank God for sandals, right?"

Reed grinned. "They are cute, practical, stylish…"

"And completely not boring." Amy finished with a wink as she fell into step beside him and smiled up with a sparkle in her eye.

****

The Birth

Lucinda E. Clarke

The young woman gave a scream and fell back on the bed. The pain was terrible, so bad – so intense. The other two children she had given birth to had never caused her such agony. They had both been delivered quickly and almost painlessly. This time was very, very different.

She took a deep breath and gasped as the sweat poured down her face, and whimpered as the next contraction sent pains shooting throughout her body. She almost passed out with the searing agony, but no longer had the strength to shout out.

The pains had begun early in the morning and it was now almost dusk. Wave after wave after wave of pure hell.

When Alois got home from work, surely he would send for the local midwife. But it was more than likely he would stop off at the bar where he sometimes stayed for hours drinking with his friends. Then he would come home drunk, and he would be angry if his supper wasn't ready on the table for him. He would fly into one of his terrible rages. He was known throughout the whole town for his vicious temper, his shouting and swearing. Once, he had smashed every dish in the house and kicked the table to bits, just because she'd kept him waiting.

When they first met, she'd adored him, worshipped the ground he walked on. What could an important customs official see in a poor, simple housemaid? Twenty three years older than her, he was a man of the world and she was only a simple peasant girl who cleaned other people's houses. She had admired and respected him. She couldn't believe it when he proposed. She walked on air for weeks.

But it wasn't long before she saw the darker side of him. His bitterness at being born illegitimate, his frustration after two previous marriages at not producing a string of fine, strong, obedient sons.

The only son he had was proving to be such a disappointment to him. She had a strong suspicion that the boy was stealing from the local merchants. He was seldom at home and she had no idea where he was now, or she would have sent him to fetch the midwife.

Alois once had such high hopes for the children he was sure she would bear him, but all she had managed to do so far was produce two sickly girls who showed no signs of surviving. Maybe this one would be different. Maybe he would be ambitious, make his father proud of him, temper his father's moods and bring peace to the family. Please God let this son, if it was a son, make his father truly proud.

Another contraction wracked her body as she lay there in agony. No chance of getting up to fix supper, or see to the two young ones who were playing in the ashes of the fire which had long since gone out in the hearth. They were filthy dirty and fretful with not eating all day, but she couldn't see to them now. She didn't have the strength.

A cold chill was creeping though the room and despite the perspiration that was breaking out all over her. She shivered and pulled the blankets higher.

She must have passed out at some point, for when she came to, she was aware of Alois' face close to hers.

"What you doing in bed at this time of day?" he snarled at her.

"Alois, my time has come," she gasped, "Please help, please... the nurse." For once Alois did not argue with her.

She passed out again so she was not aware that the nurse was there, nor did she see her shake her head and whisper that the doctor must come. The nurse could not cope with this; it was beyond her skills. She had never encountered a child so reluctant to enter this world.

The pain came flooding back as the doctor shook her hard.

"You must help, Klara. You must push, push hard, ignore the pain; it will all go away after. Come on, come on – push."

She floated in and out as the pain built to a crescendo and then receded, and all the time the doctor was urging her to push. She was not aware that Alois had left the room, nor that the midwife had scooped up the two younger ones and, despite their wide-eyed interest in what their mother was doing on the bed, taken them into the kitchen to give them their first meal of the day.

The doctor remained with her all through that night and into the next day. He was beginning to wonder if this would set a record for the longest labour ever. He was grateful that Alois had stormed off to work, grumbling that he couldn't understand why the whole silly issue was taking so long. Women were made to have children weren't they? But even he had respect for the doctor, and for once kept his temper under control.

It was almost 6:30 in the evening when the baby finally completed his entrance into the world. Both the doctor and Klara were exhausted, but the boy looked strong and healthy. Klara offered several words of thanks to God as she cradled him in her arms.

The doctor sank onto the chair by the bed.

"That was the most difficult birth I have ever attended," he smiled at his patient. "But you have a fine boy there, with a good set of lungs on him. So what are you going to call him?"

"I know Alois wants to call him Adolf," Klara replied.

"Adolf, Adolf, yes, a fine name Mrs Hitler," agreed the doctor.

****

Lotta Blum

Barbara Doran

They parked their car on the outskirts of Cologne and headed for the city centre. Deirdre, the Irish woman with the dimples and the auburn hair, who was also the oldest, had just turned fifty the previous week. This outing was Jane's present to her.

Jane, a bubbly, blonde English woman, had booked tickets for the three of them to see the Michael Jackson musical which was touring Germany at the time. Roni, a dark-haired, petite spitfire of a woman, hailed from New York. You could almost hear a joke coming on. What happens when an Irish woman, an English woman and an American go to see a Michael Jackson concert? They had been living in Germany for several years, and fate had thrown them together when they had signed up for the same German class many years previously.

In front of the main square, Jane stopped to peer into one of the windows of the Dom café. "Why don't we go in here for an hour or so?" She looked at her watch. "We've got a couple of hours to spare before the show starts." A customer opened the café door and piano music floated out onto the late afternoon, autumn air. The others nodded with enthusiasm.

Inside, a warm bouquet of aromas, chocolate, cinnamon and freshly-ground coffee, enveloped them as they took in the impressive, stylish interior.

"Smells delicious," Deirdre said, as she peered around the spacious and tastefully-decorated room. Little alcoves with upholstered banquettes formed intimate spaces around small, wooden tables, creating a sense of privacy despite the busy atmosphere. The décor, which looked newly renovated, still retained the style of days past. The plush, pink velvet and dark wood complemented the neo-gothic architecture. A glass-domed winter garden added a modern touch to the traditional space.

While the trio stood searching for seats, one of the waitresses came over and beckoned them to an alcove off to the left. Cocooned by a gentle buzz of conversation, the familiar soft, melodic chords of *'Some Enchanted Evening'* created a pleasant backdrop and added to the genteel atmosphere. It was like a step back in time.

"This takes me back," Jane said, as she removed her coat and gloves. "I remember listening to that on the old radio at home, as my mother sang along. It was one of her favourite songs." Her eyes glinted. Although it was not yet dark outside, the room was filled with chandeliers, and candlelight flickered on the tables creating a magical atmosphere.

As they settled in, hanging up their coats and trying not to disrupt the mood, a tall, elegant lady, looking to be well into her eighties, tapped Roni on the shoulder.

"Would you mind terribly if I joined you?"

"No. Not at all." Roni turned to the others and shrugged. Jane and Deirdre nodded their approval and turned their attention to the old lady, helping her with her bag and her coat. Within minutes, one of the waitresses, dressed in the traditional black dress and white frilly apron, came over with her pad.

As the others gave their orders, Roni envisioned herself back in New York, in one of the dance cafés that used to be popular once upon a time. She closed her eyes for a moment and pictured Cary Grant walking up to her with that warm sparkle in his eye, and asking her to dance.

A few couples swayed to the music on the polished dance floor.

***

In her mind's eye, Deirdre looked into the past and saw ladies dressed in their finery, sipping their coffee or daintily eating their cake as they fluttered their eyelashes at the suited, handsome men across the room. She was awoken from her daydream by the older woman, who spoke almost perfect English, although her German accent was strong.

"So, where are you from, ladies?" She resembled a queen on her throne as she sat straight-backed and held an ivory cigarette holder in her hand. This was part of the prop. "Don't worry," she joked. "There's nothing to light. I just can't break the habit and need to have something in my hand."

They introduced themselves, extending welcoming hands. The old lady's sharp gaze focused on them, one after the other, smiling.

"It's so kind of you to let me join you," she said. "My train was a bit late today. I'm Lotta Blum, from Bonn originally." One had the impression she had rehearsed this speech many times. On second glance, one couldn't help but notice the powder and lipstick had been applied with a heavy hand, either that or the lady had bad eyesight. Her Dame Edna-type glasses were attached by a glittery chain. She used them only to read, it appeared, for in the midst of talking she had hooked them behind her ears and browsed through the menu. When she released them, they dangled on her voluminous chest. Her watery eyes held depths of wisdom and a certain challenging look too. She pointed her empty cigarette holder toward the musician. "Don't you adore Dorjan? He's a true master, old school through and through. A virtuoso on the violin and piano, but his voice is..." Her voice trailed off as the waitress came to take their orders.

Lotta rested the cigarette holder on the table, and ordered a cup of Earl Grey and some *Apfelstrudel* with warm vanilla sauce. While the others gave their orders, the old lady leaned in closer to Deirdre, who was sitting next to her. She pointed her red-lacquered finger in the direction of the podium, where the entertainer was playing his violin with extreme artistry. Her hands were slim with long tapered fingers. There were no typical arthritic knots on her finger joints.

"See that woman over there," Lotta said, in a low voice. As the waitress marched off with the orders, all three younger women's heads turned simultaneously to look in the direction of Lotta's waving hand.

***

The subject of interest was a woman who appeared to be in her mid-sixties. She was leaning into a velvet armchair, head back and eyes closed. With her shoulder-length, titian-coloured hair, glossy lipstick and champagne-coloured dress, she looked like a movie star of bygone days.

Lotta continued. "She's his lover, or so they say. A millionairess, who married money, I believe. There are rumours that she had a hand in his sudden death." A smile played upon her lips. "But far be it for me to spread them."

Roni nudged Jane and tried to stifle a laugh.

"Dorjan comes from Budapest. A poor musician, all clichés filled. She keeps him in good suits and dotes on him while he panders to her wants and whimsies." Her infectious laughter rang through the salon. "Whenever he sees me, he plays my favourite song."

As if on cue, the entertainer finished off the last number, smiled over in their direction and began playing *I Only Have Eyes for You.*

"He's splendid, isn't he?" The three women's eyes softened as Lotta's face flushed with pleasure.

"So, how did you learn such good English?" Deirdre wasn't sure what to make of this old lady. Who used words like *splendid* these days? She suspected she'd learned most of her English from old films.

"Well, I worked for the British Embassy for years. Back in my day it wasn't common to learn English at school, but I was a quick learner. They used to call me 'The Parrot'." She held an imaginary telephone to her ear and said in a high pitched voice, "Hold the line, please. Ambassador White will be with you in a moment." She was obviously enjoying her audience's attention and rattled off a string of greetings. "He's in a meeting. How can I help you? Yes, it's a wonderful day today, isn't it?"

"How interesting." Deirdre said. "I bet you have many tales to tell."

"Oh, yes. Too many to remember." Lotta's eyes took on a dreamy look. "It was a terrible time in our history, but one had to make the best of it. I was lucky, I suppose." She paused for a moment to reapply her lipstick. "I never did marry, you know." Her eyes took on a wistful look again. "The man I loved wasn't for me, but the story is as old as the 'Emerald Tablets.' Like a fool I thought he'd stay with me. Women can be such ninnies sometimes."

This music changed and both Lotta and Deirdre said in unison. "'*You're dancing on my heart*,' Victor Silvester." Deirdre's eyes lit up. "I haven't heard him in years."

"Come on, let's dance!" Jane, fired up by the music, tried to pull Roni out onto the small dance floor.

"Forget it, Jane," Roni said. "Everybody's looking at us. Not that it ever bothered you," she teased. "I can't stand when women dance together."

"Well then. I'll dance by myself. My husband always said I'm missing the shame gene." Jane laughed as she shimmied toward the dance floor.

"I'll dance with you." The old lady was half way out of her seat already. Roni wiped her forehead in mock relief, and both she and Deirdre looked on in delight and horror as the old lady walked with slightly unsteady gait onto the dance floor, shaking her hips to the music in Jane's direction.

"She's some lady, isn't she?" Deirdre said. "You know, I almost feel as if we were meant to meet her. She's refreshing. I was a bit depressed about turning fifty, but now that I've met her I feel a lot better."

The room buzzed with lively conversation. Deirdre called the waitress over and ordered a bottle of sparkling wine.

***

Jane and Lotta were obviously enjoying themselves, oblivious to the audience, but a few minutes later they returned, breathless, to the table.

"That was wonderful," Lotta said, as she sat heavily in her chair. "I'm so pleased I didn't trip over my feet, but I'm much too old for this."

"Nonsense, Lotta, you're marvellous." Deirdre poured the Sekt into their glasses and raised hers. "To Lotta," she said.

"Cheers."

Lotta took a sip of her drink. "What part of Ireland are you from, Deirdre?"

"I'm from Dublin. Why, have you ever been there?"

Lotta nodded. "Yes, many years ago. It seems like another lifetime now but I remember it as if it was yesterday. It's a lovely country and true what they say about forty shades of green."

Jane had finally convinced Roni to join her on the dance floor. Lotta and Deirdre smiled as they watched their antics.

"He was the only man I ever really loved." Lotta's voice became hoarse. "I met him at an embassy dinner. He was from Kilkenny – joined the RAF during the war and stayed on for a couple of years. What a handsome fellow he was, too. More than anything else though, he was funny. He could entertain an entire room with his stories and songs. All the ladies fell for him." She paused, searching in her handbag and popped a peppermint in her mouth. She offered the tube to Deidre who shook her head. "Please go on..."

"When his father died, he had to leave suddenly. Oh, how I pined for him. I, Lotta, the one everyone thought could handle anything. Nobody knew about us. German women who went out with the enemy were despised by most of the population. Of course he wasn't the enemy, but there were still many who forgot who started that horrible war." She sighed. "People never learn, do they?" She brushed a bit of imaginary fluff from her dress. "He told me to keep it quiet for my own sake. I'd like to think he loved me too."

Deirdre placed her hand on hers. "Is that why you went to Ireland?"

The woman took the ivory holder between her index and middle finger and held it in the air near her lips. "I'm ashamed to say it, but when he never returned, I went looking for him. I'd never done that for any man before or after. You see, he had told me so many stories about his homeland that I felt as if I knew it intimately. I knew something must have happened to him and I had to find out. When I arrived there, I recognised everything. It was just like he'd told me." She paused for a moment to clap at the performer and flashed a smile at the singer, diva-like in her performance. Then she turned to Deirdre again. "I hope I'm not boring you."

"No, not at all," Deirdre said. "Did you find him?"

The old woman continued. "I tried to be discreet, of course, but I was out of my mind with worry. We'd planned to marry, after all. He'd said he'd take me back with him and we'd have a family of our own and buy a little house and a bit of land. I took a train to Kilkenny and booked into a hotel and made some enquiries. It was as beautiful as he said it was, but when I heard he'd been involved in a tragic accident shortly after his arrival, I broke down completely." She took a deep breath and straightened her shoulders as she fastened the clip in her hair. "So, Deirdre. That's my love story."

The other two were returning to the table, giddy from the exercise. They were already zipping up bags and putting on scarves.

"I'm so sorry, Lotta." Deirdre admired the old lady's stoicism. Despite her tragic tale, she had survived and thrived.

"Cheers," Lotta smiled at them, and raised her glass as Dorjan played *We'll Meet Again, Don't Know Where, Don't Know When, but I know we'll meet again some sunny day.*

****

Never Too Old

Angela Lockwood

Patricia Turner's children had wanted her to do it years ago. They said they were worried for her, all alone in that big house. They didn't realise that you can't just sell a house that holds forty-five years of memories and move to an apartment.

Forty-five years of seeing the children grow up, thirty-five years of blissful marriage with Frank, and in the last few years seeing the grandchildren enjoying the garden all over again. But Patricia had to admit that the garden Frank had always kept so pristine now looked a little overgrown.

Then one morning, Patricia slipped on her bedside rug; fell and broke her hip. She lay there in agony for four hours. A concerned neighbour with a spare key let herself in, having noticed that at 11 a.m., the curtains were still drawn.

Once Patricia had recuperated from the hip replacement surgery, she told her children that she wanted to sell the house and move to the sheltered apartments on the other side of the village. They told her they were relieved she had taken the decision. They pledged their help in tidying up and packing. Carloads of superfluous goods were dispatched to children and grandchildren until all that remained was what she needed in the new rooms.

***

Patricia had moved into the apartment yesterday. Once all the furniture had been put in place by the removal men, a small army of relatives started opening boxes and putting her possessions in the empty cupboards. She quickly exhausted herself by running after everyone, trying to direct her things to the right places. She gave up. Out of breath, she sank into a chair.

Let them be, Patricia... she told herself. They mean well and you've got the rest of your life to put it right.

***

"This is a lovely view," said Patricia to her new neighbour, Sheila Smyth.

The two were standing in the bright hallway outside their apartments, looking through the large glass windows at the village below. When Patricia stretched onto her toes, she could see the roof of her old house. She hadn't moved far and even the new neighbour was someone she had known for years; their children had gone to school together.

"I'll take you down for coffee hour. Management puts some tea, coffee and biscuits on every weekday. Residents can go down if they want," informed Sheila.

Patricia nodded her approval and the pair set off down the long hallway.

"It's great you've moved here. I heard Mavis Barnstable might be coming too," said Sheila.

"That would be nice; she's an excellent Bridge player," said Patricia. Then after some thought she added, "Mind you, her husband Colin likes his whiskey. Frank and I used to play the Barnstables, but by 10 p.m. we would make our excuses, as his play didn't make much sense anymore."

"What, you haven't heard?" said Sheila, surprised. "Colin died a month ago from a heart attack."

Patricia found it hard to say something nice about Colin Barnstable. Instead she just left a respectful silence. Then when it seemed appropriate she asked cheerfully, "Do they have a Bridge club here?"

"I think they meet every Friday in the recreation room."

The two women stopped in front of the lift and Sheila pressed the call button. When the door opened there was already a man in a wheelchair inside.

"Morning Mr Walker," said Sheila cheerfully. "This is Patricia Turner. She just moved in."

"What a delight to have another lovely young lady in our residence!" he said, beaming.

"Gosh, no one has called me a young lady for a very long time," laughed Patricia.

"Mr Walker is going to be ninety-nine next week; at seventy-five we're just mere spring chickens to him," explained Sheila.

Just then Patricia felt her bottom being pinched. She looked at Mr Walker in his wheelchair. He sported a grin stretching from ear to ear. To her relief the lift stopped and the door opened. The man in the chair left through reception and the two women headed to the recreation room.

"I think that Mr Walker just pinched my bottom," whispered a shocked Patricia to her friend.

She roared with laughter. "Ninety nine years old, in a wheelchair, but still a randy bugger."

They entered the recreation room and found about a dozen residents already there. Most of the people living at Lower Hallerington sheltered housing were female, and

Patricia only spotted two men in the room. Sheila first introduced her to them.

"This is George Willoughby," she said to a bald-headed heavy set man. "Did you not work at British Gas, George?"

"I did indeed," he answered, shaking Patricia's hand.

"So did my husband. You might have known him – Frank Turner?"

"Not very well as he was in a different department, but yes I've heard of him. Delighted to have you with us, Mrs Turner."

Then Sheila introduced a thin grey-haired man as Victor Lambert. Patricia and Victor shook hands and the ladies moved on to the women in the room. Most of them, she already knew from church or via her children's old school. After the introductions were done, she noticed that the men were having an argument and she leaned in to listen.

"I'll tell you it was a fellow called Corleone," George argued.

"I'm not sure that was the fellow who played Fredo in 'The Godfather'," replied Victor doubtfully.

"It was! Donald Corleone. I think he even got an Oscar," said the bald one with certainty.

Victor shook his head sadly. "Maybe it was. It frightens me how forgetful I am these days. I used to know all the Hollywood actors."

"Well, my mind is as sharp as an eighteen-year-old's," stated George proudly and without a shred of sympathy for the other man.

Patricia did sympathise with Victor. Alzheimer's was the disease that she was most afraid of. Every time she caught herself forgetting something, she would smile wryly and think: *I'll be able to hide my own Easter eggs soon!*

Patricia turned her attention to the women. One particular lady had caught her eye because she was wearing bright red nail varnish and her cheeks glowed with pink blush. Sheila noticed her staring.

"Betty here is all dolled up for her fancy man," she explained.

Grey-haired pensioner Betty giggled like a little schoolgirl.

"Paul is taking me dancing later at the town hall," she said bashfully.

"Well done you, going dancing! I couldn't imagine doing that with my replacement hip," said Patricia, full of admiration.

"That shouldn't stop you, dear. I just had my second one done last December," retorted Betty cheerfully.

"How about your fella, Harriet?" said Betty turning to the woman on her left.

"We're meeting up this Thursday," replied Harriet, smirking like a Cheshire cat.

"Harriet met Nigel on the internet," explained Sheila, winking.

"Aren't you afraid to meet a complete stranger you found online?" asked Patricia.

Harriet smiled. "I hardly think that the man, who told me all about the heartbreak of losing his wife to cancer, is going to rape and kill me."

This isn't what I expected... Patricia began to think in the lift, on her way back upstairs to her flat.

***

She had expected talk about grandchildren and knitting patterns, not Skype, online dating, which Scholl shoes are best for dancing, and which of the men in their sheltered housing complex were single and not going senile. She hadn't realised how far from the modern world she had become removed, rattling about alone in her big house. She felt happier than she had done in a long time.

When she got in, she phoned her son. She asked him if he had a spare computer; an old one the grandchildren no longer needed.

"I thought you didn't want any of those 'contraptions'?" he said in surprise.

"Absolutely everyone is on the internet now. I'm not just some grandmother that knits socks all day," said Patricia expertly.

She was still puzzled however as to how you could send letters through a computer.

"I hope you know what you're doing," said her son, concerned. "Promise me you won't do any online shopping and give people your bank details."

"I won't, and my friend Sheila has offered to help me with Skype. Apparently you can then phone the entire world for free," explained Patricia innocently, her mind buzzing with the possibilities of the internet.

Her son promised he would set her up with a computer and an internet provider.

She sat back in her chair after she had ended the call and looked out of her living room window. From the fourth floor, she could just see the river and some fields with horses behind the trees.

The garden in front of the flats was well tended and Patricia thought with relief that she no longer had to do the gardening herself. So far, she had not regretted moving in there. She would get a computer set up next and try and become one of those... oh what did they call it downstairs? Oh yes – a 'silver surfer.'

She decided it was time to take the next step and to move on from all the wonderful memories her husband Frank had given her – time to make some new ones.

****

Ooh, Air Margrit

Rebecca Bryn

"We are gathered here today to celebrate the life of Margaret..." Dai Davies, lay-preacher at the cathedral, pillar of the community, stands beside the coffin in the crematorium chapel as if carved from the same Welsh oak: he rolls the 'R's in Margaret and lilts in a rich, melodic baritone about my mother, a woman he's never met.

My mind rebels at the platitudes for, although I loved my mother, and I know she loved me, my relationship with her was ambiguous, even difficult at times; there was never that mother/daughter closeness between us, and the older, and more dependent she became, the more restrictive and binding were the apron strings.

I'm ashamed to say I felt relief when she died; relief at finally being free - tinged with familiar guilt. She died on her eighty-seventh birthday and, though I'd taken her present-hunting only days before, I hadn't visited her on her special day.

With her death, the spectre of my own mortality drew me to dredge through family history, and I've begun to understand Mum's relationship with her own mother, Grandma's relationship with her parents, and the impact they've had on my relationship with Mum.

Northamptonshire born and bred, Grandma was a tailoress, nimble-fingered whether sewing or knitting, and nimble-tongued in the broad dialect peculiar to Kettering. If a garment needed taking in, it was 'A bit over-fully.' If she scrimped to make the most of a piece of cloth it was because, 'I ets to goo accordin.' And if she worked until the early hours to finish a suit, it was because the customer 'Ets to ev it.' Devotees of the Evening Telegraph cartoon *Air Ada* will know what I mean.

***

Grandma had never had an easy life. She was the oldest of eleven children and brought up ten siblings when her mother died young; her maternal grandmother having already been found dead in a stream at Yardley Hastings, her family home. Grandma's father, Ebenezer, Mum told me, was no help at all. He was an alcoholic wife-beater who drank his wages on a Friday night in The Woolpack unless Grandma met him at the works' gate and begged enough cash to feed his family.

According to the 1901 census, Ebenezer was a coal-whipper, a labourer who worked in the goods yards unloading coal wagons onto carts and, after that, a stoker at the gas works in the days when coal produced town-gas: hard, filthy, sweaty jobs that drove the stoutest men to drink. Mum said he was a horrible man, but maybe the hardships of life made him that way. Although I never knew him, he is my first certain memory.

I'd crawled into the middle bedroom of Grandma's back-street terrace, where an old man lay in bed. I remember that I stood up, and we stared at each other, but no words were exchanged between us. According to his death certificate, he died when I was 22 months old.

Whatever the reason for my great-grandfather's drinking and violence, Grandma never learned to show love or affection—or to spark the gift in her daughter.

I wonder how Ebenezer got on with granddad, his son-in-law. I adored my grandfather; he'd fought in the cavalry in the Great War, and a sepia photo of him in uniform, on his horse, took pride of place in the front room in Regent Street. I have his army fork and the two purple-topped cowrie shells he brought home, and a silver spoon he won showing a Dutch rabbit at Olympia in 1928. The rabbit won best in show and he was very proud of it: its name was Maurice... odd the things that stick in your mind.

I had an empathy with Granddad, as well as a shared love of horses and nature. He'd gone to war a farm boy and came back from Palestine with a wanderlust that never left him. But he'd promised Grandma that, if he survived, they'd get married, and he kept his promise—took a job in the shoe factory at the end of the terrace, and moved in with Grandma and Ebenezer.

But he'd changed, he confided: the dream he'd come home to no longer existed. The love Grandma craved was never allowed to blossom, and instead withered into a mind-set of mild disapproval and a sense of shame, of failure. I can't remember one word or look of affection between them. Mum too would repel any public show of affection Dad made towards her.

How history repeats itself. How the shock-wave of emotional repression and guilt ripples outwards to touch generation after generation. Grandma suffered from depression most of her life; understandable now that I realise the disappointments with which she contended. It was a disorder that haunted my mother's mind and I see clearly now, how she fostered in me the same feeling of responsibility for her unhappiness that her mother had fostered in her. Photographs taken between the wars show stiff figures, with sombre expressions, and served only to revive bad childhood memories for Mum. Maybe the next generation, or the next, will live untrammelled by the after-effects of war, the violence of a coal-whipper and the depression of a young woman robbed of her childhood.

***

Dai Davies raises his voice, bringing me back to the service I'd almost forgotten about. I notice that the owner of the care home has come, and two of Mum's carers are sitting by her. "Margaret had an interesting life. She joined the WAF in 1939 and was stationed at RAF Holt in Norfolk, a county for which she retained an abiding affection. She drove the blood lorries..." Light from the stained-glass window paints the pale oak red, blue and green and kisses Dai's right hand. He's getting into his stride now, even though the crematorium service isn't a religious one.

Odd, or maybe not so odd, that Mum couldn't... hadn't been able to stand the sight of blood. Dad's war service consisted of working as an electrician at Stewarts and Lloyds, the steel works at Corby. He and Mum had met through their respective brothers, who were close friends. Mum told me that when she took Dad home to meet her parents, Grandma's disapproving comment was, "Ooh, air Margrit, couldn't yuev done better en *that*?" True, Dad was small and wiry, balding, with a hook nose, a scar the length of his forehead, and was blind in one eye due to an altercation between a wooden trolley and a two-ton truck at the age of eight… which was why he escaped being called-up… but, well, Grandma spoke as she found.

She died just before my first son was born and I always regret that she didn't get to meet him. She and Dad never really got on. Dad was a quick, impatient man, and Grandma not the brightest candle in the room, though she loved a game of cards, or a bet on the horses and a gin and tonic… She once won seventy-five pounds on the football pools and made a pot of tea with no tea in it, she was so excited. I find myself getting more and more like her as I get older, though my speciality is standing in the middle of the kitchen wondering what I went there for.

***

After their marriage, Mum and Dad moved in with Grandma, Granddad and Ebenezer, and lived there until I was a year old, and my brother was four. Seven people and four generations in a three-bedroom terrace; with only an outside 'lavvy' and one cold tap in the kitchen. Is it any wonder they bottled their feelings and there were few outward displays of affection? Is it any wonder Mum became a target for Grandma's discontent and "ooh, air Margrit" a frequent rebuff?

Dad died twenty-one years ago, only eighteen months after he and Mum followed my second husband and me from Northamptonshire to Pembrokeshire. I'd escaped… briefly… from the uneasy cords that bound me to my mother. What is it they say, *a woman is a daughter first, a mother second, and a wife third.* It was a constant juggling act with those three clubs, hands constantly slippery with guilt feeling I failed at all three.

Dad had prostate cancer and the hospital sent him home to die. The nurses, who visited daily, were fantastic and our family doctor spent the whole of Christmas Day with us. Dad died peacefully at ten minutes to midnight on Christmas night. "I know your mother can be difficult," he'd said. "It hasn't always been easy, but I love her. Look after her for me."

"I will, Dad. I promise." I did my best... Did I? Did I, really? I put her in a home when she lost her sight, became wheelchair-bound, and demanded more time and love than I could give her. I *could* have gone to see her on her birthday.

"Margaret loved her garden, and nature." Dai's gentle purring voice lulls me back from my guilty past. "She bred Swallowtail butterflies which she released on Wicken Fen in Cambridgeshire..."

My eyes rest again on the polished oak coffin with its shining brass handles. Soon the curtain will draw across in front of it and Mum will be gone forever, her ashes floating free on the air like her beautiful butterflies. Her great-grandchildren, although doubtless bored, are behaving themselves remarkably well. There's some shuffling of feet and rustling of paper from the younger members of the congregation, and some asthmatic breathing and the odd cough from the older generation, but otherwise Dai holds his audience wrapt. Ken the Box, the undertaker recommended by the care home, sent Dai to speak to me soon after Mum's death. He arranged the order of service at the crematorium, and for Mum's ashes to be interred with Dad's, in the windswept churchyard on the hill above Solva, overlooking the sea. He asked me about Mum's life, what she was like, so he could say something about her at the funeral. We got chatting... Dai was a man with a twinkle in his eye and a wicked sense of humour. He laughed a deep belly-laugh as he related the tale of the man who'd insisted his parrot attended his funeral. Halfway through the service the parrot had piped up. "Fuck off! Fuck off!"

His irrepressible humour relaxed me and drew me out. We got onto the subject of family history and I told him I was researching mine. Black sheep, rumours of who had always intrigued me, leapt the imaginary hurdles to freedom. A great-great-great aunt had been the 'bad girl' of Warkton village and was deported to Australia. A great-great-great uncle and his two cousins had been convicted of killing a gamekeeper in Yardley Chase. None would admit to murder, or finger either of the others, so, rather than being hanged, they'd found themselves on a prison hulk in Portsmouth harbour before setting sail on the convict ship HMS Tortoise, bound for Hobart, Tasmania, in 1841.

And then there was Aunt Ellen, I went on, warming to my subject. She was Grandma's younger sister, who'd run a tailor's shop in Glasgow, lost her only son in the Second World War and lived in a tenement in the Gorbels. As children, we took bets on what colour her hair would be when she visited. I can definitely remember blue, orange, red, green and purple, and once a mixture. We kids loved her, but Grandma said she was a kleptomaniac and you couldn't take her anywhere: she'd even come out of a restaurant with half the cutlery shoved up her sleeves. Pressed for more of Aunt Nell's misdemeanours, Grandma had clamped her lips disapprovingly shut. On reflection, I'm surprised she'd admitted as much as she did.

**

Dai pauses for breath, head bowed respectfully, as Mark Knopfler plays guitar with wordless eloquence. I glance across at my older brother, who lost his partner not long ago; she and Mum shared a birthday, and today will be hard for him. Then there's my uncle, my father's younger brother, who's in his 80s and now the last of his generation. My sons and their families are behind us, and behind them Mum's brother's children and their partners. Family, some I haven't seen for years, have travelled from Northamptonshire, Leicestershire, Kent, France and Germany to be here to honour Mum's life.

I catch my cousin Libby's eye as 'Theme to a Local Hero' plays quietly, and she smiles comfortingly. I last saw her at her wedding almost twenty years ago. It was a lovely service, held in a Catholic church in the woods somewhere near Trier, Germany. The English contingent was small compared to the groom's side of the family, but we did our best to follow a ceremony that was entirely in German. We did sing one English hymn, somewhat feebly, and our minds eagerly latched onto the odd German word that sounded marginally English. It was all going fine until the priest said, "Jesus farted."

At least, that's what it sounded like to English ears. In front of me, rows of shoulders heaved with suppressed mirth. I suspect those behind me heaved as well. Like the bride, I daren't turn round to look; catching someone's eye would have been disastrous. She, too, knew exactly what her family and friends were thinking.

Dai clears his throat and looks directly at me; I straighten my face as the wedding darkens into a funeral—white to black. "Margaret came from a good family." The timbre of his voice commands our full attention, with a majestic rolling of his 'R's' and his lyrical Welsh accent. His eyes move to the assembled mourners and he smiles broadly, benignly, embracing us all in his appraisal. "Of murderers, thieves and prostitutes."

The silence behind me deepens until a vast pit opens and swallows all sound, all asthmatic breath, all rustling paper, all shuffling feet. Time hangs suspended, and into that silence, as I will the floor to swallow me whole, my late grandmother voices her final disapproval, her final humiliation and shame, though for once she targets the wrong sinner. "Ooh, air Margrit!"

****

Babes

Max Power

There is a place out beyond Bakers Point, high up on the rise of the road, where you can see the ocean on one side and the high majesty of the mountains on the other. That quiet little spot is remote and there is only a fifty yard stretch of track where you can really appreciate the beauty of the spot. Jacob brought me there on our second date and it struck me as odd at the time. Now I know it was just a Jacob thing to do. We have become such an integral part of each other, that I can't imagine a world where we don't know every intimate thing about each other. When I held his hand yesterday, he barely even knew me.

I always said that I wished we had met when we were younger. That way we could have had longer together. Jacob never agreed.

"Nah," he'd say, "We were meant to be together. Maybe if we had met when we were young, you would have had time to get fed up with me."

I never agreed. I still wish we had more time before and especially now. We have always been happy and so much in love. I have never met a man quite like him. He often jokes and makes fun of me. But Jacob has never been able to be mean to me and he always apologises, kisses and hugs me immediately afterwards to make amends.

"Besides, the way we veg out, you'd be the size of a blimp by now if we'd met when you were twenty."

Only my Jacob could get away with such a remark. Importantly, he would never say such a thing in front of others. I recall him saying those words and then he grabbed me, hugged and kissed me. Even though I knew he was joking, Jacob was and is, always afraid to hurt me.

"I love you, Babes. Only joking, and even if you were a blimp, I'd still love you. "

He calls me 'Babes' and I call him 'Babes' back. It sounds silly, childish almost, but he is my Babes. How on earth can I let my Babes go? I don't want him to leave me. What will I do without him?

Whenever the subject of death came up, he used to joke that he'd go first. I told him I would go first and that when I died, I wanted to be cremated.

"Keep my ashes safe and when you die, make sure that you're cremated and then you can come in with me."

That was my plan anyway. I said I didn't want to be put in the cold ground and that I didn't want to be alone. He told me I'd never be alone and I believed him. For his part, he joked that I should take the cheap option.

"Ah just dump me in a ditch at the side of the road. Sure I won't care."

I hated it when he said that. He stopped saying it when he fell ill. Not at first, but once he knew how serious it was, he never joked about it that way again. Jacob knew I wouldn't want to hear him say those words anymore. I cried and cried when I found out that I was going to lose my precious man, my sweetheart, my love. For the most part I kept my tears from him. They were not for sharing those selfish, salty drops of sadness.

Jacob cried once. That's not true I know, but he only cried once in front of me. I held him in my arms and he

238

sobbed until I could bear it no more, and until he had let out his despair. But that was it.

"I'm sorry."

He apologised ten times in the space of two minutes, for letting me see him that way. There was no need. His doctor told Jacob that he couldn't put a time frame on it, or at least he tried. Jacob pushed and squeezed until we somehow settled on six months. It wasn't the Doctor that came up with the number; it was really Jacob. It was a notional number without much meaning, but Jacob created meaning. He needed meaning. He needed something to help him cope with the tragedy that was about to invade our lives. Six months. That would see him through my birthday in November and out the other side of Christmas. If he made six months, then his February birthday was his next target. I knew exactly what he was doing. My birthday was two days ago. I know he won't make Christmas. Jacob kissed me softly on my lips and told me that he loved me.

"Happy birthday, Babes." I held his face as he lay there in his bed, and he said, "Didn't get you a present, doll. They won't let me out to the shops."

Even now he makes jokes. But I know how sad he was. He was sad for me. Jacob was sad that he was dying and that he was leaving me alone, and he knew I didn't want to let him go. The problem, of course, was that I had no choice.

***

My first husband was a mistake, plain and simple. I met him when I was sixteen, we married when I was twenty-two, and he treated me like dirt for the next fourteen long years. There is really nothing more to be said about him.

Why would I want to waste any more time thinking of that man, when time is the one thing I desire most now?

Jacob came from Ireland. His accent swayed me the moment he opened his mouth. People say the Irish are charmers – well, Jacob always says that anyway. I was charmed. For a woman feeling a bit past her prime, after the damage inflicted by years of chipping and picking by the man I want to forget, Jacob was a delight and I felt sixteen all over again.

"Excuse me, love, I don't suppose you could tell me if there is a good dry cleaners in town?" It was the worst chat up line ever, but he smiled at me and I felt the first tremor.

"I'm new in town and I haven't a clue where to find anything."

Then he apologised.

"Jesus, I'm sorry if I took you off guard. You look a little shocked. Don't worry, I'm not a mass murderer or anything." Before I could say a word he apologised again. "Sorry for the bad language, wasn't thinking. Pardon my French. That's the problem with us Dubs; we can't finish a sentence without slipping in even a baby curse... sorry."

He was so handsome and he talked at one hundred miles an hour. Every syllable was like a musical note. His words flowed through me and I was staring at him. I blushed and he spotted it I know, because he told me.

"Didn't mean to embarrass you, love, but seeing as how the damage is done and you can't go any redder, I have to say I'd have come to America sooner, if I knew the girls were so pretty." Then as brazen as you like, he broke into song right there on the street.

"*In Dublin's fair city, where the girls are so pretty, I first set my eyes on sweet Molly Malone*" Then he laughed and said, "Ah look it, do ya hear me singing to the best lookin' girl in the town. You must think I'm an awful eejit and I haven't even introduced myself yet. The name's Jacob, Jacob Cronin."

He held out his hand for me to take, which I did, and he shook it with a firm grip but also ever so gently. I hadn't even said a word at that point.

"Caroline." I know that's all I offered because he interrupted me almost immediately. I should have known I would spend the rest of his life trying to get a word in edgeways. But I wouldn't have had it any other way.

"That's gas... my first ever girlfriend when I was a young lad was called Caroline. She was from Cavan; Jesus, what an accent. I mean she was gorgeous, but my God she was best with the sound turned down. Think she married some millionaire. Sorry, I'm forgetting why I stopped you in the first place. Do you know a good dry cleaners?"

He was overwhelming, but in a wonderful way. Jacob bounced from one thing to the next, happy to offer a complete stranger snip-bits about his life, and always with a smile on his face. I directed him to the dry cleaners; he thanked me and said he might bump into me again. Jacob left me a little dizzy and I couldn't stop thinking about him for days.

It was one week later that I bumped into him again. I was filling up with gas when he pulled up beside me.

"Now before you say anything..." were his first words as he got out of his car, brushing his hair back, "...I haven't been stalking you for the last week. The judge told me he'd lock me up the next time."

We both laughed and he thanked me for pointing him in the right direction the last time we met. Then he asked me another question.

"I don't suppose you know where I could get a decent cup of coffee around here... do you, Caroline?"

He remembered my name. It sounds silly looking back and knowing him like I do now, but I thought all men were players. Jacob was funny, handsome and so very charming. I suspected he was a player and I couldn't have been more wrong. But there was something about him. He was nice, and the way he said my name in that soft musical accent, made me feel a little flattered.

"There's a nice little café just across the street past the bank." I pointed.

"I don't suppose you'd let me buy you a coffee to thank you for being so helpful the other day?"

He was hitting on me. I knew it, he knew it, and normally I wouldn't have said yes to such a proposal from what was pretty much a complete stranger.

"Thank you," I accepted. The words fell out of my mouth before I could engage my brain and I'm so glad now that they did.

"That would be nice." What was I doing? I had barely accepted when I was regretting it immediately.

Jacob bought me coffee. I learned that he was from Dublin, had three sisters, no brothers and he was the youngest in his family. His parents were dead, he was thirty nine years of age, he was an engineer and he used to play a game called hurling, and could have played for Dublin, if he hadn't had a car accident that put him out of the game. I learned so much more, in what turned out to be a marathon coffee session. Jacob loved to talk.

To be honest the weeks that followed have all blurred for me. He swept me away in a tide of romance, long walks and endless hours of conversation. He never ran out of something to say and he was constantly interesting and funny. I have always been shy, but when I was with Jacob he drew me out.

That such a love could exist was beyond my imagination. He adored me and told me every single day. My girlfriends were jealous. Everyone loved Jacob. He was infectious. You couldn't help but like him and for a long time I was waiting for the crash. There had to be a catch. Only there was no catch. For whatever bizarre reason, the Gods had chosen to smile down on me and repay me for years of unhappiness, by giving me this wondrous love. I should have known that it was all too good to be true. Twelve years of happiness was all that I was allowed. The Gods weren't smiling on me. They were mocking me. They set me up to believe that I could somehow deserve this life and that I could be happy. The day we walked out of the doctor's office with Jacob's diagnosis, they stole it all away again.

***

I watched my mother die. It was slow and sad and I miss her still. Death has hung about me the past few years. It started with father. We weren't close, but my mother loved him and it broke her heart when he passed away. To say I was indifferent would be a push, but we hadn't really had a relationship for twenty years. He disapproved of my marriage and we fought about it often. It got so bad he refused to come to my wedding and I never forgave him for that. Turns out he was right, but he shouldn't have abandoned me like that. Lately I wonder if I shouldn't have just forgiven him and let it go.

Poor Mom tried her best to get us to put our differences aside, but we were both as stubborn as each other. Besides, after my marriage broke up, I didn't want to live under his 'I told you so' for the rest of my life. One day he went to get the paper and he never came back. The police called to our door and broke the news to my mother. He had dropped dead in the street. It was a massive heart attack and he didn't suffer, we were told. Typical of him, he got off lightly. My father never met Jacob, but he would have liked him.

My mother had a whole host of problems. She developed Parkinson's disease and she was a diabetic smoker, with a dodgy heart and emphysema. That is only the headlines. There was more, but her other ailments were minor by comparison. Mom was miserable after my father died. Only Jacob could get her to laugh.

"If I thought I'd get enough interest, I'd open a book on what you're gonna get next."

She used to laugh at him. Jacob could say almost anything to her. When she was taking steroids, he told her she was getting fat; well, not in such a cruel way.

"Jesus, Janey..." He called her Janey. Her name was Jane and she once told him that her first boyfriend called her Janey and that was that from then on. I'm sure she had a crush on him. "...you're slipping on a few pounds there. I'll have to bring you out dancin' to burn it off." Then he'd grab her and give her a kiss. He could say anything to her.

When she passed I think he was as heartbroken as I was, but he made sure to look after me. My grief was paramount and he took a back step. Jacob was quiet and supportive. He made all the arrangements, the church service, the funeral, the flowers, the music, everything. It was perfect, if you can say that about a funeral.

Not long after that, in the space of two years, my mother's only brother and sister died within days of each other. They were the last remaining family that I had. My father was an only child like me and I never had the children I so wanted.

When Jacob came along, I was close to the point of it being too late and there was always a reason not to have children. I was afraid at first. After my history, I thought it was too much of a commitment, too much of a risk. I desperately wanted a baby with Jacob, but stupidly there was always something. There was my concern about my age, my mother's illness and of course, the stupid concern over what other people might say. By the time Jacob became ill, it was too late. I was destined to be left alone. How stupid could I have been, to worry about what others thought?

But it wasn't the thought of loneliness that upset me most. I wanted a piece of Jacob. He wanted us to have a baby together, but he never pushed me too hard. We were both a little on the wrong side of forty when the conversation came up and he knew of my concerns. I had lived in the same small town my whole life. Everyone knew my business, my history and they were a judgemental lot.

"I'm just a blow in."

That's what he used to say and he was right. Jacob couldn't care less what people thought or said, but he hadn't lived in my shoes. I couldn't explain to him how it felt to be judged when my marriage broke up. I know now that he was right. The what if's, the regrets are all things that have haunted me lately. But I can't turn back the clock.

I have tried to summon up the courage to accept the fate I cannot control. But I can't. I know he is dying, but accepting that, is admitting defeat. It's much worse than that.

In the last couple of days, his breathing has become critical. The nurses keep monitoring his oxygen saturation, but I see how he is struggling. He asked me to bring a fan from home. Jacob knows it makes no difference, but the feel of the air blowing on his face gives him hope in his breathing. He says it feels like he is getting more air. It's no more than a placebo, but neither of us cares. The nurses keep trying to reassure me, to be realistic, yet their natural instinct is from a place of kindness and they give off positive signals that don't always help.

He has had enough. I know that now. But I don't want to let him go. How on earth can I do this? Every time I sit with him, which is pretty much all day and night for the last week, I try to tell myself that it is time. I hope I can accept that when the moment comes, I will be relieved for him. Only it still doesn't feel that way. The same question runs through my head over and over again. What will I do without him? I'm tired and exhausted from the last couple of months looking after Jacob, but I don't care. A piece of me would keep doing this forever, to have him for the shorter and shorter spells of time he is awake, just to be able to talk to him. I am desperate to keep him.

An hour ago I awoke from a dream. We were together up by Bakers Point and we were younger and I could feel the sea breeze on my face. I closed my eyes and he was suddenly there in front of me. Jacob kissed my lips.

"What's that for?" I asked him and gave him my biggest smile.

"That's for you," he said. "That's because you are the most beautiful girl in the world. That's because I love you."

He kissed me again, and I could smell him as I woke. His smell was so familiar, so comforting, but I found myself looking at the last remnants of the dearest man, as he lay slipping through my fingers. He moved in the bed and turned to look at me. Jacob smiled through the oxygen mask and struggled to take it off. I rose and tried to stop him.

"Give us a kiss, Babes."

His voice was barely there. It was a hint of my giant of a man. I climbed onto the bed beside him and kissed his lips. I held my lips to his for a long time and we both closed our eyes.

"Put your mask back on you, darling."

He couldn't of course, so I fixed it for him and I lay beside him and held him. Jacob turned his head and looked at me with his soft green eyes.

"How did I ever pull you?" He made me laugh.

"I still don't know, Jacob." He asked me for another kiss like he needed more kisses and I couldn't deny him. I lifted his mask and pressed my lips to his one more time. We both closed our eyes. Jacob was leaving me, I knew it and so I held him. I held him and I kissed him. My darling. My love. My Babes.

****

Last Goodbyes...

Paul Ruddock

"Ready for our adventure, Lucy?" I asked. A gentle squeeze of her hand in mine and the almost imperceptible smile on her lips was all the answer I needed.

"Do you remember the last time we were there, just the two of us?"

She did remember; it had been a glorious weekend—one where we enjoyed all that nature had to offer, and lost ourselves in each other's arms and company. This time, though, all the immediate family would be joining us: Lucy and me, our two grown up children, Cody and Nicola, and Gemma, Lucy's younger sister. We knew it would be the last time we would all be altogether.

"I'm sure that's where we conceived our Cody," I added with a wink and a wry smile. Cody chuckled at my last remark, old enough now to no longer be embarrassed at the thought of his parents having once enjoyed all the passions of youth that his generation were presently taking for granted. But time enough for all that, we'd best be on our way...

We started off at a nice easy pace. No need to tire Lucy unnecessarily, I thought. I mean, neither of us were still in our first flush of youth. Leave the mad scrambles to the youngsters, I laughed – not that Cody was likely to move more than a few feet away from us; our six foot two hulk of a son had always been his mother's boy. I remembered when he was a nipper. Whenever he wanted something, needed help, or anything for that matter, it was always *'Mum, can I...'* or *mum this, or mum that...* and when she wasn't around it was simply *'Dad, where's mum?'* or *'Dad, when's mum back?'* I didn't mind of course, how could I?

Navigating the majestic scenery of Rannoch Moor was something we had all enjoyed many times before, and even though Lucy knew the landscape and features as well as any of us, I couldn't resist my usual running commentary.

"It is like having Scotland's answer to Wainwright tagging along." Cody chipped in.

"Mum loves the sound of me voice," I chuckled in my defence, adding as I turned back to Lucy: "Don't ya, Luv?"

I reminded her of every site and feature we'd ever come across, so yes, I probably did sound like some over enthusiastic tour guide. But it was more than that; what made it special was its proximity to Leum Uilliem, a nearby mountain where I had first proposed, and where we might well indeed have conceived at least one of our two children during subsequent visits.

"I remember that time Dad tried to show you how to use a compass," Cody was saying to his mum. "He nearly went mad trying to explain mag to grid, grid to mag, taking bearings, and the differences between grid north, magnetic north, and then *true* north – that really got you going... 'So what are you saying – that the other two are *untrue*?' you would ask, just to wind dad up even more."

Nicola, my eldest daughter, smiled adding, "Yes, I remember that... 'What are you on about? How can you have three different norths? North's north. It's like saying there are three different Glasgows or Scotlands,' you would say."

"I remember too," I said jokingly, as I turned back towards Lucy. "It was your way of getting your own back for all those times I came back with completely the wrong things so you wouldn't send me out shopping again, or mixing all the colours when you had me to do the laundry... you knew I hated owt like that."

"Well, for what's worth, I was always with you on that, mum," Nicola said defiantly, holding her hand, adding: "I never could see the point of all that map and compass stuff when you can click a button and see exactly where you are on a coloured screen."

"Don't be daft Nic, we didn't have all that back then, and what if we had? Not much cop if the bloody batteries die on you or can't get a signal is it?"

"Well that's made the day complete, ain't it Luv?" I said to Lucy.

"Sorry Mum, sorry Dad," the two of them said with a smile, almost in unison.

"Nowt ta be sorry for kids. I mean, what would a day out be without you two getting into a row over something?" They both smiled.

"Does anyone remember the time we turned up at Corrour railway station and we saw all the camera crews, and thought there must have been an accident?" I asked, changing the subject.

"Um?" Cody grunted.

"Well, it was when they were filming a scene from that movie, what was it? ...Trainspotting... And the catering guys shared some of the film set food with us, and you scoffed three hamburgers," I said in mock remonstration. "... And then you scolded me for letting him over-eat when he was being sick on the walk back later," I added, turning back to Lucy.

It was nearly midday now, some four hours since the start of our reminiscing adventure. Time for a break, I thought. "Speaking of scoffing, sarnie and a brew, anyone?" I asked.

"Sounds good to me," Cody agreed.

"Well, there's a surprise," Nicola laughingly added, at which point we all had a chuckle; Cody may have been the youngest but he had an appetite that matched the rest of us put together.

And so it went on, time flying by all too quickly as we swapped stories and memories of our travels together, like when we took the kids wild camping for the very first time – come to think of it, it was only the second or third time Lucy had agreed to camp out overnight as well. The kids of course took to it all like ducks to water, and had no inhibitions whatsoever when I explained about 'toilet etiquette' in the wild.

"Not like you, Luv. I swear the first time we wild camped you thought the countryside would be littered with public conveniences or portaloos."

Her curt and 'not amused' answer of 'it's different for men' was just so funny at the time, especially as just then Cody and Nicola came running past trailing toilet rolls behind them, just like the dog in the Andrex advert.

"Oh my God, yes, and Cody planting little flags all over the place to mark where he'd buried his poo."

"Okay, okay, there's plenty I remember about you as well, Nic." Again we all laughed.

"And then there was that time when we saw that Brocken Spectre – that was amazing," Nicola said.

"Brocken Spectre?" Our middle child, Gemma asked. Gemma had never been much of an outdoor sort of person so wasn't familiar with the phenomenon:

"It's a rare and lovely rainbow and cloud formation you sometimes see on a misty mountainside or cloudbank," Nicola answered.

"It's a sort of triangular or circular rainbow with a hazy figure in the centre. The figure you see is actually an optical illusion created by your own shadow reflected from nearby clouds. It's hard to explain, but your own movements can often appear to be reflected by the movement of the figure in the spectre," I added by way of explanation.

"And you and Dad convinced me and Cody all the angels in heaven were looking down and waving at us, and we started calling out to them and waving back," Nicola recalled, as she positioned herself to sit back next to Lucy…

***

Almost fortuitously, it was then that the doctor entered the room. He smiled – not a wide and beaming smile but just one of gentle sympathy. I imagine his manner and sympathetic demeanour was something he had had to perfect over many years but it was still appreciated nonetheless.

There was no need for us to wait for him to ask the question.

"We're ready," I said.

Gemma agreed. A heavy intake of breath and slight nod of the head from Nicola and a stifled cough and tear filled flicker of the eyes from Cody told me they were too. Gemma was the first to approach and lean in to take Lucy's hand and kiss her on both cheeks: "See you again, my kind and lovely wonderful sister."

It had been a wonderful day for us all, just sitting with Lucy as we chatted about our times and memories together. And credit to Cody – it had been his idea to enjoy and share those memories at Lucy's bedside while we imagined one last great adventure together.

I raised myself from the bedside seat, allowing room for Cody and Nicola to approach Lucy's bed from either side. It was the first time I had released my Lucy's hand since I had entered the room early in the morning; it was now gone half past four in the afternoon.

"Bye mum, love you always..." Nicola whispered, just loud enough for those immediately near enough to hear.

"Me too mum..." Cody added, the frailty and softness of his quivering voice totally at odds with the strong young man I knew my son to be: "You're the best mum in the world, the best anyone could have... I'll..."

I could sense Cody was welling up and could practically *see* the lump in his throat. He'd struggled to keep his feelings in check the entire day but now that the moment had come, the tears were rolling. He fell to his knees beside the bed, to place one last kiss on his mother's cheek. I in turn placed a hand on his shoulder and gave it a gentle squeeze, comforted by the return of his own hand to meet it. "It's not fair, dad, it's just not..."

"I know, son, I *know*..."

Cody rose to his feet and slowly moved backwards away from his mum's side, not once losing sight of her until he reached the window, when he finally looked away, supposedly to cough and clear his throat – but what parent doesn't know every little nuance of their children? Nicola was always more open with her feelings, and rarely tried to hide when she was upset, but Cody, ever since I could remember, would rarely let on if something was seriously bothering him, a practiced master of the 'something in my eye' ruse. I recognised all too well the truth of the matter; this time there was little disguising his stifled sobs, and I dare say it was probably only my greater years and experience of death that was giving me the strength to hold back my own, at least for now.

"Mr. Rogers," the doctor said. I'd almost forgotten his presence. Although it had only been a few minutes since he had entered the room, it was as though a lifetime of memories had come flooding back in that brief time – much as they describe how your life flashes before you when you're about to die suddenly.

"I know," I replied.

We all gathered round Lucy's bed one more time. Just the merest nod was all the final consent he needed to flip the little red switch of the respirator machine, while a nurse simultaneously switched off the various monitors. The cold reality and physical reminders of my wife's condition seemed to disappear with the extinguishing of the lights and noises of the life maintaining machinery and assorted apparatus.

"Time of death, 16:47," the doctor declared. It sounded cold and clinical but I knew he was just following the hospital's set procedures and other legal requirements.

"It was the right decision, and what she wanted..." I could hear the doctor saying. Again his tone and manner were caring and sympathetic, just as it had been these past months since the accident. Despite the finality of the moment, there was a sense of peace now, almost of closure for us all, just not for me... not yet...

***

Two weeks later we were once again reunited on the summit of Leum Uilliem, only this time for real as I looked westward to watch the setting of the sun, as we had so often before. The gentle breeze that had complemented the fading light had now grown into an angry storm, telling me it was time. I took the small urn and removed the lid. Like a celestial carriage waiting to carry my Lucy's soul to a better place where I knew she would wait for me to join her someday, the raging winds carried and scattered her ashes...

It's not goodbye, it's just you leading the way this time...

****

A Stitch in Time

S K Holmesley

For fifty-four years, the clock had lost one minute every twenty-four hours. Each morning, Miriam had added that one minute back. This morning was no different.

***

When Miriam's father gave her the clock on her sixteenth birthday, he explained that she could return the time she added each morning if she ever needed more time. Going on to explain further, he opened a small panel on the back of the clock that hid a gauge like the odometer on his car. He had started her with five minutes so she could see how it worked.

Following instructions, Miriam tapped the blue button beside the gauge five times, then hit the green button and closed the panel. Looking up from her task, she realized that her father appeared to be frozen. She also felt that he was somehow distant, even though he was within reach.

As a test, Miriam walked into the living room. Her mother was frozen too. She walked back into her room. Her father was where she had left him with his mouth open as he explained to her what to expect. Miriam heard no sound and saw no apparent movement when she looked at his lips.

The hour and minute hands on the clock were frozen. The second hand was moving backwards. Miriam opened the panel on the back of the clock and was relieved to see the 'ones' tumbler slowly rotating, then was chilled when she realized it was counting away her minutes; two minutes plus another partial minute had tumbled away. She had never realized how long a minute was until that instant. Panicking, Miriam instinctively hit the red button on the other side of the gauge, then breathed out a relieved sigh when she heard her father's voice as he finished his explanation.

Miriam interrupted, "I know, Dad."

"How do you know what you haven't been told?"

"I hit the green button. You were frozen. Then, I hit the red button."

Miriam's father reached out a hand and took the clock from her. Opening the panel, he saw that there were over two minutes gone, but not the full five. Shaking his head, he adjured, "You must let it run to the end once you decide how much time you're using, or you've wasted the minutes. If you end the count before you reach the time you've requested, then you end up where you already were. If you wait and let it count down the full amount, then you leap back the minutes you've requested."

Handing the clock back, Miriam's father ordered, "Hit the counter button once; then you'll see."

Miriam waited until the minute that had begun previously ran out.

"...know what you haven't been told?"

"Perhaps not before, Dad, but this time I have been told. It was as though time folded back onto itself and was stitched together, then we ended up back where we were about thirty seconds ago."

"It uses partial minutes first. You should have two minutes left."

"I do."

"Now, you know how it works."

***

Before that day, Miriam had never really thought about minutes. She had considered quarter hours, half hours, hours, days, weeks, months, even years, but not minutes. Minutes had seemed too insignificant. Now, she had minutes that were hers to use and no one else's. Somehow because she could see those minutes, they became more precious to her than any others.

Miriam became obsessed with time. Every morning after she wound and reset the clock she would open the back panel to see how many minutes she had accrued. She became selfish with her time. Each moment became more precious, and she did not want to lose it. Previously, Miriam had never been particularly punctual. Generally on time, but not worried if she was 'fashionably late' as her mother called it. Everything changed after she received the clock. She held onto time in the same way a miser holds onto money.

Each minute allotted to her had to count, so she did not have to use her personal minutes. When she came home from school in the afternoon, she chose to study rather than hanging out with friends. She did not want to be tempted to use her personal minutes to get her homework done before bed. Miriam completed any household chores she was given as perfectly as she could, so she would not have to use her personal minutes to redo what she should have done properly the first time. Miriam welcomed sleep each night. After a night of sleep, she was not only more efficient, but also she could reset her clock and add one more minute to her hoard of personal minutes.

Time passed. Miriam's friends gradually moved on and forgot her part in their lives. By the end of her senior year in high school occasionally one or another one time friend would almost recognize her and smile, but then the smile would fade as the friend puzzled over who she was. Miriam hardly cared. She knew the cost of each minute they wasted on frivolous pursuits.

Miriam graduated from high school with honors. In college, she majored in math, and minored in physics. Not wanting any distractions, she turned down several offers to join academic sororities and honor societies. She was never asked by the non-academic sororities, so did not lose the moments it would have taken her to refuse. She acquired both her masters and her doctorate in record time by eschewing summer vacations and working year-round to make each moment of each minute count.

Miriam did not date. She never thought about marriage. Intangible actions that depended on fate were not on her radar. Wasting time on dreams was not for her. That Miriam married at all was almost by accident, or maybe it was fate. She never thought about it, because that would have wasted time.

***

Henry was a statistician at the first research facility Miriam worked at after receiving her doctorate. He was several years older than she was, but because as well as being a statistician, he was also an efficiency expert, he admired her. Henry had never paid much attention to any specific woman before he met Miriam.

Henry was not a misogynist. He loved his mother and as the youngest in his family had grown up pampered by both her and his two older sisters. Despite that, he had never met any women who cared about numbers as much as he did. He knew they existed, but had not seen any point in wasting time looking for them. Then, he met Miriam. She was as much a freak about time as people accused him of being about statistics. They complemented each other.

Miriam had little use for probabilities. She preferred measurable results that were easily defined and broken down into significant segments. Henry liked numbers that could be stretched to identify and describe expectations. As a team, they were unbeatable. Over the course of the first six months they worked together, they began to regret when they had to separate to go home. Putting their work away at the end of each workday seemed to be a waste of time. Weekends were even worse: they would each have a moment of inspiration about one or another of the problems they were trying to solve, but no one present to share that moment with.

***

Six months into their collaboration as a team, they were packing up one Friday evening when Henry suggested, "I think we're really close to coming up with a solution." Knowing that efficiently using time was Miriam's greatest weakness, Henry offered, "I can drive us to the restaurant, then take you home afterwards. Time savings for you, since I don't stop every block like the bus does. Also, it will save you time, since we can concentrate on our current problem while someone else cooks for us."

"Save time?" Those were magic words for Miriam. She agreed immediately.

They stayed at the restaurant until nine o'clock, chatting about the problem they were currently working on or about calculations they had recently released for another project.

A few weeks after their first dinner together, their manager suggested that they attend an upcoming in-town conference to present a paper detailing their results on an earlier project.

Feeling conferences to be a waste of time, Miriam refused.

Over that evening's dinner Henry was able to convince her that collaborating with other mathematicians working in their field would save them time, since they would be less likely to repeat trials others had already successfully completed.

The next day Miriam agreed to their manager's request.

Over the following months one conference led to another. Eventually, Henry realized that he and Miriam were spending more time together than they were apart. At dinner that night, he suggested sharing an apartment would be more efficient.

Up to that time, even as their relationship moved from one of being collaborators to one that almost bordered on romantic, Miriam always insisted that Henry drive her home each night, so she was there each following morning to wind her clock.

Now, considering Henry's suggestion, Miriam realized if they were living together, she would have her clock with her.

For his part, Henry merely accepted the twists of Miriam's logic. Having sisters, he did not think it odd that Miriam's thought processes sometimes took her in directions that made no sense to him. Thus, he simply agreed with everything she said. Although initially puzzled about her concern for the clock, when Miriam told him that her father had made the clock for her sixteenth birthday, Henry thought he understood.

***

Henry and Miriam had been married four years when they were offered teaching positions at the same university. Because the job included housing, Miriam agreed with Henry that living on campus would save time. They accepted the university's offer.

They had been married eight years when Miriam and Henry had a son. Miriam was as efficient about that as everything else. Nine months to the day, she delivered the child. She worked up to the day before the baby came, wound her clock the next morning, then went to the hospital to deliver the child, a fine healthy baby boy—and came home that evening so that she was there to continue winding the clock. At Henry's insistence, Miriam took three days off, but went back to work the Monday following Chase's birth.

After Chase was born, Henry pointed out to Miriam that it would save time if they hired someone to help with the child. After three days at home trying to accommodate the chaos created by the baby's needs, Miriam set aside the schedule she had created and agreed that they needed help.

Knowing Miriam's questions would be about time management, rather than child care, Henry chose to do the interviews himself. He hired Lucy principally because she reminded him of his own mother.

***

The family muddled along as Chase grew up. Once he was grown, when asked about his childhood, Chase always remembered Lucy as his caretaker, Henry as the one who made sure he got to wherever he needed to be, and Miriam as the person who made sure that they got there on time, and whatever they were doing, it got done on time. Intellectually Chase knew that Miriam was his mother, but emotionally he always turned to Lucy for succor.

Lucy retired when Chase was twelve. The major change for the family after Lucy left was that Henry, with his son's help, took over the cooking. Other than letting Miriam pop a couple of pieces of bread in the toaster, because it had a timer and settings that were fairly accurate for light, medium, and dark, neither Henry nor Chase trusted Miriam to make anything that required she interpret time. If a recipe said forty minutes that was what Miriam set the timer for. If the roast charred or the chicken was still raw when she pulled it from the oven, Miriam was at a complete loss.

When Henry explained that some ovens ran hotter than others when baking, and that she had merely put the meat on the wrong shelf when broiling, Miriam showed him the recipe and asked how she was supposed to know which shelf to use, when the recipe did not specify. Miriam asked how she was supposed to know whether their oven was hotter or colder than the temperature she had set it to.

Henry loved his wife and Chase loved his mother, but after Miriam's first few attempts at cooking, neither would let her do more than make toast.

Cooking might not have been one of her strengths, but Miriam remembered to wind her clock each morning. She never told Henry about her minutes, and continued to hoard them.

***

Miriam was almost sixty-nine when her father was hospitalized. At one point when she and her father were alone, he asked, "How many minutes do you have left?"

Seeing her father shake his head in dismay when she admitted that she had all her minutes left, Miriam prompted, "Dad, what's the problem? I worked really hard to make sure that I never needed to use any of those minutes."

"What were you saving them for, sweetheart?"

"I don't know. I've always felt they were too precious to use."

"But not too precious to lose?" After a moment Miriam's father revealed, "My father made me a clock like yours."

Miriam was not surprised, since she knew her grandfather had been a clock maker too. She asked, "What did you use your minutes for?"

"Moments I had missed that I wanted to remember. Moments when I wasn't there when I should have been. When you were eight, you fell from the big oak tree in your grandparents' yard and broke your arm. I used twenty-five minutes to go back to five minutes before you broke your arm. I pulled the trampoline over to where you had fallen. When you fell you landed on it, and bounced a few times.

You were shaken by the fall, but not hurt, and were more careful after that when climbing the tree, so a win all around and well worth twenty-five minutes to me."

"Oh."

"When you were born, I was late getting to the hospital and just missed your birth. I gave fifteen minutes back to the clock, which put me in the delivery room ten minutes before you were born."

"You had your clock with you?"

"Not always, but we were living with your grandparents at the time. Your grandmother called, then decided that she should take your mother to the hospital. When I got home to find them already gone, I stuck the clock in a briefcase and took it with me, just in case."

"Oh." Miriam thought a moment, then asked, "How many minutes do you have left?"

"None. I knew you were on your way. I had two hours left on the clock. I haven't long left, but I used those last hundred twenty minutes yesterday to go back so I could tell your mother I wasn't feeling well before I had a final heart attack. My doctor was already here the second time, so wasn't too late and they intervened before my heart was irreparably damaged. Gave me a few days rather than just a few hours. I wanted to be here when you arrived, so I could see you one last time."

Reaching over to take Miriam's hand where it rested on the edge of his bed, her father asked, "Have you told Henry about your clock?"

"No."

"Why not?"

Miriam shrugged. "It sounds too fantastic. I always thought he would think I was crazy." Justifying herself, Miriam added, "Chase never fell out of a tree."

Miriam's father smiled lovingly at his daughter.

"After I'm gone, tell Henry about the clock. I've written a note to him to explain how it works. He'll help you figure out how to use your minutes."

She had never thought about it previously, but Miriam asked,

"Can Henry have a clock?"

Sadly her father shook his head. "No. There were only a dozen gauges, one for each of twelve generations. The last one went into your clock. Also, the clocks work for us, because we're the clock makers."

"I'm not a clock maker."

"You could have been; not Henry, though, and not your mother."

"Oh."

"Promise me that you'll tell Henry, and that you'll start using your minutes."

Miriam tightened her grip on her father's hand and promised, "I will."

***

Once he had read her father's letter, Henry understood why her clock was important to Miriam. Each day after that, Henry prodded her on how she wanted to use her minutes. This day Henry asked, "What don't you have that you could have if you had more time?"

Miriam could not think of anything. She had arranged her entire life so not a moment was wasted. She had every natural minute accounted for, and could not think of anything she might need any extra minutes for. She had been lecturing at the university for over thirty years. Henry had retired from teaching five years previously, and was working on a book on statistics. Miriam could have retired, but she liked living on the campus, and she liked tutoring Math and beginning Physics.

Chase was grown and teaching Physics at the high school in town. Chase's spouse Wendy taught English at the same school. Miriam's nine-year-old granddaughter Jennifer attended the elementary school one block over from the high school. To Miriam, that was a perfect situation, because they could all three go in together.

Miriam thought of Jennifer. She loved her granddaughter, but did not spend as much time with her as Henry did. Miriam wondered why that was. Turning to Henry, who stood beside her at the window as they waited for Chase, Wendy, and Jennifer to arrive, Miriam asked, "Why haven't I spent more time with Jennifer?"

"Maybe your schedule and her schedule haven't accommodated each other. However, they're on their way over now. You have scheduled the entire afternoon for us. Perhaps, rather than you and Chase retiring to a corner after lunch to discuss the latest advances in Quantum Physics, you could stay in the group and include Jennifer in your discussion, even if the best you can do is discuss the latest advances in adding two plus two."

"What do grandmothers usually do?"

"I don't know, sweetheart, make cookies or give unrequested dating advice when they're older—knit scarves in atrocious color combinations perhaps? What did your own grandmother do?"

Miriam thought on Henry's options, then prompted, "How long does it take to make cookies?"

"Longer than you have today before they arrive. There's always the future."

Miriam stared thoughtfully out of the window, then murmured, "Or the past." Turning to Henry, she asked, "Will you coach me in making cookies?"

"Of course, sweetheart."

"How long does it take?"

"Well, you've never made cookies before, so maybe a couple of hours."

Turning away from her husband, Miriam said, "Thanks!"

***

Miriam walked into the kitchen. Henry was putting the finishing touches to her birthday cake. Catching his attention, she said, "You promised to teach me to make cookies."

Unable to hide his surprise, Henry asked, "Did I?"

"Yes."

Staring at his wife, Henry suddenly had a moment of intuition. "You finally used some minutes?"

"Two hours. You told me it would take at least that long for a novice to learn to make cookies."

"Why?"

"You told me grandmothers make cookies for their grandchildren."

Henry smiled. Pausing to cover the cake and to move the stand to a counter, Henry pulled an apron from the pantry. After helping Miriam put on the apron, he said, "First, set the oven to 350 degrees." Innocently pointing to the oven he added, "It's that sort of box like appliance over there."

Walking over to the dishwasher, Miriam asked, "This one?" She then spoiled the effect by bursting into giggles.

**

Two hours later, when Chase with his family, walked into the living room, Jennifer declared, "Grandpa, I smell cookies! What kind did you make?"

"Pecan chocolate chip. I didn't make them, though, your grandmother did."

Chase spoke first. "Mother? You made cookies? What brought that on?"

"After talking to your father, I realized that hoarding minutes was becoming more pointless every year. I have always felt that because you couldn't buy time that its value was in saving it, but after talking to Dad—your grandfather—before he died, I realized that the value of time can only be calculated once it's spent. I decided I wanted to spend the time I've saved on all of you."

******

Day Late, Dollar Short

Eric Lahti

My grandfather told me the lightning and thunder that crashed across the skies during the summer storms was the gods of the land smiting their enemies and repairing the damaged world. I always thought he was a crazy old man. He'd lived in a shack out in the badlands for decades and I was pretty sure the light and space out there fried his brain. Still, he was my grandfather so I listened patiently to his stories of skin walkers and UFOs and wild-eyed gods of this hot, dusty part of the world.

I asked him once why he chose to live in a run-down shack in the middle of nowhere and he said, "I spent a lifetime designing weapons to kill people I've never met. I made a good living off my skills. I can't live with that anymore. Out here I can hide and try to help heal a world I tried to destroy."

Then he'd go off on his magical creatures and gods and I'd figure he was just telling stories. I'd go home and he'd wave and we'd meet again a week or a month later.

My apartment is right off Central Ave, behind a building that used to host a salad bar but now contains a Mexican restaurant. It's a converted basement not too far from the University of New Mexico. There's one heater in the place, an ambient heater that glows red and works over the space of hours to warm the living room by a couple degrees. In the winter I can see my breath when I get out of bed, but at least the rent is cheap and I haven't had to kick any hookers or heroin dealers off my dirt lawn in a couple months now. Plus, the Mexican restaurant has an amazing selection of tequila.

All in all, not a bad place to live. For an apartment not too far off one of the busiest streets in Albuquerque, New Mexico, it's surprisingly quiet. There's an alley between my place and the salad bar, so that may have something to do with it.

I like to sit in an old lawn chair that's seen better days and watch people wander up and down my alleyway. Sometimes it's a man with wild eyes mumbling about shadows, other times it's the random college students. Right now, there's a Native American guy in washed-out, dusty blue jeans and an old red shirt. If the colors weren't so faded he'd look like a superhero. Maybe he's a fallen superhero, a kind of Superman who's gone past his prime and slipped into soft middle age. When he gets home, Lois will give him a kiss and tell him about her day. He doesn't seem like the kind of guy to expect dinner to be on the table when he walks in so he'll make something simple and they'll chat over wine.

Making up stories about the world around me keeps me sane. I love to sit out here with a Captain America glass full of rum and Coke, a pack of smokes, and wonder what the people around me are doing. Anyone that comes down this alley gets the same treatment: a story, a smoke, and a swig of rum and Coke. I should write them down; it'd make for some extraordinarily strange reading.

At about 10 p.m. I shuffle off back into my apartment, lock the doorknob, the deadbolt, the chain, and the sliding lock. I love this neighborhood but it's not exactly what I'd call 'safe'. As I'm going back in, I notice one last guy shuffle down the alley. Reddish shirt and blueish jeans washed out in the lone feeble street light. Is that the same guy? Is he the retired Superman? Did Lois kick him out for the night or is she out of town on spouses of retired superhero business? Maybe she goes to bed early.

Speaking of going to bed early, I'm exhausted.

***

In dreams you can see through the holes in reality. Most people think the real world is solid and immutable, but it's actually pretty porous. At least that's what my granddad always said. He would always wax philosophical about the fact that most people could only see what was right in front of their face. I'd nod and smile and he would continue telling me that there were places where the normal world would break down and other worlds would come creeping through. Or maybe it's just that we see only a small part of reality.

For me, the real world is always the real world. Dreams though, that's where magic happens. That's where reality - whatever that is - takes a back seat to something far more powerful and primitive.

I fall asleep and wake up on a mesa, a flat-top hill in the badlands overlooking the vast emptiness of New Mexico. Even though it's night, the full moon illuminates the valley below. There hasn't been water running through this land in months but when it rains it carves scars in the ground. The scrub brush and yucca plants wait patiently for the next crash of thunder rocking the skies, the lightning flashes that burn the world into retinas, and the crashing rain.

In front of me a man stands looking out over the vista. I can't be certain how I know this, but I know he's as dusty as the world around him. He's got long black hair pulled back into a pony tail and wrapped with some kind of cord from the base of his skull down to the middle of his back. I have a strange feeling I know him, that I've seen him recently.

He feels dangerous, but not overtly so. He's like the Black Widow in your garage or the Gila Monster crouching in the shade; left to his own devices you'd never notice he was there. As soon as you see him though, you can't take your mind off him. Something about his presence echoes in my head and a fascination takes over. It's just like hearing a rattle snake and instead of doing the smart thing and backing away, I start to move closer.

As soon as I take my first step he says, "It's about time Bilagáana. I was wondering if I'd have to wait here all night."

Alcohol is still in my system and the rum suppresses my ability to think diplomatically. "You have something better to do?" I ask.

He looks calmly over his shoulder at me and snorts. "Something is always happening in my land. Just because you're not bright enough to see it doesn't mean it's not happening."

"Why are you here?" I ask. "No, wait. Why am I here?"

The man laughs quietly. "Tell you what, Bilagáana, I'll answer both of your questions. Sound fair?"

"What does that mean, Bila ... bilagonna?"

"Bilagáana. It's a Diné word," he pauses, seeing I have no idea what he's talking about. "It's a Navajo word; it's what we use to refer to white people."

"Like calling us honkies?" I ask.

"Like calling you white people," he says. "Now, your questions."

"Yeah, those. What is this place?"

"That wasn't one of the questions I agreed to answer," he says with a sly smile. He's enjoying himself, playing these little games with my head.

"Fine," I say. "Why are you here?"

"I'm here because this is me. I'm the land and the sky and the eagles."

"That's not an answer," I say.

"It is the perfect answer," he tells me. His eyes are twinkling in bright moonlight, echoing the stars above and the light glinting off the sand below. "You're just not bright enough to understand it."

"Asshole," I mutter beneath my breath.

He laughs out loud and clasps my shoulder. "At times, Bilagáana, at times. Next question."

"Why am I here?"

"A friend asked me to bring you here. It seems he wants to talk but you don't know how to listen," he says, and turns back to face the valley below.

"Who is that?"

He doesn't answer, just keeps staring out at the land. There's one of those pregnant pauses in the conversation, an awkward moment where I'm unsure if I should specifically ask again or just walk away and find a dreamland McDonald's or something. Just as I'm about to wander off, he points down into the valley.

"What's down there?" I ask.

The man turns into a thousand lizards that skitter off into the moonlit sands.

Dreams. What are you gonna do?

274

After searching around where he was pointing to - whoever he was - I find a trail leading down into the valley. The going is treacherous: slick rock, loose gravel, shifting sands; the reasons this place is called the Badlands. Fortunately the really scary critters tend to sleep at night; as long as I don't go poking around in the brush or sticking my hand into any holes I should be fine.

I make it to the bottom with only minor scrapes and a couple of bruises. A short trail leads up to my grandfather's shack. I've got a sneaking suspicion I need to go in there but really don't want to. It's kind of like Luke and the Tree of Darkness, except I don't have a single weapon and he wasn't afraid to go in. I am. Death lurks in that place, sticky and sweet and seductive.

I start to back up and find the trail overgrown with yucca and tumbleweeds. My stupid subconscious mind is forcing me forward. Since it's just a dream nothing bad can happen, right?

Sure. Right.

The wooden door creaks when I open it. Inside the shack is dark and still. I stand in the doorway desperately wanting not to go any further but the dream decides to move me forward in that way that dreams have. My feet step inside against my better judgment while alarm bells go off in my head. The shack smells like madness and decay. In the corner is a bed with a figure on it. I can barely make out the rise and fall of his chest as he breathes.

"Nicholas," the figure whispers.

I step forward gently, feet finally mine again. There's something familiar about the voice, but I can't put my finger on it. "How do you know my name?"

The figure shifts on the bed. Eyes like stars open and stare at me, bathing the dingy shack in dim light. A mirror on the wall reflects the light back on my grandfather's cadaverous face. "Nicholas," he says. "Get here with the speed of a thousand horses."

***

My alarm clock is an Android tablet that pulls a random MP3 from my "hated songs" playlist. This morning it's some loathsome rap song. My hand moves like a snake to tap the damned thing before collapsing back onto my bed. I'm almost back asleep, watching a horse of all things running around in my head, when last night's dream comes storming back in. Normally my dreams do the right thing and fade into the background but this one won't go away; it has the feel of something real and tangible.

The same hand that struck my tablet so perfectly a few moments ago suddenly can't find my phone. I grope around my nightstand until I find my digital leash. A quick check of my calendar shows I don't have anything overly pressing to do today. The nice thing about doing freelance software development is that clients have set deadlines but don't really care when you work to get things done. I hadn't really planned on going out to the boondocks today, but there was... something... about that dream.

That dream was one of those that won't leave my head. It's like a bad taste in my brain or a kicky little pop song that you need a pry bar to get out of your head. Every time I close my eyes, even if it's just long enough to blink, I see glinting eyes and a man staring out into a valley. Think about work, think about a story, think about a movie and it doesn't change anything.

Maybe I just need coffee.

I bought some coffee on sale recently, good and dark. It's from some boutique beanery called Kicking Horse Coffee and they make a heck of a cup of Java. The familiar smells and sounds of the world slowly penetrate my senses. I swear, there are times I wonder if it's the smell of the coffee that's as much of a stimulant as the caffeine. Outside, my neighbor is revving up his muscle car, some Mustang he stripped the muffler from so it would be louder. While the coffee brews I turn on the TV and hear a story on the news about kids getting hurt while horsing around.

I'm out the door five minutes after my first cup of coffee, and burn myself spilling the second on my lap when I hit the brakes to avoid hitting a Native American guy in a red shirt. He smiles, waves, and says something I can't make out over the noise of the engine. Am I just going to show up at my granddad's place unannounced? Damn Skippy, I am.

Too many horses. Normally I'm not prone to flights of fancy; I'm a programmer after all. Three mentions of horses in just a few minutes, though? Maybe it's all in my head. Maybe I'm subconsciously seeking out horses. I'm probably doing that. It's just a dream. Dreams can't become real and there's no way a dream can become reality, yet here I am, speeding out into the Badlands with coffee in my lap and babbling away to myself like a gibbering lunatic.

I take the 230B exit north off of Interstate 40 too fast and nearly roll my aging Pathfinder. Nissan's engineers were pretty talented back in the day and the old truck stays upright. Once on it, the road turns to dirt and I hit the accelerator. If no one can be bothered to name this road, no one will be patrolling it. I swear, most of the time I've driven this way I've never seen another soul.

There's a faint cloud of dust rising behind me from the sand on the track. Ahead is nothing more than a seemingly endless dirt road and clear skies. This would be a perfect day if I wasn't driving in the middle of nowhere with a dream pinging around in my head.

What the hell am I doing?

I brake hard on the dirt road and skid for a bit before my tires bite in and drag this hunk of metal to halt. The cloud of dust slides quietly past the truck and through my open window before following the breeze further down the road.

What the hell am I doing? I'm driving headlong through the badlands on... what, some kind of quixotic quest to save my grandfather from something, because I had a strange dream and saw some horses? I must be losing my grasp on reality.

A storm is brewing in the distance; giant thunderheads, like fingers of some mighty god protrude from the sky to caress the ground. My head is throbbing.

Seriously, what the hell am I doing out here? I could turn around, drive home, heat up my coffee and enjoy a quiet day of coding and people watching. The truck slides neatly into reverse but my foot won't go down on the pedal.

My grandfather is at the end of this journey. He was more my father than my actual father and I'm sitting here debating what to do.

Screw this. I put the truck into first and floor it. If I'm going to be out here I'm at least going to drive angry. I wish my stereo worked. I've got some Ministry in the tape deck (yes, I have a tape deck) and it's great for getting pissed off and driving the back roads. Great plumes of dust feather out behind me. Jackrabbits and road runners skitter off into the brush.

The storm is still bearing down on me. Damn, but those are big clouds. The whole sky lights up when the lightning arcs. The first huge drops of rain hit my windshield like locusts, just as I arrive at my grandfather's shack. By the time I'm banging on his door the drops hurt when they hit and the thunder shakes the world.

No matter how much I bang, the door doesn't open. The rain turns to hail and my reticence to open his door fades when the stinging starts. The shack is dark inside, dark and quiet and far too still. I fumble for the light switch, but the storm has knocked out the power.

"Granddad," I call.

No response.

A flash of lightning briefly illuminates the dark shack enough to make out a mound on the bed.

"Granddad," I whisper.

Lightning flashes, thunder rumbles, but the mound doesn't stir.

A part of me will always wonder if stopping in the middle of the road slowed me down too much to get here on time. A day late and a dollar short.

As usual.

Goodnight granddad. I wish I had made it here earlier.

***

The storm rages for half an hour or so, and all I can do is stand in the doorway of the shack and watch the world rattle and hum with energy. The shack is empty of any energy it had and there's a black hole in my heart. When the rain stops I'm still leaning on the door frame, smoking a cigarette and wishing there was some Bourbon nearby. That's when he walks out of the desert. Same Native American guy, same red shirt and faded jeans. Superman, walking tall and proud like he owns the damned place.

"Who were you smiting?" I ask.

He cocks his head to the side.

"My granddad always said storms like this were when the gods were smiting someone," I add. "I'm pretty sure that's what you are, isn't it? Some kind of god. You were in my dream last night. Not a memory of you. You."

"Figured it out, eh, bilagáana?" he asks.

"I'm slow but not that slow." I say. "So, which god are you? You don't look like Coyote."

"He's a punk, but fun at parties," the man says. "I'm the spirit of this whole land."

"Got a name?"

"John Begay," he says. "You?"

"Aalto. Nicholas Aalto."

"Well, Nicholas, let's see to your granddad. Ukko will be waiting."

"Who?" I ask.

"Never mind," John says.

A tear rolls down my cheek and I wipe it away with a sleeve. To cover up the tear I try to act tough. "I'm considering burning the place to the ground and being done with it."

"He'd be glad you're here," John says. "He talked about you a lot. Let him go back to the land. He found peace out here; it only stands to reason he should stay with it."

All I do is nod.

John and I carry my granddad's corpse from the shack and set him on the ground. I get in one last goodbye before the soil rises like a wave and swallows him up. A strange sort of peace flows over me. Somehow, I think my grandfather would have found all this fitting. His grandson and some kind of god returning him to the soil would have tickled his funny bone.

"That's a better thing," John says.

"What's that?" I ask.

"Letting him go home," John says.

We eye each other briefly before John finally says, "Well, Nicholas, it's been a pleasure. Don't be a stranger."

With that, he turns on a heel and starts walking out into the desert.

"Need a lift?" I call out. "I can take you home."

"I am home," he calls over his shoulder.

"Begay!" I call out.

He turns and looks at me calmly.

"Who were you smiting?" I ask.

"The God of Dreams," John says. "He wanted to use my land, but I had other thoughts. We finally reached an agreement of sorts."

I have no idea what that means so I just say, "Okay."

"Don't worry about it, Nicholas," he says. "There are things brewing that you don't want anything to do with. Go home. Go home and remember your grandfather."

He turned again and stepped calmly into the desert like he owned the place. Actually, come to think of it, he probably does.

On the drive home I wonder how my grandfather managed to fall in with the ... what did he call himself? The Spirit of the Land. Those must have been some incredible conversations.

One more thing I'll never get to ask my granddad. All this time out here and I never asked the important questions or told him the important things.

And it took a god to point that out.

I'm so dense sometimes.

****

Love In An Elevator

S E Meyer

"You don't even know what passive aggressive means," Katie argued, shaking her dandelion hair away from her plain, but attractive face.

"Yes I do!" replied Tom. "I know exactly what it means. Passive aggressive is when someone you live with sticks a toothbrush in their ass and then puts it back in its place without telling anyone," he explained, waving his hands in front of him for greater effect.

Katie's eyes grew wide. "What? Gross. You've done that?" she asked.

"No, I haven't done that." Tom replied shaking his head before looking into his wife's storm-gray eyes. "I was just giving you an example, that's all."

Katie's face was still twisted into a look of disgust. "And that's the example you came up with? Obviously you've thought it over." Katie shuddered. *Note to self, pick up a new toothbrush on the way home.*

"And you know, the therapist said having sex once in a while could help us get along better," explained Tom.

Katie winced at the thought. "Maybe I would if you didn't suck at it so bad." she tipped her head to one side in thought.

"You know, maybe you'd suck less in bed if you were willing to try something new once in a while," Katie pleaded. "Like try a toy or something."

"What? No, come on honey, you know I hate messing with those things. They make me feel like Inspector Vagit or something."

Katie rolled her eyes. "That's exactly the problem. You have to stop treating my vagina like it's a broken machine that needs fixing. You can't just go digging around in there like you're under the hood of a car and hope you'll find a resolution."

Katie clenched her jaw, trying to remain calm.

"I can't help you," Dr. Thomas Townsend finally replied, having listened to the couple arguing in front of him for thirty minutes. "We've taken this about as far as we can, I should think."

"Wait, what?" asked Katie, temporarily distracted from making her next point to her husband.

"I can't help you," the therapist repeated, before leaning back in his chair.

Katie felt the disappointment and hope that the good doctor was just kidding, creep into her chest simultaneously. She knew the former was the most likely feeling to be dealing with, and her heart sank.

"Really? You really think our situation is hopeless?" she asked the bald man, shying away from his piercing blue eyes and focusing instead on the degrees that hung in neat rows on the wall behind him.

Katie and Tom had been religiously attending weekly therapy sessions with a psychiatrist for six months. It had taken Katie the six months prior to that to talk Tom into going with her.

Their marriage had started out like most. The whirlwind romance of two lovers; gushing with life and young love. Like a spring river swollen from melting snow, rushing down an emerald hillside and sloshing over its banks with no regard for anything in its path; deeply connected to one another in a multifaceted and intricately blended relationship where they experienced everything together. One could say they were joined at the hip, or often joined somewhere near it. But life came charging in like a raging bull and Katie felt like she was the one holding the red flag: college, and then a gruelling work schedule for both of them, added to the stress of buying a house. The bills were late, and then one day, so was Katie.

Their new daughter was a wonderful addition to their life, but another distraction to their relationship. And so their marriage, that had started out as many do, also ended up like most; a mix of repressed emotions, lack of connection and a feeling of general discontent. Katie wanted nothing more than to fix the problems and change her and Tom's marriage back to how it had begun, or some semblance thereof. She had been trying everything. Before therapy, there were the advice columns in magazines and relationship books, but nothing seemed to work. Katie and Tom loved each other deeply, of that Katie had no doubt, but she was tired of the fighting and constant arguing.

"Things need to change. Our marriage needs to change." she remembered telling Tom. "I just can't do it anymore." So at the risk of divorce, Tom agreed to therapy, Katie's final desperate effort to save something they both knew was special.

So after a year, we're still exactly where we started, Katie thought, returning her gaze to the doctor's navy-blue three-piece suit, but still avoiding his eyes.

"No, I never said that. I just said I can't help you," explained Dr. Townsend and then shrugged before continuing. "You both have a habit of running away before you resolve anything. You feel hurt so you hide. Short of locking you two up by yourselves in a room somewhere for a few days so you can sort everything out, I don't know what else we can do."

"You can do that?" Katie asked.

"No, I can't. Not without putting my license at risk."

"Well that's good news at least," Tom said in disbelief. "There's no way you're locking me up with her for a few days anyway. That would be torture."

Katie felt tears of rage begin to sting her eyes. "What?" she roared. "I can't believe you just said that." She crossed her arms and crept deeper into the opposite side of the couch from Tom. She glanced back to Dr. Townsend. "So there's nothing we can do?" she asked quietly. "I would do anything to save our marriage. It's so obviously broken."

"Well, there is only one person I can think of that may be able to help, but..." his voice trailed off.

Katie's heart leaped inside her chest, pounding itself against her rib cage like a gorilla trying to escape its barred cell. She uncrossed her arms and leaned in towards the doctor with renewed hope. "I will do anything; whatever it takes." She reached over and grabbed her husband's hand. "No, *we* will do anything," she finished.

"Within reason, of course," added Tom.

Dr. Townsend stared at the young couple in quiet contemplation for a moment before answering. "Okay, I'll give him a call. He doesn't always have an opening right away, but I'll check." The doctor picked up the phone and dialed. After a moment he began to speak to someone on the other end of the line. "I might have a couple for you here." There was a pause. "Yes. Okay, three o'clock you say?" the doctor looked at his watch. "Very well, I'll send them down," he finished, and hung up the phone. "Good news. His three o'clock appointment canceled and he can see you right now. You'll have to hurry though. Just go down to the main floor lobby and let them know you need to get to Dr Dun Dat's office. Okay?" Dr Townsend stood up and walked to his office door, placing his hand on the knob. "That's Dr Bin Dar Dun Dat," he said before turning the handle and opening it.

"What? No way!" Tom replied, getting up off the couch and turning towards Katie. "Are you serious? We're going to go see Dr Bin Dar Dun Dat? It sounds like a made up name." Tom raised both eyebrows and held his hands out in front of him. Katie raised herself from the sofa and made her way to the door. "Come on Tom, what have we got to lose?"

Dr Townsend walked back towards Tom and proffered his hand for Tom to shake it. Tom reluctantly placed his hand in the doctor's. "Believe me, Tom, Dr Bin Dar comes highly recommended and is the very top therapist in his field. Trust me," Dr Townsend finished, as he hurried Tom to the door. "Just don't be late," he added, with a final wave of his hand.

***

"We're going to be late," Tom complained, looking at his watch as he and Katie walked to the main floor reception desk.

"It's almost three."

Katie ignored him while getting the attention of the receptionist, an elderly lady with horn-rimmed glasses nestled beneath a bouquet of blue hair.

"Excuse me, we need to get to Dr Dun Dat's office. Can you help us?" she asked.

"Just a moment, I'll get the elevator attendant. We're having trouble with the main elevators, so you'll need to take the service one to get to the lower level offices," the receptionist explained, and then pushed a few buttons on the control panel in front of her.

Within a few minutes a man dressed in a red bell-hop suit arrived at the desk. He was a portly porter with walnut eyes and midnight hair that stuck out from under his crimson cap in straw tufts. He was the kind of man that exuded trust and carried a contagious amount of joy in his heart.

"Allo! Follow me," he said in a bubbly East Indian accent, and then attended to straightening his jacket.

He led the couple down a corridor and through a double doorway to a bank of three elevators. "Ah, here we are," the porter said, with a broad grin and smiling eyes. He then gestured with his hand for Katie and Tom to proceed to the elevator on his right.

"I don't think we're going to make it," Tom announced.

"Do you have to be so negative? I'm sure we'll be fine, it's barely three o'clock right now," Katie sniped.

"Don't worry, I will make sure you get to Dr Dun Dat's appointment on time," the caramel skinned attendant promised. He gave Katie and Tom a reassuring smile then pressed the silver button next to the elevator door.

The doors suddenly opened to reveal a younger man pulling on his underwear, the only article of clothing within arm's reach. Next to him was a woman who immediately crossed her arms in order to cover her bare chest.

"Allo, and woopsie daisies," the attendant announced with a grin.

Katie looked away as the couple hurriedly got enough clothes on to cover themselves adequately. *Well, at least someone is having sex,* she thought.

"I'm so sorry," the woman in the elevator said to Katie, as the couple stepped out past them and headed down the hallway.

As soon as they made it a few feet away they began giggling to themselves and exchanging 'I love you's'.

Katie let out a sigh. Must be nice to be that happy.

"Oh, please excuse me," said the porter. "You can take the other elevator instead," he explained while pushing the button in front of the elevator on their left. This time the doors opened to an empty car and the porter ushered them inside. "Just a moment," the Indian gentleman called before sending Katie and Tom on their way.

"This is the supply elevator and we need to re-stock the vending machines on the lower levels. Is it okay if send a few things down with you?" he asked.

Katie shrugged. "I don't mind," she replied before looking at her watch.

"We're not going to make it," Tom repeated.

"Stop saying that," Katie snapped as the porter rolled in two large cabinets filled with supplies, then gave them a nod.

"Finally," Katie said, tapping her foot on the industrial low pile carpet beneath her shoe.

The doors closed and the numbers on the display began to change. Katie felt the familiar difference in speed as the elevator slowed and then stopped. A few seconds went by, but the doors didn't open. The car made a sudden jolt and then went dark.

Katie stiffened. She reached out for Tom's hand with trembling fingers and upon finding it, squeezed hard in panic, her knuckles turning white from the effort.

"What the hell was that?" she asked.

Tom sent his gaze around their small capsule, squinting through the dim light of the emergency light in the corner. "I don't know," he replied. "It appears the main elevators aren't the only ones having trouble today."

Katie glanced at her watch again. "Great!" she hollered. "Just fantastic! Now we're never going to get to Dr Dun Dat's office in time." She placed her back to the wall and allowed herself to slide down the cold metal sheeting. Katie, and her wounded heart, both sank to the floor in despair.

"I told you we weren't going to make it," said Tom before slapping the elevator doors with the flat of his palm.

Katie's anger boiled over like a forgotten pot of pasta left unattended on high heat. "Well I guess we should all be grateful that Tom can see the future!" Katie bellowed with her hands in the air.

She continued to unload her feelings on Tom, the sarcasm dripping from her lips like battery acid. Tom fired back and a heated argument ensued over the next several hours. The angry shrieks and back-and-forth ranting echoing up the dark shaft above them should have ensured a rescue any moment, but none came. On and on, the fighting continued, in a pattern that started with flinging hurt words and ended with a retreat to their perspective corners to lick their wounds.

By the end of the fifth round, Katie was sitting quietly in the corner with her back against the wall. "I guess we're just destined to fail Tom. What happened today confirms it. I mean come on, getting stuck in an elevator? That has to say something about fate, don't you think?" Katie peered at her watch through the dim light. "Jeez, it's been six hours. Someone has to be coming soon, right?"

***

The next day.

"Um, hello, my name is Jim. My wife and I, we have an appointment to see Dr. Dun Dat. Can you tell us where his office is?" Jim asked. He was a middle aged man with graying hair and blue eyes. The woman with horn-rimmed glasses behind the desk simply nodded and pressed a few buttons on the switchboard. The enthusiastic porter arrived momentarily and escorted Jim and his wife to the service elevators. Upon arriving, the elevator doors opened, startling a young couple inside. They were barely dressed and their faces were flushed from both the act, and the embarrassment of being caught.

"Allo and woopsie daisies," the attendant called out in his cheerful accent.

The woman reached over and pressed the 'Close Door' button and when the doors re-opened a minute later the couple came strolling out, holding hands and now fully dressed. Jim peered into the elevator car to see several empty water bottles and snack food wrappers littering the floor.

Katie sheepishly glanced at Jim and his wife. "Sorry about that," she apologized with a bright smile, then held back a giggle. She looked at Tom with dreamy eyes as they headed down the corridor away from the elevators.

The attendant smiled. "I'm sorry you were not able to make it to your appointment," he apologized. "These elevators have had a mind of their own lately."

Katie looked back over her shoulder. "Oh, don't worry about it, sir. Getting stuck in that elevator was the best thing that has ever happened to us. We spent hours fighting, crying, laughing, and in the end, making up. We were able to address and resolve more issues in one day then we did in therapy over the last six months!" Katie walked back to where the porter was standing and shook his hand. "I know it was an accident, but thanks to you, our marriage is no longer broken," she explained with a bright smile and glowing complexion.

Katie turned and walked back to where Tom was waiting for her.

"I love you, Katie," Tom said, returning her smile with his own wide grin.

"I love you too, Tom," she replied, squeezing his warm hand as they made their way back to the lobby.

Katie realized that it was not her marriage that needed changing, but rather it was her own heart and mind that needed a fresh perspective. As in most relationships, she and Tom finally understood what it meant to be happy together. It took courage to sort through the pile of untidiness that was their union. The pair figured out that it takes a long hard look at oneself in order to heal with others. A coupling now mended through personal self-reflection and coming to understand the meaning of 'What can I do today to make my spouse's day a little brighter?'

and how far that one thought will take two people who are profoundly in love.

Katie now understood that they couldn't change one another, they could only change themselves.

The porter escorted Jim and his wife into an empty elevator car and then made his way back to the reception desk. "Oh, we have had another busy week Mrs. Potts."

"I should say so," replied the receptionist. "I'm not sure how you do it," she wondered, scratching the back of her head and then fidgeting with her blue hair.

"I have about a ninety per cent success rate," he replied nodding, making the bill of his cap wobble like a Mallard's foraging along the Thames.

"Nicely done, Dr Dun Dat." the woman commended, and then gave the man a wink.

"Oh yes, not too bad for a poor boy from Mumbai," he replied.

"Not bad indeed sir, not bad indeed."

******

No Longer Broken

Nico Laeser

As a contractor, I find myself at the mercy of many exterior elements. Seasonal weather shut-downs are rarely due to any concern for the workers, but are necessary when product installation cannot be guaranteed. A project can be shut down for the smallest change in weather; the change of a few degrees can ruin a paint job, crack caulking, warp or stress wood, change the bonding success of glue and the list goes on, and on. An economic storm can shut everything down completely, and for months at a time.

Months without work and talk of another recession have equally recognizable results on a marriage. I watched as small cracks formed under the added stress, and as our once strong bond began to weaken. When it was just the two of us, money was never a problem; all we had to do was love each other, and that was easy. When our daughter was born, everything changed.

We had agreed, during the pregnancy, that my wife would take leave from her employment to be a stay-at-home mom, and I would work. As a husband and father, it became my duty to bring home the money, and as a wife and mother, it became my wife's duty to take care of the house and our little girl.

With the addition of a baby came added stress. When business suddenly dried up, so dissolved my ability to provide as a father; it meant that my wife could not fulfil her now most basic need—the need to protect her child. I spent two months looking for something to fill in the gap until my company finalized the big contract they'd been promising; the kind of *big job* that promises a couple of years of security, but *that* job always remains just around the corner, held up with the acquisition of endless permits, morphing the job into a dangling carrot for all those workers sitting at home. You have to believe in the carrot, or believe in it enough to convince your wife, but after a while, you realize that there is no carrot, the company just doesn't want to lose its entire workforce before it lands a new contract.

Our savings were all but depleted, and money worries coloured every conversation. The most trivial conversations quickly turned sour and led to petty arguments that would last all night. It was never about money on the surface, but money was always the root cause. In my mind there was blame in my wife's tone, and there was guilt in my own, which made me fight harder out of frustration.

What could, and should, have been quality time spent together as a family, devolved to bouts of tense silence, or loud snapping and jabbing matches. I would leave, take a walk to calm myself down. My wife would take extra time in the bathroom getting ready, washing the streaked eye makeup from her cheeks and starting all over again. I felt like a loser, a lazy dead-beat dad, a lousy let down of a husband and father. For a time it seemed that all that remained of our marriage was resentment; it was my failure, my fault, and there didn't seem to be anything I could do about it. It was after another petty argument about nothing at all that my wife burst into tears and sobbed that she was pregnant again.

During the pregnancy, my wife's family stepped in to offer financial support, and although the rational part of me was thankful, I still held a deep resentment over the fact that my wife had shared our problems and accepted their generosity. I had no say in my own resulting emasculation, and what could I have said? Don't take their money, it makes me feel like less of a man? It was no longer about me, and very soon I would be another step lower in our family hierarchy.

At last, jobs began to trickle in, eventually growing steady again, and I took all the overtime I could, working thirteen or fourteen-hour days, six days a week. I begged for my wife's family to let us pay back the money they had given to us, but they refused to appease my pride, and continued to offer support in anticipation of our family's new arrival. My role as the provider was no longer threatened, but by no means secure; the job was set to last for at least a year, beyond that was anyone's guess.

The ultrasound showed us what we hoped it would. Our baby was a boy. Soon, we would have the family we'd always talked about—the perfect nuclear family: Man and wife, a daughter and a son. All that was missing was the white picket fence and a dog. In the beginning, we always talked about the future, our family, about what we would do if we had two boys or two girls, if we'd try again. Back then, we never worried about money, we both worked and had fewer responsibilities; we were in love and wanted to be together forever.

The bond between a mother and child is way greater than that of a father and child or husband and wife. While I was getting to know this strange new addition to our family, my wife was continuing a relationship that started over nine months before he was born. They felt each other's movements no matter how subtle. They shared the same space, food, oxygen, chemicals and emotions. It was not love at first sight for me; I had to get to know both of our children after they were born. I hadn't carried them around or shared any intimacy with them prior to birth, and hadn't thought about the future, beyond the practical aspects of how we would pay for our expanding family, and how much overtime I would have to put in to ensure that we wouldn't end up in the same financial freeze during the slow-work months of winter. I don't mean to sound cold, but I've always chosen logic over emotion, actually it was never a conscious choice, but more the way I'm wired. I *grew* to love my children.

Once my daughter's personality started to shine through, I fell completely in love, and expected that the same would be true for my son. Our little girl was always ahead of the curve. She walked early, talked early, hit or surpassed every check-point on my wife's developmental calendar. She was so far ahead that it became cause for a great deal of jealousy among our friends with children around the same age, and I revelled in it. I felt a swell of pride over the fact that my little girl was gifted. By the time our son was born, our daughter could count as high as her attention allowed, recite the alphabet, had an amazing vocabulary and used it to question everything.

Our pride over our daughter's development, and our attention to those developmental check-points made us watch eagerly as our son progressed. He too, stood early, walked early, and his speech was incredible. He spoke right away in complete sentences – all lines from his favourite TV shows. His facility to memorize whole scenes and recite them back word-for-word was staggering. Our son was to be a genius.

Beyond the first year of our son's life, my wife started pointing out not only how many check-points he was hitting or surpassing, but how many he was missing completely. She told me that, while shopping for a birthday gift for one of our friend's kids, our son had shown no interest in any of the toys in the store. She pointed out a fire truck, but he didn't respond. She pushed the *try-me* button to set off the siren and still got no response, and she continued to push every *try-me* button on all the fire trucks in the aisle to get his attention, but he remained still, staring straight ahead as though oblivious to the sights and sounds. When she told me about it, I thought it pretty trivial and said that maybe he just didn't like fire trucks, but that had not been the point. My son's personality was not coming through. He showed no interest in toys, wouldn't look up when called, or respond to his name. His speech continued as lengthy scripting from television shows, with no original language other than the word 'mom.' He used the memorized phrases or songs to communicate his needs, but wouldn't answer a question with a simple yes or no.

I kept denying any problems, in spite of my wife's pleas for me to take her concerns seriously. My wife knew that something was wrong, and deep down in the pit of my stomach I knew that she was right, but refused to admit it to myself, let alone to her. As my wife pointed out various behaviours that had become cause for her concern, I began to see them all the time. Red flags were popping up every day, and the pride I once felt for my boy genius quickly turned to an anxious dread of what could possibly be wrong with him.

We were offered brief reprieve when the paediatrician said that he was perhaps a late developer, and that some kids just develop slower than others, but a sideways glance at my wife's expression on the drive home let me know that she wasn't convinced, and my own hope dissolved.

My son began to flap his hands like a bird, and I found it cute at first. I would ask him, "Are you a bird?" My wife saw this behaviour as a flag. He would spin in circles with his eyes pinned to one side; I reasoned that all kids spin in circles, they get dizzy, they fall down, that's just what kids do, but to my wife it was another red flag.

I tried to convince my wife that his language was improving all the time, referencing full conversations that I'd had earlier in the day with my son, but she would repeat his responses back to me word-for-word and tell me what television show they had come from. I followed my wife, reluctantly, into acceptance, and relented to follow her instincts as a mother.

After several months of examinations and tests, and relentless effort on my wife's part to have them examine the possibility that had become a certainty in her heart and mind, we got our answer, and my wife got the confirmation that she was dreading.

***

Statistically, nine out of ten marriages fail within a year of a dependant receiving an Autism diagnosis. Over the phone, they suggested for us to consider marriage counselling to help us through it. Our odds of surviving as a family had dropped below one in ten. It seemed like we were already well above the load capacity for the glass floor that supported our family, and the cracks were now spreading under our feet.

My wife cried for weeks, not anywhere that she would be seen, but the proof was in her once beautiful blue eyes, which both of our kids had inherited, and which were now always glassy, pale and framed with varying shades of red. She worked tirelessly to secure funding, to register him into programs, to find therapists and a behavioural interventionist. Everything that she did was focused on giving our son the best chance of a normal future. While my wife moved forward, planning our new lives around improving our son's life, I became lost in unnecessary endeavours, scouring the internet for the causes of autism, trying desperately to find a target for my anger, and someone or something to blame. There are so many theories about what causes autism. They include everything from vaccines, to food allergies, to electrical pollution, but mostly what my research came back to, over and over again, was genetics. The long-standing view and general consensus is that, genetically, autism comes from the man's side; my son had been diagnosed with autism, and it was *my* fault. I was the cause. I was to blame.

In retrospect, I know how much work my wife put in on the phone and in consultations, but at the time I was oblivious. I was too busy blaming myself to stand back and look at the bigger picture; to quit looking at myself and pay attention to those who needed me.

In an attempt to kill two birds with one stone, my wife had me take our son for nightly walks around the townhouse complex. One of her biggest fears was that our son would run out in front of a car, or just run and never stop; he was a flight risk, a 'bolter.' He seemingly gave no thought to his personal safety, and wouldn't come when called, so I would take him out for a walk each night to burn off some of the energy that made him 'stim' and to train him to walk beside us. It also gave my wife a thirty or forty minute break from both our son, and my temper.

One Wednesday, I returned home from work to my wife in tears. Wednesday was the day that the landscapers came to mow the yards and common areas, blow and collect fallen leaves, trim lawn edges, and all the other tasks involved in maintaining the grounds. My son had spent the whole day in melt-down mode, devastated by the sound of the lawn mowers, leaf blowers, trimmers and trucks, and nothing my wife could do would calm him down. This wasn't an uncommon occurrence, but for some reason, on this particular Wednesday, our son had refused to wear his ear defenders, and had dealt with the sensory overload by spinning, flapping, screaming and crying non-stop for the entire time.

I put on his shoes, his weighted backpack, complete with attached leash, and we left for our nightly walk. I can't count how many contemptuous side-glances the leash had earned in the short time we'd used it, but it was no more than the looks garnered in public from his odd or loud behaviour.

The landscaper's impact on his day hadn't ended with their departure. In the wake of their hasty egress, several gates had been left open. This was a major change in our routine, and a major upset to my son. At the first open gate, he began to spin and flap his hands, and every time I called his name he yelped like an injured hound. After a few dirty looks from passing dog-walkers, I let frustration get the better of me, took my son by the hand and dragged him away from the gate. Within a few steps, he went limp and I scooped him up under my arm and carried him away.

I set him down when the gate was out of sight and asked if he wanted to try again, and he relented to walk by my side, all the way until the next open gate. He began the cycle again, spinning in circles, yelping when I called him, and I cursed under my breath, perhaps at the landscapers, or maybe just at the situation. I didn't know what to do. I thought that maybe if I just let him get it out of his system that he would get over it, get past it, and we could carry on with our walk. I sat on the grass by the side of the road and waited. I called his name. He yelped, spun, and flapped. I called him again, and noticed that his response was exactly the same, the same yelp, the same number of spins, and the same number of flaps. It looked like a response to some programming error, on a seemingly endless loop.

As I stared at my son, he didn't look like a boy misbehaving, being silly or difficult. He looked like a boy trapped in a sequence beyond his control. I broke down into tears as I watched him wind down. When he finished, he came back to me and curled up on my lap like a baby. We cried together for longer than I'd care to admit, and then my son began to sing a song from one of his shows.

"It's okay to feel sad sometimes. Little by little, you'll feel better again."

I held my son tightly, and sobbed my apology. I had spent so much time dwelling on the insignificant details of money, cause, and blame that I had failed to see what really mattered. My son didn't need to be avenged. What he needed was my love and support, and so did the rest of my family, just as I needed theirs.

***

My son has continued to improve in his language and comprehension, and is every bit as loving as our daughter. Some children diagnosed with autism will never say I love you, will never show emotion, and my heart goes out to the parents of those children. My son *does* say I love you, and when he does, it is honest, complete, and with no ulterior motive. It is that unconditional love that he brought back into our house that kept our family together. He taught us to love one another again, without money or relatively insignificant problems working their way between us.

I realize now that my son was not broken, and there was nothing *wrong* with him. He was the angel, sent to fix our broken marriage, and to fix what was broken inside me. I am thankful for the lessons my son has taught me. Of the things I have learned, there is this: A house that has enough love will never be poor, because love is the only currency needed to pay for a family. I am grateful to my son, for I no longer feel broken.

****

MEET THE AUTHORS

All contributing authors were asked a single question –
"Why have you given your time and work to this cause"
Below, you will find a list of their individual answers and links
to their books or websites, to help you discover more about them
and their other works.

Lisa Shambrook: Carmarthenshire, Wales

My family life has been touched by cancer with two of my children's
grandparents suffering. We've seen both those who've won and lost the
battle, and this is a chance to do something to help.

http://www.lisashambrook.com

http://www.thelastkrystallos.wordpress.com

Sallyann Phillips: Swansea, Wales

My dad died of cancer, but his strength and determination amazed me.
This is my way of honouring him, and the nurses who helped keep his
spirits up.

http://www.Angelsblood.co.uk

Penny Luker: Cheshire, England

I wanted to contribute to this anthology because of the dear friends I have
lost to cancer and because the Macmillan nurses gave them such help and
support.

http://www.pennyluker.wordpress.com

https://www.facebook.com/pennyluker.writer?

Anthony Randall: Dorset, England
Both of my Grandmothers died from cancer. My maternal Grandmother
spent her last week in a hospice where she received brilliant care, the
nurses were formidable. It's an essential charity that I am more than
happy to support in this humble way.
http://www.amazon.co.uk/English-Sombrero-Nothing-but-run-
ebook/dp/B00IHH209W
https://www.facebook.com/pages/The-English-
Sombrero/555658614480373

Katharine Hamilton: Texas, Unites States of America
In memory of my cousin, Melissa. One of the most hilarious, kind-hearted,
and genuine women I have ever known. Fifteen years later, I still wish I
had taken that crazy car ride around Murfreesboro with you. But thank
you for making my awkward, teenage-self feel cool... even if it was in
Arkansas.
http://www.katharinehamilton.com

Christoph Fischer: Carmarthenshire, Wales
I lost both of my parents to cancer and also a few close friends, so I'm
naturally committed to the MacMillan cause. I have seen the MacMillan
nurses in action and couldn't be happier to support their marvellous
work.
http://www.christophfischerbooks.com
http://www.amazon.co.uk/Christoph-Fischer/e/B00CLO9VMQ

SK Holmesley: Colorado, United States of America
I contributed because Ian asked, and it was a way that I could say: "Sorry
you lost a loved one."

Rebecca Bryn: St David's, Pembrokeshire, Wales

My mother was a volunteer cancer nurse, and also nursed my father who died from prostate cancer. This is my chance to honour their courage, love and strength.

http://www.rebeccabrynandsarahstuart-novels.co.uk

http://www.independentauthornetwork.com/rebecca-bryn

D Avraham: Hebron Hills, Israel

When I lost my mom, it would have been that much harder if there hadn't been caring people supporting us at the time. Ian's project reminded me of need to thank them. I have donated my piece in their honor, a small gesture to say thank you.

The Shepherd King Chronicles: Foundation Stone (Beith David Publishing, 2010).

Off-Wire (Lulu 2014), and the author/illustrator of the children book, Squared (beith David Publishing 2013).

Tom Benson: Scotland

I lost both my father-in-law and mother-in-law to cancer before I really got to know either of them.

http://www.tombensonauthor.com/

Ian D Moore: North Yorkshire, England

I began and contributed to this anthology to support the work that the Macmillan Nurses do. My father, Grandfather and Mother-in-Law were all taken by cancer. This is a tribute to them all.

https://www.iandmoore.com

http://www.facebook.com/yourenotalone2015

Andy Updegrove: Marblehead, Massachusetts, United States of America
I have dedicated this story to the memory of my father, mother and sister, all of whom died from cancer.
https://updegrove.wordpress.com/

Lesley Hayes: Oxford, Oxfordshire, England
I've been alongside several people affected by cancer. One familiar emotion is powerlessness. Contributing here seems a concrete way of continuing to be alongside, and to show that I care.
http://www.lesleyhayes.co.uk

Nico Laeser: British Columbia, Canada
I took a brief hiatus from writing my third novel for the opportunity to work alongside the many incredible authors taking part in this project, and to offer whatever help I could to such a worthy cause. You can find my novels on Amazon by searching 'Nico Laeser' or by visiting my author page:
http://www.amazon.com/Nico-Laeser/e/B00SF3C732/

Max Power: Maynooth, Republic of Ireland.
Having lost my father through cancer, when asked, I had no hesitation in making a contribution through my writing, to this most worthy cause.
http://www.amazon.com/author/maxpower
http://www.facebook.com/maxpowerbooks

Eric Lahti: New Mexico, United States of America
I joined the anthology, at the time, because another story was needed. As I started to write, my story became a kind of goodbye to my dad and grandfather who died in 2001 and 2008 respectively.
Arise: http://www.amazon.com/dp/B00PX710Y0
Henchmen: http://www.amazon.com/dp/B00GRXB5Ik

Phyllis Edgerly Ring: New Hampshire, United States of America
In memory of my father, I am grateful to contribute to this healing resource of hope and compassion.
http://phyllisedgerlyring.wordpress.com
http://www.amazon.com/Phyllis-Edgerly-Ring/e/B001RXUFD6/ref=ntt_dp_epwbk_0

S.E.Meyer: Wisconsin, United States of America
I made the decision to donate my time to this cause for my brother-in-law, Paul, who just recently fought and won the battle against testicular cancer.
Facebook: http://www.facebook.com/semeyerbooks
Amazon:http://www.amazon.com/S.-E.-Meyer/e/B00CFRHL9Y/

Christine Southworth: Lancashire, England
I am involved in this project as a thank you to those who cared for my husband.
Twitter: @bearprintstudio

Sylva Fae: Cheshire, England.
Helping with this anthology allows me to show my appreciation for those who cared for my dad.
Sylvanian Ramblings http://www.sylvafae.co.uk

Barbara Doran: Munster, Westfalen, Germany
I submitted my story, Lotta Blum, to this Anthology because it's for a good cause. Ian D Moore wrote a moving statement on the wonderful works of the Macmillan cancer nurses in a recent post on an Indie Review Group and I responded. You can find my musings here:
http://www.eclecticwrite.wordpress.com
http://www.serendipitydoit.wordpress.com

Kayla Howarth: Queensland, Australia

Knowing it was for a good cause, I decided to try something I'd never done before: write a short story. This experience has been uplifting and therapeutic, and I'm glad I took up the challenge.

http://www.kaylahowarth.com

https://www.facebook.com/KaylaHowarthTheInstituteSeries

Angela Lockwood: France

Never too old, has been inspired by my mother, who lost her husband and my father to cancer in 1993. I wanted to add a positive story about life afterwards.

Website: http://www.cruftslover.adzl.com

Blog: http://languageintheblood.blogspot.fr

Katerina Sestakova Novotna: Honolulu, United States of America

It was just an automatic response to a post that I saw. If my thoughts may support a good cause, it's a great honor to get involved.

http://www.amazon.com/Hawaiian-Shrunken-Katerina-Sestakova-Novotna-ebook/dp/B00OYUSO1Y/

BL Pride: Slovenia

After a close encounter with cancer I decided it was time I started pursuing my dreams. Being a part of this project is a tribute to a life-changing experience.

http://www.blpride.com

Mike Billington: Reus, Spain

I wrote this story for the anthology because, as a cancer survivor myself, I know first-hand just how important the kind of support MacMillan Cancer Nurses provide is. My hope is that "Dolphins Dance" reminds readers that life is better when we are connected to other people.

http://www.amazon.com/-/e/B001KCABGK

http://www.amazon.com/author/billington

Felipe Adan Lerma: Austin, Texas, United States of America.

The simplest answer is of course because I wanted to share some of what I feel when writing. The question of whether we are ever truly alone sharpened my focus for this story, shifting the action several times. I am very grateful for the impetus to bring my thoughts to expression in this very short work.

Amazon author page: http://www.amazon.com/Felipe-Adan-Lerma/e/B005XCUUK0

Author website: http://www.felipeadanlerma.com

Paul Ruddock: London, England

Having witnessed cancer first-hand I was absolutely delighted to contribute to such a worthwhile project in support of Macmillan Nurses.

Author site: http://www.paulruddockauthor.com

Blog site: http://www.echoesofthepen.com

Lucinda E. Clarke: Spain

My father died when I was two years old, from cancer. When I was diagnosed with the same insidious disease in 1999 I was terrified. I have enormous respect and gratitude for the medical team that saved my life and I hope this is a small way of saying thank you.

http://lucindaeclarke.wordpress.com

http://www.lucindaeclarkeauthor.com

Made in the USA
Lexington, KY
06 April 2016